Mrs. O
Hometown Patriot

A WWII tale of chicks and chicanery, suspicion and spies.

An Elaine Faber Mystery

Elaine Faber
2021
Enjoy!

Elk Grove Publications

Mrs. Odboddy: Hometown Patriot

Published by Elk Grove Publications

© 2016 by Elaine Faber

ISBN-13: 978-1-940781-13-6

This novel is a work of fiction. Though based on actual WWII historical events, involvement of the novel's characters are purely fiction and the product of the author's imagination. Any resemblance to actual events, locales, organizations,or persons, living or dead, is entirely coincidental and beyond the intent of either the author or publisher.

Cover photos: *Can we talk?* © Everett Collection, Shutterstock.com image 227271556 and *48-star flag* © nazlisart, Shutterstock.com image 148131515

Cover layout and book formatting: Julie Williams, juliewilliams.us
Printed in the United States of America

Dedication

To the veterans of World War II and to the hometown patriots who fought the war from the home front.

Chapter One

There, see? It's just not…" Agnes wound the black yarn around her knitting needles. The yarn slipped off the end, causing the stitch to fail.

A smile crossed Lilly Chang's face as she took the needles from Agnes. "No, no. See? You've dropped another stitch. Like this. Knit two, purl one, knit two…" She handed back the knitted sock to Agnes. "You can do it. Our boys overseas deserve the best. You don't know how much they appreciate warm, dry socks."

Agnes glanced around the Newbury County Hospital conference room where Lilly taught Red Cross knitting classes. The U.S.A. and California flags hung on poles at the front of the room. She and Mildred sat across from Edith, their knitting paraphernalia spread over the table.

"I just don't get it. You've explained it three times already. What's the use?" Agnes tossed the needles down, stood, and planted her fists on her hips. "Maybe I'll leave the knitting to you gals and see if I can round up a pot of tea from the cafeteria."

Mildred looked down and muttered, "Good idea."

"I heard that, Mildred Haggenbottom. Don't blame me. You insisted I join the Red Cross knitting class. I told you I wasn't good with my—"

Crash!

The ladies jumped as the door crashed against the wall. A soldier burst into the room, his rifle drawn as though he was facing down a battalion of Japanese soldiers armed with heavy artillery. "Lilly Chang, stand up!"

Lilly's face paled. She glanced from Mildred to Agnes's anxious faces and slowly stood. "I'm Lilly Chang. What's wrong? What do you want?'

The soldier hurried forward. "Get your personal belongings. You're coming with me."

Agnes rushed to Lilly's side. "What's going on here? Lilly is our knitting teacher. She's not some backroom drug dealer."

"Sorry, ma'am. I have my orders." He pulled a paper from his jacket pocket. "This is an order to pick up all Japanese persons and bring them to Boyles Springs Military Base for questioning. Get your things together, Mrs. Chang. You have five minutes."

Agnes stepped in front of Lilly. "I don't care if your orders came straight from God. This is the United States of America. Lilly is an American citizen. She has rights. Show me an arrest order with her name on it. Just because she's Japanese doesn't mean you can—"

"'Fraid you're wrong there, lady. This here is direct from President Roosevelt's Executive Order 9066." He stared at his paper and read aloud. "By order of President Roosevelt, any Japanese persons located within fifty miles along the Western coastline are hereby ordered to submit to examination and subject to removal from any area susceptible to espionage or sabotage, for the duration of the war." He turned toward Lilly with a sneer. "You Japanese?"

Lilly nodded. "Yes, but I was born in Sacramento. My family has been here for thirty-four years. We own a home. My husband runs a nursery and—"

"I don't care if you came over on the Mayflower," the soldier sniggered at his inane joke, "You could be married to Tokyo Joe for all I know. You're Japanese and you're coming with me!" He jerked his rifle toward the door.

Lilly burst into tears as Mildred brought over her jacket and purse. "It's alright, dear. This must be a mistake. I'm sure things will be sorted out in a few days."

Tears pricked Agnes's eyes. How could her beloved President Roosevelt do this to an American citizen? Sure, they were at war with Japan, but hadn't Lilly wept at the news of the Pearl Harbor attack? Wasn't she horrified by the action of her ancestral country? Hadn't she also bought war bonds, collected papers and cans, cooked meatless meals, and sacrificed for the benefit of the boys on the battlefield?

Where had their freedom gone? What were they fighting for, if it wasn't for justice and due process to determine the guilt or innocence of anyone charged with a crime? Lilly's only crime was her heritage and the color of her skin.

"What about my husband?" Lilly sobbed "What about my pets? Where are my children?"

"We picked up your husband at his business," the soldier said. "They're sending someone to the school for your kids. I...I don't know what you'll do with your pets!" The young soldier's chin quivered. Had he finally realized the pain his actions were causing this gentle woman? Was he ashamed of his part in this injustice, unparalleled in American history since the way Indians were treated during the days of the Old West?

Agnes regained her composure at last, rushed to Lilly and wrapped her arms around her. "What can I do? Oh, Lilly, I'm so sorry..."

"My dog, Piffles and my cat, Ling-Ling... Can you go to my house?" She opened her purse and pulled out a keyring. "Here's the house key. I hate to ask, but... Can you find a home for the pets?" Tears glistened in her eyes. "I don't know for how long... Thanks." She turned toward the stricken faces of her friends. "Well, I guess there's nothing more to say. Good-bye ladies..." Her lips quivered. Lilly lifted her chin and faced the soldier, who now looked foolish, holding a rifle on this tiny, proud woman. "Okay, I'm ready. Let's get on with it."

"Don't you worry, Lilly Chang!" Agnes's glare could melt the stickers off a cactus. "This injustice shall not go unchallenged! I'll get to the bottom of this if it's the last thing I do."

The soldier's face was now crimson. He opened the door and stepped back. Lilly walked through the door as through she was emerging from a limousine into a gala event. The soldier quietly closed the door. Oh, how differently than the way he had opened it only minutes before.

Agnes stood silently, staring at the door.

Mildred pulled out a handkerchief and dabbed her eyes.

"I think we're done here today." Agnes's words were almost a whisper. She reached for her purse. "Mildred, would your brother take Lilly's dog out on his farm? I'll take the cat home with me."

Mildred's face brightened. "Under the circumstances, I'm sure he would. He and his wife have lots of room. I'll go with you. We can pick up the dog and drive him right over there now."

Within several hours, Piffles was scampering around the farm with Mr. Haggenbottom's dog, and Lilly's cross-eyed Siamese cat, Ling-Ling, was curled on a blanket beside Agnes's kitchen stove.

Content, and with her tummy full of warm milk and a yellow yarn ball clamped beneath her dark brown paw, Ling-Ling could not know that her old life with Lilly had ended. Her new life with Agnes Agatha Odboddy, a warrior on the home front and the self-appointed scourge of the underworld, had begun.

"Yoo-hoo, Grandmother, I'm home."

"I'm in the kitchen, *punkin'*."

Katherine dropped her purse on the table. She drew in her breath as her gaze paused at the silver framed photograph sitting on the china cabinet; a picture of her and Stephen taken at their engagement party. The following December, he was stationed on the USS Arizona when Japan attacked Pearl Harbor. She shuddered, thinking of his body, still somewhere in the sunken ship along with thousands of his shipmates.

Katherine breathed in the scent of oatmeal, raisins and nuts. Like a soothing balm, the scent of warm cookies eased the pain in her heart. "*Umm.* Oatmeal. My favorite."

Agnes pulled a cookie sheet from the oven and set it on the counter. "You can have a couple, but I baked them for the boys at the USO tonight. Everything okay down at the beauty parlor?"

Katherine nodded. "I finished my last client for the afternoon, so Myrtle let me leave early." She glanced at Grandmother. "What's wrong? You look worried."

Agnes nodded toward the blanket by the stove. "I've had a very trying day. Wait until you hear. This is Ling-Ling." She stooped and stroked the little cat. She purred and wound her toes in and out. The wrinkles deepened in Agnes's face. She sighed. "My friend Lilly got scooped up this morning and hauled away. Can you believe it? Just because she's Japanese, they've taken her away. I swear, it's hard to believe we live in America these days."

"That's terrible! I heard something like that happened in a couple other towns, but I didn't think they'd bother us here in Newbury."

"Well, it's true. I guess it's happening all along the California coastline. We took Lilly's dog to Mildred's brother. I brought Ling-Ling home with me. I don't know what else to do."

"Well, I'm surprised. I didn't know you liked cats."

"Why did you think that? Of course, I like cats. It'll be good to have a pet again."

Katherine shrugged. "It's fine with me. I always liked cats." She glanced out the kitchen window. "I don't like the look of those storm clouds. Are you still planning to drive to the Boyles Springs Military Base tonight? Perhaps you shouldn't go out this evening. I hate the thought of you driving that crooked ocean road all the way in the rain. What if you have a flat tire out there all alone?"

"It wouldn't be the first time, and likely not the last. I was hoping I might find out something about Lilly tonight. That's where they said they were taking her.

"Why don't you come with me? The young men are so nice and

they always want to dance with pretty girls." Agnes fluffed Katherine's red hair. "And, there's no one prettier than you, *punkin*. Say you'll come this time, please? It would be so much nicer driving with someone."

Katherine shook her head, her heart stirring as her fiancé's face filled her mind. "I'm not ready for another romance. It's only been a few months since Stephen died. I don't think I could bear it if I met another man and he went off to war. Please don't fuss at me about it, Grandmother."

Agnes gave Katherine's hair another pat. "I understand. I felt the same way when I lost your grandfather and your father. I couldn't..." Agnes turned away but not before Katherine saw tears sparkling in her grandmother's eyes.

"You, me, and Ling-Ling. Just a house full of old maids. And, it's fine for now. At least until the war is over. Maybe then..."

"Taste one of these oatmeal cookies. What do you think?"

Katherine nibbled a cookie. She raised her eyes toward Heaven and sighed. "They're just wonderful. With cookies like this, the boys at the USO won't even notice if there aren't any girls to dance with." She stroked the kitten's nose with one finger.

"Oh, I'm not so sure about that. Cookies have never been able to compete with young men and girls, and I doubt they're going to start now."

Decked out in comfortable walking shoes, a chic white blouse and a blue surge calf-length skirt, Agnes carried a tray of oatmeal cookies into the garage. She opened the driver's side door of her 1930 Model A Coupe and laid the covered tray on the cushions. She slid into the driver's seat. *Old Nelly is getting on in years, but weren't we all?* Aging had nothing to do with spunk and ability. She and Nelly had plenty of both.

She turned the key, tapped the dashboard dials to check the fluids, pulled the timing lever down, pushed the starter button on the floor, and gave it a little gas. The engine rattled to life. She adjusted the timing lever. When the engine purred, she released the hand brake, pushed in the clutch, shoved the floor shift into reverse and let out the clutch. She smiled. *That was easy! Not like in the old days.*

Driving Old Nelly always took her back to her adventures during WWI when she had to hand crank the engine before the car would start, then jump into the driver's seat before the engine died again. There were so many ruts in the road, most assignments included at least one blown tire. Jacking up the car and changing a tire on a dirt road while wearing an ankle length skirt and a corset took perseverance and skill. Like dancing backwards in high heels, everything in life was harder for a woman, thanks to costume issues.

Old Nelly rattled off down the street hung with American flags. She was near the edge of town when the first drops of rain splatted across the windshield. The single wiper swished across the glass. *Whish-Yoo! Whish-Yoo!* Old Nelly's way of starting a conversation.

Whish-Yoo! Just what did she wish for? A quick end to the war and a devoted husband for Katherine. She wanted nothing for herself. She had her memories, a nice home, good friends and a loving granddaughter. What else did she need at this stage of her life?

A drizzle of rain seeped through the window of the door and dribbled down inside the glass. Agnes leaned forward and peered into the gloom. Rain sloshed against the windshield, blurring the images alongside the road, not unlike a night like this when she had followed a suspect through the streets of Paris. Admittedly, it was so many years ago it felt more like a dream than a memory.

Once out of town, the road narrowed as it climbed higher up the cliffs beside the ocean. Like the White Cliffs of Dover, the road along this section of the northern California coast rose and fell high above the ocean.

Agnes flipped on her headlights. She slowed the car, adhering to the 35-mph speed limit set by the government to save fuel and tires.

Not that she would have driven any faster on this crooked road anyway, but it made her smile, thinking how adhering to the speed limit made her a law abiding citizen.

At 6:00 P.M., the sky had already darkened and the rain sluiced down in torrents. A touch of panic crept across Agnes's chest. She swallowed a lump in her throat. *Katherine was right. I should have canceled tonight. What was I thinking?* She pulled the car to the side of the road and stared into the rain. *Should I go home?* She hated to disappoint the boys at the USO, but other local volunteers from Boyles Springs would be there; volunteers who didn't have to risk their life in the pouring rain on a crooked road along the ocean.

A large black Packard roared up the road behind her, honking vehemently. The glare from its headlights lit up Nelly's interior.

"Fool! At the rate he's going, he'll end up in the ocean." Why on earth would someone be in such a hurry on a night like this?

"Well, Nelly old girl. What should we do? Go on to Boyles Springs, or turn around and go back to Newbury?" The idea of curling up with her new cat and a good book appealed to her. She gazed through the rain, squinting at the Packard's tail lights. The pinpricks of light seemed to blink on and off as the vehicle dipped out of sight and appeared again where the road rose up. And then the tail lights stopped, somewhere near Brighton's Landing, similar to the beach where she and Douglas had picnicked that last day before he deployed to the European war zone many years ago.

In spite of his age, when war was declared, the fool had volunteered. Too old for the battlefield, the army loaned him to Britain and put him in charge of training young fliers. An unexpected air raid on an English air field took Douglas's life.

Then, there was John. Determined to exact revenge for his father's death, he enlisted, in spite of having a young wife and baby Katherine. In less time than it took for his first letter to reach home, John joined the thousands of young men who died at Ypres on the Western Front in Belgium, leaving a widow and baby Katherine without a father.

Overhead, tears from the sky matched those flowing down Agnes's face as her heart wrenched at the memories. World War I took both of her boys. Thank God for Katherine, with John's flaming hair, golden brown eyes and sweet nature. She reminded her so often of John.

By all that's holy, I won't let the Germans get away with it again. What am I doing, sitting here in the rain running on in my mind, like some sentimental old fool? Turn the car around and go home before you run off the cliff road and kill yourself. You won't be any good to the war effort dead, nor to anybody else.

Her gaze moved across the black sea. There, far off the coast, a light flashed, barely visible through the mist and rain. And up ahead, the Packard still sat on the beach; its headlights blinked. Once. Twice. Three times.

Agnes gasped. "Call me a suspicious old woman if you want, but that's a Japanese submarine out there signaling to that Packard or my name isn't Agnes Agatha Odboddy. If that's not a spy sitting in that black Packard, waiting to pass off secret information, I'll be a monkey's uncle twice removed."

Now what? Rush back into town and call the authorities? By the time they got back out here, the Packard and the submarine would be long gone. She wasn't exactly equipped to take on a spy ring and an enemy by herself. There was a day she might have given it more thought but the reality was, that time and an additional forty pounds had taken its toll. On the other hand, she wasn't about to let the spy get away with his nefarious doings. She could get closer and record the license number and alert the authorities with vital information. They could apprehend the spy after the fact and she could testify to what she had witnessed.

Agnes clicked off her headlights and released the hand brake, jammed the Ford into gear and chugged down the road, inching her way through the darkness. Anxiety surged through her chest and sharpened her senses. What might happen if they caught her, alone, out there on the beach? She shuddered. Best not even think about that. Her heart pounded and her pulse quickened at the thought of the risk, just like in the old days. Oh, how she had missed the thrill of the chase. Any red-blooded ex-under-cover agent would feel the same, right?

Agnes's Model A rolled up on Brighton's Landing. The rain stopped and from the light of the quarter moon, she could just see a dark shape on the beach. The Packard! From this angle, the submarine was no longer visible. Likely the spy had left his car and was already rowing out in a small boat to deliver his contraband or stolen documents to the Japanese captain.

Agnes opened the door, got out and closed the door without a sound. She drew off her shoes, leaned over and crept toward the Packard, running in short spurts between clumps of ocean grass and driftwood logs blackened by lover's bonfires. A run in her stocking zipped up the back of her legs. *Rats!*

The moon slid behind a cloud, preventing a good view of the Packard's license number. She crept closer. Each breath burned in her throat. Over the past twenty-four years, since she retired as a WWI agent, never had she experienced an adrenalin rush such as swept through her body as she crept toward the Packard. The information she was about to glean would bring a spy ring to its knees. She'd be a national hero. At the very least, she'd get a medal. If she survived to tell about it.

Her chest rattled with short, raspy breaths. She paused. She had to control her excitement. It wouldn't do to rush headlong into the fray and do something foolish and get caught. What would Katherine do without her? *One thousand one, one thousand two...* Her breathing eased. *One thousand three...*

She crept closer. The moon slid out from behind a cloud. The numbers on the license plate were easily visible. 6X2358

Beep!

Agnes's heart lurched. She threw herself face down into the sand. Another signal to the submarine? Or had they seen her?

Tiny shells bit into Agnes's cheek. She spit sand and wiped the back of her hand across her mouth. The door on the Packard creaked. *What am I doing? Am I crazy? If they catch me, I'm dead!*

Agnes closed her eyes. *Yea, though I walk through the valley of the shadow of death, I will fear no evil.*

Psalms. Good to remember, but doubtful the Archangel Michael would be hovering on the beach tonight after she had knowingly put herself under the *shadow of death* on purpose.

Thoughts of home almost made her weep. What was an old woman doing out here, all alone in the dark, sneaking up on murderous spies when she could be in her own bed with her new little cat curled by her? Was there still time to back away and leave before someone got out of the car and shot her?

Best peek at that license once more before she left. Had to memorize it. Was it 6X 2353? No, that wasn't right. She lifted her head and peered at the vehicle. The clouds had passed from the front of the moon. There sat the Packard, quaking and creaking under the light of the moon, the squeak of the springs loud in the stillness. Steam clouded the car windows. Soft moans came from inside the car.

What the Sam Hill? Was that…? It was.

Apparently, whoever was in the Packard wasn't passing secret messages back and forth. Even reaching back into her distant memories, creaking springs and fogged up windows could only mean… "Oh!"

Agnes scooted backwards through the sand. She stood, brushed the twigs and leaves from her skirt and tiptoed back toward her car. Her stockings sagged and her shoes were full of sand. With luck she could creep away and get Old Nelly started unnoticed.

Not far off shore a boat drifted from a fogbank. Fishing poles jutted from its sides and large buckets hung off the back. The engines churned and its running lights blinked until it disappeared into another fogbank.

Guess I'll pass on taking cookies to the USO tonight, go home, turn on the radio and go to bed.

Chapter Two

W hy, Mildred Haggenbottom. What on earth are you doing in the park at this ungodly hour?" Agnes ambled toward the bicycle wheeling toward her, a smile crinkling her cheeks.

The scent of roses from the bushes beside the pathway wafted across the cobbled stones. Agnes put up her hand to stop Mildred's bicycle.

Mildred stepped off and dropped the bicycle to the ground. Several oranges tumbled from a bag in her bicycle basket and rolled across the grass. She staggered, gasping, toward the bench where she flopped down, her chest rising and falling.

"Are you alright?" Agnes squinched her brow. "You look positively tuckered out." She patted Mildred's arm.

"I'm just winded. Not as young as I used to be, dear. Seventy, next month, you know."

"*Huh!* Don't I know it? Wasn't my birthday last March? We're just not as spry as we used to be. Remember WWI? Weren't we a caution? Though I'm perfectly content to be the age I am. Gaining in wisdom and all that claptrap…"

Mildred gazed around the rose garden. "Isn't it lovely here this time of day? I'm on my way home from Wilkey's Market. Had to pick up a quart of milk. Took my last coupon." She took in a deep breath and let it out. "My, the roses are beautiful this year. Look at that one. It's almost the color of your hair."

Agnes's hand flew to the mass of hennaed curls piled on top of her head. She touched the two sterling silver chopsticks stuck crosswise through the thickest part of her bun, a gift from her late husband, Douglas, the day he left for the European front ever so long ago.

A warm glow crept up her neck. She had worn the chopsticks every day for the past twenty-three years, a constant reminder of her betrayal, and an outward sign of penance to Douglas's memory, a concept that not even she could have explained if asked. "At least *my* hair color is natural. Not like that new woman at the knitting circle. What's her name?"

"Sophia Rashmuller?"

"That's the one. She dyes her hair or my name's not Agnes Agatha Odboddy. It's obvious that she's trying to hide her true identity. Most likely, she's a Nazi spy. Why, remember back in 1918? How we caught that guy red-handed stealing supplies from the commissary? Mrs. Rashmuller dyes her hair that same color and—"

"Yes, dear," Mildred nodded. "I believe we've had this conversation a few dozen times before." She squeezed Agnes's hand and smiled. "Here it is, barely twenty years later and the world is at war all over again. And, you're still seeing the same Nazi spies everywhere you turn." She stifled a little snicker. "Agnes, Agnes. You know, people are starting to talk."

Agnes dropped her head and closed her eyes. *She's right. I'm just a foolish old woman.*

"Aggie? I'm sorry. I didn't mean to hurt your... Wait a minute." Mildred glanced at her watch. "It's only 8:30 A.M. What are *you* doing in the park this early? Is everything alright at home? Did you and Katherine quarrel?"

Agnes gazed across the lawn toward the pond. A mother duck with a string of babies paddling behind her, passed from view behind the willow branches dipping into the water's edge. The willow tree swayed in the light breeze, stirring the water with its trailing tendrils. She waved her hand. "Nothing like that. Today is my son, John's, birthday. I come here when I want to feel close to him…I…" A sob caught in her throat. "I used to push him in his perambulator to a park like this when he was a baby. He loved to feed the ducks."

"Oh, Aggie. I'm so sorry. Happy birthday, John," Mildred whispered.

Agnes sat for a minute, her heart full of memories and her thoughts miles away. She pulled a hankie from the neck of her dress and blew her nose. *First, I lost Douglas and then John. Move on Agnes. Ancient history.*

She turned to Mildred and smiled. "So, are you coming to the hospital with me this week? We need more volunteers to roll bandages."

"Agnes, you never cease to amaze me. How do you do it all? Knitting socks for the Red Cross… Well, sort of. At least you try. Then, you work on the paper drives, volunteer at the ration office, serve on the coastal watch, and you still have time to roll bandages?"

"I like to volunteer. It's 1942! This time around, you and I are fighting the war from the home front. I just don't feel that I can do enough for the war effort. All those young men…"

"Don't sell yourself short. You do more than most of us." Mildred chuckled.

"Not like in WWI. Weren't those the best days?" Agnes's smile faded and her cheeks warmed as the reference to 1918 turned her thoughts back to a night in Paris when she was on a secret assignment with a handsome and attractive man who was…not her husband. She dismissed the disturbing memories.

"Isn't tomorrow your day at the watchtower out at the ocean?" Mildred leaned down and picked up the oranges that had rolled from her shopping bag. She laid them on the bench between them.

Agnes shook her head. "I'm at the ration office tomorrow. Albert has me addressing envelopes. I'm at the watchtower later this week. I'm glad the weather's finally warming up. I nearly froze my patooties out there last month. Today, I'm off to the paper drive. I'm meeting Clara at 10:30 A.M. this morning."

"How's the cat doing? Heard anything more about Lilly?"

"It took Ling-Ling about an hour to feel at home. Nothing about Lilly. I'll make a few calls later and see what I can find out, but I don't think there's much we can do for her."

Mildred rubbed her pale cheeks. "I should be going, too. I haven't felt well since the potluck at the church last Tuesday." Her hand trembled as she stood, picked up her bicycle and set the kickstand. "It's my stomach. I feel queasy in my stomach and light-headed for several days."

"You've been sick since last Tuesday? What did you eat?" Agnes dug through her purse, pulled out a peppermint and handed it to Mildred.

"Not much. I ate the lemon tart the new lady brought. You remember. Sophia Rashmuller?"

"You mean the red-headed floozy? Didn't I say she was a spy? Probably a Nazi undercover agent. Anyone with that fakey-colored hair… You know those people pretend to be just like everyone else, but they're not. They sneak around and join churches and clubs and try to fit in with honest folks. You know what they say, *loose lips sink ships*. They'll buddy up to someone and when they hear something important, they tell their Nazi masters."

"Oh, Agnes. There you go again. Everyone you meet isn't a spy. I've probably got the flu, pure and simple. That's all there is to it." Mildred burped. "Excuse me. My stomach… I have to go. I have Chinese plumbers on my roof and—"

"You have what?" Agnes set her purse back on the bench. "What are you talking about? What do you mean; you have Chinese plumbers on the roof?"

"That's not what I said. I said I got some *prize cucumbers* from Rufus, you know, the old man who lives next door?" Mildred chuckled. "Agnes, dear, you get harder of hearing with every birthday."

Agnes peered into Mildred's face. *I know what you said, Mildred. There's nothing wrong with my hearing.* "Are you sure you can ride home alone? You don't look well. I could run and get the Model A and drive you home. We could toss your bike in the rumble seat."

"I'll be fine. Besides, you have your own errands to take care of." Mildred tied her scarf under her chin and climbed onto her bike. "See you later." Leaves, picked up by the breeze whipped around her wheels as she pushed off.

"Guess I'm off, too. So long." Agnes started down the path around the lake.

"Millie is a dear friend," she muttered to herself, "but we don't always see eye-to-eye about affairs regarding the war effort. I'll call Pastor Lickleiter. Maybe he knows something about that red-headed Mrs. Rashmuller. She doesn't fool me. She's a Nazi German spy, or my name's not Agnes Odboddy."

When Agnes arrived home, she hurried into her library and pulled a book from the shelf. *You and Your Garden, the Home Owner's Friend.* She thumbed to the chapter called Poisons Around Your Home: Symptoms and Signs. Her finger ran down the page and stopped on the words: *Cyanide—Symptoms and Signs.*

Headaches, nausea, confusion, shortness of breath (dyspnea), vomiting, elevated blood pressure (hypertension)

Agnes stared at the book. *Good gosh and little fishes! Mildred's been poisoned. Who would have thought?*

Mildred demonstrated all the signs and symptoms: Headaches. Nausea. Confusion. The cyanide had already addled her mind. *Prize cucumbers indeed! I know exactly who poisoned her. That redheaded floozy, Sophia Rashmuller from the First Church of the Evening Star and Everlasting Light Benevolent Society.* Everyone knew that acidic flavors, like lemon tarts, would mask cyanide's bitter taste! "Well, I'm certainly not going to let her get away with it. I couldn't help Lilly. I'll not stand by this time. Not without a fight. Not to my best friend since grade school."

Agnes donned her sweater and hurried out the kitchen door. Poor Mildred. The victim of a mad German killer. Poisoned! Right in the middle of the church potluck and knitting circle.

Clara and the weekly paper drive would have to wait. She had to report the attempted murder immediately. Cyrus Waddlemucker, Chief of the Newbury Police Department would know what to do. He'd keep everything quiet and arrest the spy. Probably wouldn't even put it in the paper, so as not to frighten the local citizens.

As President of the First Church of the Evening Star and Everlasting Light Benevolent Knitting Society, Mildred was the obvious target for an undercover agent. It stood to reason that preventing the boys overseas from receiving their knitted socks would put a considerable cramp in morale. What better way to foul up the production of knitted argyles than to kill the club's president? The ladies would be in such a tizzy dealing with Mildred's death, they likely wouldn't knit a sock for weeks! Morale on the European Front could grind to a halt.

Agnes pushed her bicycle into the rack outside the police department and entered the building. She poked the elevator button. *Come on, come on! Should have taken the stairs.*

The doors slid open. "Good morning, Mrs. Odboddy. Back again?" Jackson, the dark-complexioned elevator boy grinned.

Agnes swooshed into the elevator. *Smarty pants. You'd think I was here every week.*

Jackson reached for the elevator button and paused, his finger hovering over the button. He raised a bushy eyebrow toward her. "You want I should push the button, ma'am, or do you want to?"

"*Humph.* Don't get fresh with me, young man." She nodded toward the button panel. "Do your job! I'll do mine. I have a civic duty to report any and all suspicious activity in our town, and that's exactly what I intend to do. We have a Nazi killer living right in our midst and I won't stand idly by and let her poison my best friend." Agnes's foot tapped the tile floor.

"You're kidding. A Nazi killer, right here in Newbury? Whatever will they think of next? You'd think them Nazis' would have enough folks to kill over in Europe without comin' here and picking on our citizens. You going to report this to Chief Waddlemucker, ma'am?"

"Perhaps this time he'll take me seriously. I know what folks say behind my back and I won't stand for it. No sir, I won't. This time I've got proof."

What proof she possessed was hard to define, other than Mildred's symptoms that somewhat coincided with the symptoms of cyanide poisoning she'd read about in her garden book, but forewarned is forearmed. Dear Mildred's life could very well hang in the balance. If she was right, perhaps there was still time to save her. *If I'm wrong... well, I'm never wrong. Well...mostly never wrong.*

Chief Waddlemucker sat at his desk, puffing on a cigar. As Agnes came through the door, he laid it in the ashtray. "Have a seat, Agnes. What can I do for you?" He gestured toward the chair in front of his desk. A wisp of smoke rose from the cigar and drifted toward the circular fan overhead, then disappeared in the wake of the fan blades.

Agnes covered her mouth and coughed. *Nasty habit, cigars.* She sat, her knees primly together, her handbag perched on her lap. She wrinkled her nose.

"I'm a busy man, Mrs. Odboddy. What brings you in *this time?*" A sigh escaped his lips. He reached for his cigar, took a puff and leaned back in his chair, his hands behind his head.

Now isn't he just the epitome of officialdom? I know darn well he'd sooner have a root canal, than talk to me. Agnes pursed her lips. "I've come to report an attempted murder. I—"

"Indeed! Attempted murder, you say? Well, I think this is the first attempted murder you've reported. So, tell me? Who is trying to murder who...whom?" He waved his hand dismissively and scowled, pulled the cigar from his mouth and blew a perfect smoke ring over his head.

Agnes sniffed. "Before you so rudely interrupted me, I was about to tell you that Sophia Rashmuller has poisoned my dear friend, Mildred Haggenbottom."

Chief Waddlemucker rolled his eyes, crinkled his forehead, and then shook his head. "Just exactly what makes you think Mrs. Rashmuller has poisoned Mrs. Hoggelbottle?"

"Haggenbottom! Mildred Haggenbottom! President of the First Church of the Evening Star and Everlasting Light Benevolent Society! She's been sick since last Tuesday, ever since she ate Mrs. Rashmuller's lemon tart. I'm sure Sophia put cyanide in it. She set one of her tarts on Mildred's plate. I clearly remember her saying, 'I baked this just for you.' And she grinned. Such an evil grin, not unlike how one would suspect a Nazi undercover agent would grin as she poisoned her victim. Poor Mildred has nausea and confusion. All the symptoms of cyanide—"

"Now, hold it!" Chief Waddlemucker stood, holding his hand out like a traffic cop. He circled his desk and hovered over Agnes's chair, forcing her to bend her head back to look him in the face. "I happen to know that Mr. and Mrs. Rashmuller were *polish sausages, pork and beans*, and there's no way—"

"They were what? Polish sausages and pork and beans? What does that mean? I just reported an attempted murder, I wasn't ordering lunch!" Agnes pulled a lace-trimmed hankie from her bosom and blotted the perspiration off her upper lip. *Is everyone being poisoned by that ruthless woman? Now, poor Chief Waddlemucker is showing signs of confusion. Maybe the cyanide wasn't in the lemon tart, after all. Maybe she's put it in the town's drinking water.*

"I didn't say Polish sausages and pork and beans. I said, 'Polish refugees, poor things.' Now, it sounds as if you're the only confused person in this room. Quite frankly, Mrs. Odboddy, you've come to the station almost every week, making wild accusations about just about every good citizen in Newbury. Have you considered professional help?"

Agnes sputtered and threw back her shoulders. "Well, I never!"

"I'm not an expert, but I'm afraid you're suffering from delusions and a persecution complex." Chief Waddlemucker ran his fingers over his mustache and covered his mouth.

He's laughing at me. Agnes jerked to her feet, almost toppling her chair over backwards. "Haven't you read the papers or listened to the radio lately? We are at war, sir, in case you hadn't noticed, and the public is advised to report any suspicious activities. I'm doing my duty. We, at home, are the backbone of this country, fighting from the home front. I thought you should know about a potential Nazi killer."

"Why would a Nazi killer want to harm Mrs. Higglemeyer...er...? Hogglemuller?"

"Haggenbottom..."

"Yes, her. Why would she want to harm her? How would Mrs.... er...umm... How would her death advance the Nazi cause?"

Agnes stood taller and glared at the chief. "Think how much comfort and aid our knitted socks give the boys in uniform. With Mildred dead, we...um...well, how could the ladies keep coming back week after week to...um...knit? Mildred said our socks were a vital contribution to the war effort, and..." Warmth crept up Agnes's neck. She bit her lip. *Socks? Vital contribution? Now I even think I sound like an idiot.* "It doesn't change the fact that Mildred has symptoms of cyanide poisoning. And, she ate the woman's lemon tarts."

Chief Waddlemucker sat back down and leaned his elbows on the desk, made a tent with his fingers, drumming the tips together. "Are any of the other ladies sick?"

"Of course not. I brought my famous chocolate pecan pie with orange glaze, which I must say, cost me dearly in ration stamps for the sugar. Naturally, everyone chose my pie over Mrs. Rashmuller's lemon tarts. Mildred wouldn't have eaten one either, if the woman hadn't practically forced it on her."

"How did you determine the tarts were poisoned? With cyanide, I mean." Chief Waddlemucker raised an eyebrow.

"I suspected the tarts as soon as Mildred told me she was sick. I looked up poisons in my garden book. It said that cyanide is available in multiple gardening products. The symptoms of cyanide poisoning are headaches, nausea and confusion, and...and...shortness of breath, just like Mildred."

"Sounds like the flu. Has Mildred seen a doctor?"

"Well, *er...uh...*I...I couldn't say." *My. It's getting warm in here.* Perspiration trickled between her bosoms. *Could I be wrong about the poison?* Her cheeks were on fire. "Perhaps I should be going. I'm chairwoman for the Newbury paper drive today, you know. They're expecting me..." Agnes stood and hurried toward the door, her back to Chief Waddlemucker.

"Oh, Mrs. Odboddy?"

"Yes?" Agnes's hand was on the doorknob. She turned her head.

"Tell your friend to see a doctor. If she does have any evidence of cyanide poisoning, let me know and then I'll stalk the lawnmower."

Stalk the...? "You'll do what? You'll stalk the lawnmower?"

Chief Waddlemucker sauntered across the room and laid his hand on Agnes's shoulder. "Mrs. Odboddy, my dear. I said, if your friend has any evidence of poisoning, I'd *talk to Mrs. Rashmuller.*" He shoved his hands in his pockets and tipped his head toward her. "Have you considered changing the batteries in your hearing aid?"

The back of Agnes's neck prickled. "I don't wear hearing aids."

"Perhaps you should look into that. Come back anytime, Mrs. Odboddy. You always make my day more interesting when you drop by."

Chapter Three

Yoo-hoo! Clara!" Agnes called as she wheeled her bicycle down Gem Crest Avenue. Across the street, Clara pulled a small wagon piled with newspapers.

Clara turned and waved. "I didn't think you were coming. You're late. I started without you. Really, Agnes, if you're not going get here on time, I should think you might have called."

She's mad. Well, too bad. No way would she tell Clara the reason for her delay was talking to Chief Waddlemucker at the police station. Clara already thought she was a dunderhead.

"I was unavoidably detained." Agnes circled her bicycle around the street until she was even with Clara's wagon. She stepped off and leaned the bicycle against a tree. "Looks like you've already accumulated quite a load. Where's the collection truck?"

Clara gestured down the block. "It's back on Middle Cress Avenue. Several ladies are working that street. This is our block. I've already covered most of it." She pinched up her nose. Her lips drew together in a tight line. "What kept you?"

"It was those Chinese plumbers, you know, the ones that go door to door and tell you they'll fix your roof when you have a leak in your kitchen?"

Clara's left eyebrow hitched up higher on her forehead. "Chinese plumbers? You're crazy. Who are you kidding? Chinese plumbers, indeed. If you don't want to tell me why you're late, just don't." Clara hurried down the street with her cart.

Agnes had to step lively to catch up. "You're right. Maybe they weren't Chinese. Maybe they were…*um*…gypsies. Yes. They probably were gypsies. Anyway, have you checked over on that side of the street yet?" She pointed toward a house with a cream colored flag in the window.

Nearly every house on the block possessed a cream-colored flag with blue stars, representing a family member in the military. Agnes shuddered. Any day, those blue stars could change to gold, to indicate the loss of their loved one.

Clara shook her head. "Just this side of the street."

"I'll run over there and check out the house next door." Agnes stopped at the curb as a Mercedes touring car chugged past.

Clara gazed at the green house. "I don't see anything on the front steps."

"They might not have heard we were coming today. I'll knock and see if they have anything to contribute. I'll meet you at the end of the block." Agnes scurried across the street before Clara could question her tardiness further. *I must still have Chinese plumbers on my mind. And, I don't care how much Mildred denies it. I know what I heard her say…*

The lawn at the green house was full of weeds for lack of care. Agnes strolled up the pathway toward the rickety steps. Several brown-tinged rolled up newspapers lay on the front porch. The place looked as if no one had lived there for ages.

Her gaze drifted to the wooden carved house numbers by the side of the door. 21018, as though it was the date, February 10, 1918. How could she ever forget the date Douglas left for the war zone and she never saw him again?

She knocked.

Silence.

She peeked through the window, careful to avoid the spider web clinging in the corner. The house looked empty. She stooped and picked up the old newspapers on the faded doormat. *I'll just take these two with me.* She scuttled down the steps and hurried down the street.

Clara waited on the corner with the wagon. "Any luck?" She jerked her head toward the empty house.

"Just these two old newspapers. I guess no one lives there now." Agnes tossed the newspapers on top of the stack. "This is all we can carry this load, anyway. Should we head back to the truck? Katherine's driving today."

"We might as well." Clara glanced at her wristwatch. "We're just about done. It's almost noon." She started down the sidewalk at a fast clip.

Agnes hurried to her side. Katherine had promised to meet her for lunch. *She probably made sandwiches with the liverwurst I bought the other day. Can't wait for the day when we can have ham sandwiches again.* Just thinking about ham sandwiches and hamburgers sizzling on the patio grill made her mouth water.

"And, Agnes…" Clara's voice chilled Agnes's blood.

"If you can't be more prompt, perhaps you shouldn't commit to the paper drive. We have enough to worry about without waiting around for you."

Chapter Four

Katherine turned at the sound of a footstep. Chubby, lovable, Myrtle stood in the doorway leading into the shampoo room, rubbing up and down her arm. Worry lines creased her forehead.

"Oh. Myrtle! You startled me. I thought you went to the bank. What's wrong? You look worried." Katherine pulled a shampoo bottle from the top shelf.

"I didn't want to trouble you, but I have to tell you. I've been trying to think how I can bring in some extra income. If something doesn't change soon, I'll have to close the beauty shop." Her bottom lip trembled as tears glistened in her eyes.

"You know I'll do whatever I can to help." Katherine's shampoo bottle hovered over a container in the sink, where the last drop drained into the larger bottle. "Do you want me to work extra hours?" *As if I don't have enough on my mind.*

Life was supposed to be easier here in Newbury, away from Sacramento. Away from the memories of Stephen everywhere she looked. Nothing had changed. Just getting through the day drained all her strength. Thanks to Grandmother's urging, she had just returned from *doing her part* and driving the paper drive truck this morning. As if losing her fiancé wasn't giving enough to the war effort. Must she give more? Apparently so!

Myrtle continued to whine about the rent and taxes with an, *I-knew-I-could-count-on-you* look on her face. "Bernard Whistlemeyer called this morning. His wife left him last week. Poor man. I couldn't help but feel sorry for him."

Katherine screwed the cap back on the shampoo bottle and set it on the shelf over the sink. "I'm sorry to hear that. Please don't ask me to go out with him on a pity date. I'm willing to help out, but not that way."

"Bernard's wife was doing all of his client's hair and makeup at their establishment. Now that she's gone, he asked if our shop could take over. I'll even split the income with you fifty-fifty if you'll do it. He only has one or two clients a week, maybe three. You'd have to go to his place in the evenings, though, to do the work. What do you say?"

"I don't see why not. A couple nights a week should be okay. Why can't the customers come here instead of me going there?" *Why does the name Whistlemeyer sound so familiar? Photographer? Maybe a wedding consultant.*

"*Um...* Is that the phone I hear? Excuse me." Myrtle shot out of the shampoo room like she'd been snake-bit. She disappeared into her office and slammed the door.

So now, on top of working all day and volunteering for the Recycling Center, she'd spend another couple of evenings every week doing hair and makeup. She wanted to help Myrtle and if she was willing to split the fee fifty-fifty, what was the harm? *I can start saving for my own place. As much as I love Grandmother, I can't live with her forever.*

Katherine dragged her weary body out of the salon at 5:30 P.M., achy feet and stuffy-headed from permanent wave fumes. She slid into her old Chevy and started the engine.

About half-way home, she passed a building she'd seen hundreds of times. This time, a sign in the lawn caught her attention. She slammed on the brakes and the Chevy screeched to a stop. Katherine stared at the building. "I'll be a ring-tailed raccoon."

A big black Packard pulled up behind her. *Aaoogaa!*

Katherine turned as the big car pulled around from behind and passed her car.

The woman behind the wheel made a vigorous hand gesture.

How patriotic! Katherine's gaze jerked back to the pale beige stucco building. Pink plastic flamingos perched on each side of a bubbling fountain near the front entrance. A neon sign blinked on the lawn:

Whistlemeyer Family Mortuary
Bernard Whistlemeyer—Proprietor

Katherine gasped. *Hair dressing! Makeup!* At a mortuary? That's the extra work Myrtle wanted her to do? She drove the rest of the way home in a daze.

Yellow roses lined the driveway alongside Grandmother's bungalow. Katherine parked the Chevy, gathered her belongings and entered the house through the back door. "Grandma. I'm home."

Grandmother sat on the sofa with a blue skirt lying in her lap. Mrs. Roosevelt's voice blared from the radio. "In here, dear. I'm listening to Mrs. Roosevelt's weekly radio program." She twisted the dial and turned down the volume. Mrs. Roosevelt's voice lowered to a mumble.

"What wrong with your skirt. Did the hem come out?" Katherine sighed, tossed her purse and sweater on the floor and flopped into the maroon flowered sofa chair.

"I'm shortening my skirts. They're wearing them a little shorter this year. Back in the day, when I worked for the government, if a lady's skirt was more than an inch above her ankle, she was considered *fast*. Now, with the war shortages, they've shortened the hemlines all the way up to the knee to save material. If I want to stay fashionable, I'll have to alter all my hems, although I'm not at all convinced a woman of my age should show off so much of her limbs."

Katherine smiled. "Grandma, you're the bee's knees, no pun intended. Everything you do for the war effort and you still manage to keep up with the latest fashions."

"Oh, bother! It's easy enough if you look through the fashion magazines once in a while. Lucky for me, I have a closet full of blouses already, or I'd have to wear dickies under my jackets. As it is, I feel guilty whenever I wear my beige blouse with the puffy sleeves. The way folks look at me, you'd think I'd cut a hole from a soldier's parachute to make it."

"Nobody makes silk blouses and slips this year. Every scrap goes to the military for parachutes." Katherine kicked off her shoes and drew her legs under her. She picked up the *Ladies' Home Journal* and thumbed through it. Near the center, Katherine folded the magazine and held it up, displaying an article about Mrs. Eleanor Roosevelt's work with the Red Cross.

"You can't turn on the radio or open a magazine without seeing or hearing from Mrs. Roosevelt. You'd think she was the President."

Agnes glanced up from her sewing and nodded. "She's quite in demand these days. Before you tell me about your day, are you hungry? I made some split pea soup. It's still hot on the back of the stove."

"Were you able to buy ham hocks?"

"Oh, no. I used a little fat back and an onion, and I found a sale on cheese down at the green-grocer. I can make you a sandwich to go with the soup." Agnes laid her skirt on the edge of the sofa and stuck the needle into the doily pinned to the padded arm.

"Don't get up! I'll get something later." Katherine frowned, ran her hand through her auburn hair and flipped it over her shoulder.

"You look upset. What's wrong?"

"Myrtle asked me if I could do some extra work for the shop and I volunteered before I knew what she had in mind."

Agnes turned toward Katherine. A faint smile crossed her lips. Her eyes glowed with a gentle expression of love. "That's nice, dear. So, what's the problem?"

Katherine returned the smile. *No matter what goes wrong at the shop, I can always count on Grandma.* "Just wait until you hear. She wants me to do the hair and makeup down at Whistlemeyer's Mortuary! What do you think of that?"

Grandmother's eyes opened wide. "Really? How exciting. I always envied those ladies who made up the bodies. Can I come down some day and watch? I don't suppose he'd let you watch the embalming too, would he?"

Katherine put her hands over her ears. "Grandma, really! You can't be serious. Or are you just trying to jolly me into feeling better? It's not funny. Imagine. Me? Putting makeup on a dead person? Oh, I can't even think about this right now. I'm going to my room and read for a while." She flung herself out of the chair and dashed toward the kitchen door. "Do you want anything before I go?"

"You run on. Help yourself to whatever you want. I've already eaten. I was going to write to your mother tonight. Do you want to tuck in a letter before I seal it up? I'd like to get my three cents worth." Agnes shook her head. "Stamps are dear these days. They've raised the price twice already this year. Just the cost of three stamps and I could buy a whole loaf of bread. I suspect the government is financing the war on the backs of us citizens."

"Go ahead and mail your letter. I wrote to mother yesterday. I don't have anything new to tell her, anyway."

"You could tell her you're going to start putting makeup on the dead ladies down at Whistlemeyer's." Agnes winked and grinned.

"That's just it, Grandma. It's not just the ladies." Katherine put her hand on the kitchen door jamb. "If they send the boys home to be buried, I'll have to put makeup on them, too." Big tears puddled in her eyes. She hurried into the kitchen. *No one even got a chance to put makeup on my Stephen, there in Pearl Harbor.*

"Oh, Katherine. I'm sorry. I didn't think…"

Katherine picked up the phone in the kitchen, stuck her finger in the round faceplate and turned the dial in a circular motion. MU3-4114. The phone rang three long and a short jangle, the signal for the Nesbitt residence.

"Hello? Myrtle speaking."

"Really, Myrtle? Dead people? You want me to put makeup on dead people? You might have told me what was involved before you got me to agree."

"*Uh*—oh. Hi, Katherine. Yes, *um*…you're right. I should have mentioned it. But, I was afraid if I told you, you'd refuse and I so desperately need the money. Please say you'll do it."

"Why don't you do it? You're as good a hairdresser as I am. *Humph!*"

"I just couldn't do it. Dead bodies? I'd be too scared. You know I have a nervous condition."

"Nervous condition, my Aunt Fanny! But, it's okay for me to do it?"

"Pleeeeeze! Say you'll do it. For me? I helped you move in with your grandmother."

Oh, sure, time for the guilt trip. "Alright. I'll give it a try. But, if it's just too creepy…" Katherine sighed. "The things I do for you. You're going to owe me a big favor."

"Thank you, thank you. You're a peach. Anything you say. I'll babysit your puppy."

"I don't have a puppy." The telephone cord knotted as Katherine moved toward the icebox. She turned and gave the cord a shake, untwisting the knot. She opened the icebox door and peered inside. *The ice man should have delivered today.* She pulled out the hunk of cheese.

"Weren't you going to take one of my puppies? I still need to find homes for two."

"Don't even start with me, Myrtle. You're already on thin ice. I had never considered taking one of your puppies and you know it! Besides, Grandmother just brought home a cat." She glanced toward the box beside the stove where Ling-Ling lay curled in a ball.

"Alright. Thanks for agreeing to do the…you know. I gotta go. See you tomorrow?"

"Good bye." Katherine untwisted the remaining kinks in the cord and hung up the phone. As she turned toward her bedroom, it rang three short rings, the signal for their residence.

"Hello? Odboddy residence."

"*Ahem... Um...* May I speak to Mrs. Odboddy."

"Grandmother. It's for you." Katherine leaned into the living room and held out the phone.

Agnes put the phone to her ear. "Hello? This is Mrs. Odboddy." She listened for a minute and then snapped her fingers, getting Katherine's attention. "Hold on. You've got the wrong Odboddy. I'm Mrs. Odboddy. You want to speak to my granddaughter, Miss Odboddy." She handed the phone back to Katherine and whispered, "Mr. Whistlemeyer, from the *you-know-where*." Katherine's hand trembled as she reached for the phone. "This is Katherine."

"Miss Odboddy? Myrtle tells me you've agreed to work with us here at the mortuary. I can't tell you how pleased I am to hear it. I just called to tell you that, sadly, Mr. Clyde Hoffelmeister has taken a rather serious tumble off the roof and he's...well, to put it bluntly, he didn't live to tell about it. *Uh*...If it's not inconvenient, we need your services tomorrow evening."

Chapter Five

*A*gnes stabbed the silver chopsticks into her mass of curls, stepped back and glared at her reflection in the bedroom mirror. *Not bad for an old broad.* She ran her fingers over the curving lines beside her mouth. *Laugh lines.* She'd had them for years, long before anyone ever called them *wrinkles.* She pulled her shoulders back and turned sideways to view her profile, then pulled down the bottom of her jacket. *I'm still a fine figure of a woman, if I do say so myself.*

With a quick glance at her watch, she grabbed her lunch sack and two shopping bags, and then scurried through the kitchen door into the garage where her bike leaned against the wall. The wire pocket beside the back tire was just the right size to hold her lunch and the folded bags.

On nearby shelves, she stored jars of tomatoes, cabbage, beets, dill and bread and butter pickles, applesauce made from the tree in the back yard, plus two kinds of jam. *Fruits of my labor.* The sight of the colorful fruits and vegetables from the Victory Garden always made her proud. At times, she'd resist opening a jar of tomatoes or cucumbers because it was too pretty. She turned the label on a small jar of fig jam. *Summer—1940.*

We really must eat this jam before it goes bad.

According to the newspapers, every concerned citizen had a Victory Garden. Even the children from the local eighth grade class volunteered after school to tend the Newbury City Park garden and sold vegetables at the Farmers' Market on Saturday. Not only did it offer vegetables at reduced prices to the war widows, it conserved food needed for the troops overseas. The money earned was earmarked for the eighth grade year-end class field trip to San Francisco.

Agnes's canned vegetables brought to mind last week's movie newsreel showing a garden in front of the Andrew Carnegie mansion in New York. If Mrs. Carnegie could have a garden in her front yard, there was no reason every citizen shouldn't have one, too. In fact, it was downright unpatriotic these days if you had a lawn and shrubs in the front yard instead of tomato and squash vines. According to a recent Saturday Evening Post article, even Mrs. Roosevelt had planted zucchinis in the White House Rose Garden.

Wheeling her bike through the side yard, Agnes pedaled down the street. Albert Finklebaum, manager of the Ration Book Office, had called last night to ask if she could work extra hours at the Ration Office, mailing out emergency ration books this morning. Working at the office was not very high on her list of favorite past times, but war was *H-E-double toothpicks* and somebody had to do it.

This was supposed to be her morning at the Ladies Benevolent Society at the First Church of the Evening Star and Everlasting Light. *I should have called Mildred to let her know that I wasn't coming today.* I'll get in trouble with her next, for not calling. Agnes tried to push last week's little episode at knitting circle from her mind.

After lunch, when Sophia practically forced Mildred to eat her lemon tart, even though, given a choice, she would have chosen Agnes's pecan pie, Mildred taught the ladies a new cable stitch for the tops of their argyle socks. Agnes couldn't quite get it right. When Mildred insisted Agnes should pull out the stitches and do them again, Agnes had spouted some colorful language, tossed the socks on the floor and stomped out. *Not that I have a temper. No, not I!*

She pedaled faster down the street. *People just go out of their way to rile me.*

Mildred had followed her into the restroom. "What's wrong with you? Stop being such a cantankerous old biddie!"

"I'm not cantankerous. I'm…high strung." Agnes lifted her nose, crossed her arms and tapped her foot.

"My stars! High strung? You're acting like a puling brat and you know it. Now, get back in there and pull out those stitches. Edith Braithwaite can't knit her way out of a paper bag and she figured out the stitch. If she can do it, you can too." Agnes had returned to the whispers of the knitting circle, mastered the stitch and left early.

Agnes leaned into the handlebars and pushed up the hill behind the grocery store, a new route she'd found to the Ration Office, making the trip several blocks shorter. They wouldn't miss her at the knitting circle. *Let 'em think I'm still having a tizzy-fit over the socks. Maybe I am.*

Agnes pulled up her chair across from May Ellen. The table stacked high with ration books, supplies and lists of addresses. She glanced at the clock. 8:30 A.M. The stacks of envelopes needed to be stuffed, addressed, stamped and mailed to Greenbrier, a coastal town thirty miles north, before their shift ended at noon.

She nodded to May Ellen, then bent her head to tackle the first envelope. Tonight, she'd likely dream about stamps armed with ball point pens marching across fields of ration books.

The whole concept of rationing was a pain in the patooties. So much was needed to feed and clothe the troops. With shortages on food, clothing and gasoline, rationing was the only way for everyone to get their fair share and discourage hoarding or grocery store arguments. *I hate it, but I'll do my part.* We're all doing our part to fight the war from the home front.

The only compensation for the finger cramps and back aches at the end of the shift, was the knowledge that in several days, Greenbrier wives would line up at their local markets, with this month's coupon books in hand. And, for a few days, they might have a variety of food to cook and something other than *meatless meals* on their tables.

"Agnes. How's Katherine?" May Ellen, her Hispanic friend slid the tray of envelopes off to the side of her work space. "She did my hair last week and I must say she looked a little down. Everything alright?"

Agnes laid down her pen and flexed her fingers. "She's just dandy. Couldn't be better. She was probably thinking about her birthday. She'll be twenty-six next week. You know, none of us likes to get a year older, no matter how young we are. I wish I could throw her a party."

"*Huh!* When was the last time we could afford to have a dinner party for guests? Even chicken and hamburger are too dear these days. Never mind steak!"

"Isn't that the truth?" Agnes leaned into her stack of envelopes, addressed three more and crossed them off the list. She raised her head and caught May Ellen's eye. "Last year, on her birthday, my friend, Mildred, and Katherine's boss and her family came over to help us celebrate. We barbecued steaks. Imagine! Beef steaks for everyone, and, strawberry shortcake for dessert."

"I haven't had a steak since they declared war last December, what with the high cost and the number of coupons needed to buy one." May Ellen tossed her dark braids over her shoulders.

"We don't have much choice of meat these days, for sure, with all the best cuts going to feed the troops." *They sell us all the leftovers. Liver, kidneys, tongue, brains and oxtails. Yuck!* "I'm so tired of kidneys and liver."

"What I'd give for a good barbecue steak!" May Ellen sighed.

Agnes smiled. "I just remembered a funny story about steaks, I heard last week at knitting circle. You should join us some time. We have a lot of fun."

May Ellen laid down her pen and stretched. "I could use a good laugh about now." She leaned back in her chair.

"It seems this lady had pushed her baby to the market in his perambulator. She had saved her ration coupons for several months and scrimped and saved her money in order to buy a couple of steaks to celebrate her mother's birthday. She even talked the butcher into saving several for her.

"She placed the steaks and other groceries in the baby's buggy. On the way home, she stopped at the park to chat with a friend. Apparently, her baby threw the steaks out of the buggy while her back was turned. She didn't even notice until they got home."

Agnes chuckled. "I don't know why I'm laughing. The poor woman must have been horrified at the loss of the steaks."

"I guess it's funny because it didn't happen to you." May Ellen glanced up as Albert stepped out of his office.

"Agnes?" He waggled his finger. "Can I have a word, please?"

Agnes started. *Aren't we allowed to laugh? We're volunteers, after all.*

May Ellen bowed her head and addressed an envelope, then grabbed a ration book and stuffed it in.

Agnes stood, shoved in her chair, strode across the room and entered Albert's office.

The office door closed with a bang. He ran a finger over his pencil thin mustache, shoved back his shirtsleeves and sat behind his desk. "Have a seat, Agnes."

Agnes wrung her hands and glanced at the shelves behind Albert's desk. Canvas-covered binders with papers bulging from the tops sat amidst tarnished golf trophies with lettering scrawled across the bottom. The largest trophy read, *Albert Finklebaum, Summer Gold Tournament—1937.*

So, the old bird plays golf. She had never considered Albert's personal life outside of the office. For all she knew, he could have a wife and six kids. Agnes smiled and relaxed. "You wanted to see me? I'm not aware—"

"I'll just take a moment of your time. I want you to know that you are one of our most productive and valued volunteers. You're always on time and a diligent worker. I wish all the ladies were as reliable. Something has come up and I immediately thought of you, but it may require more of your time. Are you interested?"

"Just what would it entail? I do have other obligations that might prevent—"

"It wouldn't be every week. Perhaps it wouldn't interfere with your other duties. Maybe just one or two extra days a month, like today. We needed extra help because the ration books need to be mailed to Greenbrier this evening for delivery tomorrow."

Agnes's gaze followed his hand as he twirled the little gold golf ball cufflink on his sleeve.

"I suppose I could work an extra day from time to time. I'd have to check my schedule."

"It would be a great boon to the war effort, Agnes. You'd be responsible for all the books going to our local Newbury citizens. Now, wouldn't you like to help your own friends and neighbors receive their ration books in a timely manner?"

"Of course, but I thought another town sent the Newbury's ration books."

"You're right. Ordinarily, a ration office doesn't distribute books in its own town, but since our workload is smaller than some others, and due to an unexpected office closure in central California, Sacramento reassigned distribution of Newbury's books to us.

"I was asked to assign this task to a worker with impeccable work ethics—one who could be trusted beyond question, due to confidentiality issues. I immediately thought of you." Albert folded his arms across his ample belly. He flashed his, it's-a-thankless-job smile. "I know you can handle it."

Agnes's cheeks warmed at the unexpected praise. More often, people called her names behind her back and pretended shock at her colorful language. Here Albert was, telling her how wonderful she was. Her heart swelled. After such praise, she would agree to carry secret messages into Poland for the CIA...again...despite her advanced age.

Agnes wiggled in her seat like a stroked puppy, straightened her back and looked into Albert's dark eyes. "How can I decline a request to do my duty when my country so desperately needs me? It reminds me of the time in World War I when the colonel asked me to volunteer—"

"Yes, yes, you've mentioned that before. Now, I'll give you the list of local addresses and you can start working on them right away." Albert unlocked his top desk drawer and pulled out a sheaf of papers fastened with a paper clip. He handed it across the desk.

Agnes strutted back to the table, grinned at May Ellen and sat down. "He just gave me another assignment."

May Ellen made a silent *O* with her mouth and returned to her work.

Agnes scanned through the alphabetical list of local residents, followed by their addresses. She flipped through the fifty-odd pages, stopped at the *H*'s and scanned through the list until she found Mildred's name. Her gaze stopped momentarily as she reached several more familiar names under the *B*'s and *L*'s; ladies from her sewing circle. She found her name listed under the *O*'s. *Yep! Everyone's name and address is right here in black and white.*

A shiver crept down her spine. Now that she thought about it, she wasn't sure she liked the idea of the government passing around a list of names and addresses of every Newbury citizen to any *willy-nilly* government office volunteer. Next thing you know, they could be cataloging phone numbers and listening in on conversations. She smiled. *Nonsense! Don't be ridiculous, Agnes, This is the USA, not Nazi Germany. That would never happen in the next fifty years. We have a Constitutional Right to Privacy, right?*

She flipped the list back to the *A*'s, grabbed an envelope and began to write. Ableman, Abbott, Albion, and on and on until cramps in her hand forced her to put down the pen and flex her fingers. The stack of envelopes rose higher as she addressed each envelope, stuffed in the coupon book, and checked the name off the list.

Sometime after her mid-morning break, almost reaching the last of the *B*'s, she scrawled the next name across the envelope *Thomas Brendall*. Her hand poised in midair as she glanced at the address. *21018 Gem Crest Avenue, Newbury, CA.*

Gem Crest Avenue? Wasn't that the street where she and Clara collected papers yesterday morning? 21018. The vacant house with the number like February 10, the day Douglas left for Europe? She clearly recalled the green house with newspapers on the front porch! A shiver ran a foot race up her backbone, played hopscotch up her neck, and set the silver chopsticks in her hennaed hair atwitter.

Why are we sending a ration book to an empty house? Perhaps the government didn't know it was empty. How would they? They'd have to cross-reference every person that moved or died against the address lists—an impossible task. No way in a hundred years would the government ever figure out a way to calculate such detailed information about each household.

Ration books were likely sent to empty houses all the time. So, then, what happened to them? The mailman should know the house was empty. Maybe he sent back the books as undeliverable. But, if that was the case, shouldn't the name be crossed off next month's list? Or, did the coupon book sit in the mailbox or on the porch, and gather dust?

Surely she would have noticed if ration books were lying about under the mailbox on the porch. Agnes tapped the pen on her lips. Or… were they delivered and picked up later that day by someone else? Someone who had no business…

Agnes's heart did a double-back somersault. Another shiver raced up her spine. Everyone suffered from a shortage of goods. With rationed items so dear, such as meat, sugar, even milk for the children, and shoes, tires, gasoline… Even the most upstanding citizen, running across an unclaimed ration book might consider it a windfall.

For that matter, suppose a dishonest person had put some thought into the situation and went from house to house after dark, gleaning ration books like fallen wheat from unattended mailboxes?

Agnes's heart pounded as she glanced around the office. Had any of her coworkers noticed the *empty house* versus *ration book* situation? Of course not! They were all addressing books for Greenbrier, twenty miles east. They had no idea that books were going to empty houses.

Everyone knew about the Black Market. It was something decent folks whispered about behind closed doors and conspiratorial fingers. Wasn't she, Agnes Odboddy, upstanding citizen and almost regular church-goer, guilty of seeking a tire coupon several months ago when her car blew out two tires after running over broken glass? With her weekly travels to the Boyles Springs USO and the poor condition of the country roads, she had already purchased her five allotted tires and used up the ration coupons. She wasn't entitled to buy another tire for the duration of the war. Volunteering at the USO didn't qualify for the special permit required to purchase extra tires.

Hadn't she paid June Marie Millpond a whopping eight dollars for one of her tire coupons? *Does that make me guilty of buying on the Black Market? I still had to buy the tire!* Without the coupon, her car would have sat in the garage for the duration of the war. She already sacrificed her allotted weekly four gallons of gas to drive to the USO in Boyles Springs. She rode her bike everywhere around town now that the weather was getting better, but what about next winter? Perhaps the rain and cold would force her to give up volunteering at the USO. Rationing brought all kinds of unintended consequences.

Think of it. The desire for sugar, coffee, leather shoes and tires had made the Black Market a viable industry, right here in Newbury. What was the world coming to when decent citizens—

"Agnes?"

Agnes jumped, her heart pummeling her chest like a punching bag at the end of a boxer's glove. She pulled an envelope over the list of names and grabbed a pen. "Yes? What can I do for you?"

It took all of her concentration to keep a guilty look off her face. Should she mention her discovery of the ration books going to empty houses? She opened her mouth to speak and then closed it. Perhaps she should discuss it with Katherine or Mildred before she said anything to her manager.

Albert walked toward her table. "Agnes, how's your perfect billy-bong?"

Agnes's hand flew to her mouth. She glanced from left to right. *Is he getting fresh?* "Excuse me?"

"I said, how's the project coming along?"

Chinese plumbers! Sausages and pork and beans! And now perfect billy-bongs? Maybe I do need a hearing aid.

Hearing aid or no hearing aid, it didn't change her discovery of a Black Market operation in Newbury, and she was *squack* in the middle of it.

Chapter Six

"I'll wash tonight and you dry, Grandma." Katherine sloshed hot water into the dishpan, added soap chips and stirred the water. "Grandma. What's troubling you? You haven't said three words since I got home. You're usually chattering like a chipmunk the minute you walk in the door."

"*Huh*? Oh, sorry, dear." Grandma pulled an embroidered tea towel from the drawer and swiped it furiously around a plate, front and back, and set it on the counter. "Something came up at the ration office. I'm trying to decide what to do. You know how folks think that I'm crazy—that I see conspiracies everywhere? Well, this time, I'm not saying a word until I'm sure." Grandmother pursed her lips and twisted her thumb and forefinger in front of her mouth.

"Perhaps you'd best tell me what it's all about. Maybe I can help you decide if something is wrong or it's all in your—"

"Katherine!" Grandma dried a glass and two cups and slid them into the cupboard.

"You brought it up. I was just saying… Tell me what's on your mind." *I should say, what is it this time?* Finishing the last dish, Katherine dumped the dishpan into the sink. Water swirled and gurgled down the drain. She wrung out the dishrag and laid it across the faucet. "Shall I make some tea? There's only enough coffee left in the jar for breakfast."

Grandma nodded. "Put it on the list. I'm going to Wilkey's Market in the morning. How much more do we have to sacrifice? First they ration the meat and sugar and now our coffee?" The color rose in her cheeks.

Katherine smiled. Rationing Grandma's coffee was the hardest concession she had made for the war effort. She'd sooner give up her laced corset than her precious coffee. "It does make our one cup each morning special. We never appreciate things until they're gone." Katherine filled the tea kettle and turned to face Grandmother. "So, will you join me with a cup of tea, or pass?"

"Sounds wonderful, dear."

Katherine set the kettle on the stove, struck a match and put it under the burner. She flipped the gas lever on the chrome bar on the stove front. A blue flame whooshed and then flickered lower as she turned the knob. Katherine tossed the match into a tin can next to the salt and pepper shakers. "Now, tell me. What's the problem?" She pulled a chair from under the table and sat.

"You'll probably think I'm being silly to worry, but today I addressed a ration book to a house here in town that I happen to know is deserted." Grandma folded her hands on the table. She glanced down at Ling Ling, batting at paper clip under the table.

"I don't understand. About the books and the empty house, I mean." *If it wasn't for the blue veins across the back of Grandma's hands, I'd never even think about how old she is.*

"Yesterday, Clara and I were collecting papers on Gem Crest Street. This one particular house was deserted. The house number was the same as the date Douglas went overseas. Two-ten-eighteen. Today I addressed a ration book to 21018 Gem Crest Street. So, I added two and two and came up with six!

So, what's the big issue? "I don't think I understand…"

"Don't you see? We're sending ration books to empty houses all over town. I've discovered a Black Market cover-up! With so many men overseas, there could be dozens, maybe hundreds of empty houses. Someone must be collecting the books after dark and selling the—"

"This all sounds a bit far-fetched, Grandma. Don't you think the government knows what it's doing? I don't think they would allow such illegal dealings."

Grandmother shook her head. "Listen. Maybe they don't even know. Those books will be delivered tomorrow and I'll bet someone picks them up tomorrow night. If they're not selling the coupons, what else would they be doing with them? This time, I'm not imagining things." She pulled her hands from her lap and waved them across the table.

"I see. If you feel that strongly about it, you should talk to Chief Waddlemucker. He'll know what to do."

"*Humph!* I've talked to him till I'm blue in the face. He's made up his mind that anything I say is crazy before I walk through the door. He never believes me."

"But you said this time is different." The teakettle whistled. Katherine poured boiling water into a teapot, added the tea ball filled with loose tea and set the pot on the table. "Do you want sugar?"

Grandmother stood, opened the icebox and brought the jar of milk to the table. "Just a little milk, this time. I'll save the sugar for the USO cookies next week. They're all such nice young men. Surely, you'd find…"

"Stop!" *How many times…? Why can't she understand…?* Katherine swallowed the bitter taste in her mouth. She put up her hand. "How many times must I explain, Grandma?" Tears prickled her eyes. "I don't want some *nice* boy who'll go off to war and get killed. I can't go through that again. Why do you keep pestering me about it?" Katherine blinked.

Grandmother ducked her head. "It's just that I want you to be happy."

"It's not your place to decide what makes me happy, Grandma. Working at the salon and living here is all I can manage right now. When the boys come home, I'll think about it, but not now."

Grandma's face crumpled. "I didn't mean to upset you, *Punkin'*."

Her shoulders sagged.

"And, I didn't mean to be so persnickety. I know you mean well. Let's not talk about it, alright?" Katherine swept her hand across her cheeks and sniffed. *Here I go again. I was so determined not to cry this time.* Her gaze moved to the picture of Stephen on the buffet. *Maybe I should put that picture away. Every morning...* Katherine turned back to Grandma.

Grandma swirled the teapot and filled Katherine's mug and then filled her own. She sighed. "So, you think I should tell Chief Waddlemucker about the ration books?"

Katherine forced a smile. "If you're so concerned about them, I would. You'll just worry if you don't tell someone."

"You're right. Tomorrow morning, I'll go back down to the police station. He'll do one of two things. Listen and do something about it, or call the paddy-wagon and have me hauled away to the looney bin. If I'm not back by the time you get home, call out the dogs."

Chapter Seven

A gnes pushed a tiny metal grocery cart through the aisles of Wilkey's Market, past a tall glassed-in cooler displaying cartons of eggs. *Sixty-six cents a dozen? Plus a precious red ration stamp? That's highway robbery!*

City limits or not, she was bound and determined to get a couple of chickens and turn them loose in the back yard, next to the cabbages. They could eat the bugs off the vegetables in the Victory Garden. With luck, she'd have fewer bugs and a couple of eggs every week. Why hadn't she thought of this sooner?

She moved down the aisle past the magazine rack and glanced at the picture of President Roosevelt on the cover of Saturday Evening Post. *I love the man but don't understand why he sent my Japanese friend away.* She shook her head.

Nearing the coffee grinder, she checked her coupon book. Yes, there was one coffee stamp still clinging to the binding. Since the Japanese invasion of Manila, coffee and sugar were nearly impossible to bring onto the mainland, causing the most distressing rationing. One pound of coffee every six weeks per adult. Wasn't cruel and unusual punishment banned by the Constitution or the Bill or Rights or something? Thank goodness, now that Katherine lived with her, they could purchase two pounds every six weeks. *Ooh, wouldn't I like to wring the scrawny neck of whoever in the White House makes me suffer so.*

As she approached the coffee section, the delightful aroma of freshly ground coffee created a symphony in her mouth. Next to the large red grinder sat a glass bin full of dark brown beans. She moved the silver scoop under the spout and pulled the lever. Beans tumbled out. She shoved the lever back and then dumped the beans into the top of the coffee grinder, then replaced the scoop under the spout and cranked the side handle.

Miniscule grains of ground coffee spilled out like chocolate sand. Agnes held a brown paper bag carefully beneath the spout, lest she lose even a grain, closed her eyes and imagined fresh ground coffee tomorrow morning.

The ground coffee bag tipped the scales to just under a pound. At seventy-four cents a pound, that would cost just about seventy cents! Incredible! Price gouging! *My! What we have to pay to indulge our guilty pleasures.*

A pound of flour, margarine, a pound of potatoes, six oranges, three cans of Campbell's tomato soup, a dozen eggs and a quart of milk completed her shopping. Agnes rolled her cart to the check stand and laid her groceries and shopping bags on the counter. "Mrs. Wilkey? How are you today?"

"Fine, thank you. Yourself?" Mrs. Wilkey weighed the coffee, potatoes and oranges. She punched buttons on the cash register and pulled the register handle after each entry. "I'll need your coupons for the coffee, sugar, potatoes and oranges." She turned to her son, stacking cans of peaches into a pyramid on a nearby counter. "George, come and give a hand."

George stepped up to the counter and loaded the groceries into Agnes's fishnet shopping bags.

Agnes handed Mrs. Wilkey her ration book. "What news do you hear from your other…?" Agnes sucked in her breath as her gaze fell on Mrs. Wilkey's left sleeve. Only this minute did she notice the black armband around her upper arm!

She turned toward George, shoving items into her bags. An identical black armband circled his arm. "Oh, George. Your older brother?"

Mrs. Wilkey nodded. Her mouth trembled. She lifted her chin and punched in the last item. "That will be $3.26 please, and I'll remove your ration coupons." She lowered her eyes.

A chill trudged through Agnes's stomach. *One more lost son. When will it end?* She gave Mrs. Wilkey a five dollar bill.

Mrs. Wilkey laid the bill on the register and tore the appropriate colored coupons from the ration book.

"Groceries are dear these days, aren't they? I didn't even buy any meat. I'm thinking of getting some chickens." Agnes's gaze leapt between Mrs. Wilkey's bloodshot eyes and the pimples on George's nose. "Then I won't need to buy eggs. Of course, I'd buy everything else here…" Agnes licked her lips and swallowed the lump in her throat. *I'm babbling.* What can you say to a grieving mother and a grief-stricken boy, too young to volunteer? *Platitudes at a time like this are as worthless as warts on a frog.*

Mrs. Wilkey counted the change into Agnes's hand. "And four cents makes thirty." Four pennies lay on Agnes palm. "Forty, fifty." Two dimes joined the pennies. "And fifty cents makes four dollars." She laid down a half-dollar. "And one makes five." A dollar bill lay across the coins. "Having chickens won't save you much money. You still have to buy chicken feed, you know."

Agnes opened her coin purse, dropped in the money and snapped the latch. "I expect the chickens can eat the bugs in the back yard."

George placed the last can of soup in her bag and snorted, "Good luck with that."

Agnes gathered her shopping bags, nodded to Mrs. Wilkey and strode to the front door. "Sure sorry about your son," she called over her shoulder and stepped onto the sidewalk.

Agnes marched to her bicycle, determined to do even more for the war effort. With the shopping bags stashed securely in the side baskets, she straddled the bicycle and pushed off toward the police station. *What is the world coming to? How many more sons do we have to lose before it's over?*

The wheel of Agnes's bicycle fit snugly into the metal rack in front of the county courthouse. Her heart paddled faster as she steeled her resolve to confront Chief Waddlemucker—again.

Maybe I was mistaken about Mrs. Rashmuller and the poisoned tarts, but, by golly, I'm not wrong about the Black Market ration books. It was her civic duty to report illegal activity to the authorities, whether Chief Waddlemucker believed her or not.

Agnes straightened the hem on the jacket of her blue two-piece surge suit, squared her shoulders, and marched up the broad courthouse steps carrying her fishnet shopping bags full of groceries. She shoved open the glass door and stepped inside. Cool air from electric fans mounted on each side of the door wafted across the entryway. The breeze cooled Agnes's hot cheeks as she marched down the corridor. She stopped and took two deep breaths.

Just ahead, the elevator slid open. The attendant poked out his head. "Hey, Mrs. Odboddy, you're out and about early this morning." Jackson Jackson's toothy grin flashed across his dark face.

"Indeed! What's that supposed to mean?"

"It just tickles me ta see ya here again so soon. What brings ya this time?"

"I've come to talk to Chief Waddlemucker. I know my duty to the war effort, even if you don't. You're a strapping young man. Why aren't you in the military?" Agnes glowered at Jackson as she stepped into the elevator, and then nodded toward the buttons on the wall.

Jackson pressed the button to the third floor. His smile faded as the doors slid shut and the elevator ascended. His shoulders slumped. "I tried to enlist, ma'am. They says I got a heart condition. Wouldn't take me."

"Oh! I see." *Agnes Odboddy. If there's not already an epidemic of foot-in-mouth disease in this town, one will start with you.* Agnes gulped. "Never you mind. There are plenty of ways to be a home front warrior. Many worthwhile organizations need volunteers." Not a very good *save*, but the best she could think of on the spur of the moment.

"Yes, ma'am. That's what I does early Sattidy mornings. I volunteer over at the Boys and Girls Club, sweeping and cleaning up the building before the children come. From time to time, I does odd jobs for the town's widdas."

Agnes smiled. "I apologize, Jackson. I'm always spouting off about something I shouldn't say. I'm glad you're still here in Newbury with us. What would we do if we didn't have some good men around to help out at home?"

"That's just what I figgered. I'm mighty pleased to do my part. You need anything at all, just give me a call."

"Thanks. I'll remember that. *Humm…* Come to think of it, there is a project I need some help with. I'm thinking of getting some chickens. Perhaps you could help me build a little house and a fenced yard." The elevator slid to a stop. The door opened. Agnes stepped out onto the polished green asphalt tiles. She paused and turned back.

"I'd be mighty happy to help you with that, Mrs. Odboddy. My Sattidy afternoons is usually free, after the Boys and Girls Club. I could come by next Sattidy, if you like." Jackson's muscles bulged as he gripped the edge of the elevator door to hold it open.

"That would be fine. Say about 12:30 P.M?"

"Yes, ma'am. See you then." Jackson touched his cap, pulled his head in and the elevator door snapped shut.

Good idea or not, looks like I'm committed to getting those chickens now.

Chief Waddlemucker's office loomed just ahead. Agnes took another deep breath and reached for the doorknob. *Full steam ahead.*

Agnes opened the door. Inside, the Newbury Police employees were hard at work, keeping the city safe from jaywalkers and people throwing gum on the sidewalks. Typewriters clacked and telephones jangled. A uniformed officer looked up. "Morning, Mrs. Odboddy.

Come to see Chief Waddlemucker?" He stood and walked to the counter, a grin plastered across his freckled face.

Agnes stiffened her back and set her bag of groceries on the counter. "I suppose you think I have nothing better to do than come downtown to perform my civic duty reporting potential crimes? Am I the only citizen who keeps watch while others turn a blind eye? Well, listen here, young man, in my day, back in WWI, when I was—"

"I'll let the Chief know you're here…again." The officer turned his back and knocked on Chief Waddlemucker's door.

"Well, I never!" Agnes ran her hand over the back of her head and shoved the silver chopsticks firmly into her hair.

"Enter!" A muffled voice behind Chief Waddlemucker's door.

The officer poked his head inside. "She's back, Chief. You busy?"

A moment of silence. "I don't suppose I have to ask who. Send her in."

Agnes marched across the office, head held high, her fishnet grocery bags bulging with a pound of flour, margarine, a pound of potatoes, six oranges, three cans of Campbell's tomato soup, a dozen eggs, coffee and a quart of milk, gripped in her hand. "Good morning, Chief, fine morning. Hope I'm not intruding."

"And, if I told you that you were intruding, would you leave?"

"Not on your tintype. I have a matter of singular importance to report." Agnes's shoulders reared back.

"Like last time? Is Mrs. Rashmuller up to her tricks again? Someone else drop dead? Or should I say, to what do I owe the pleasure of your company twice in the same week?"

"You don't need to get snippy. I could be baking cookies for the Veteran's Hall bake sale this evening, but I'm here instead. I have a matter of national security—"

"You always do." Chief Waddlemucker tipped back his head and blew a smoke ring toward the ceiling. He laid his cigar in the ashtray. His jowls pulled down in a scowl that made Agnes think of a pedigreed bulldog.

She put her hand to her mouth and coughed. "Do you mind? In my day, a gentleman did not smoke cigars in the presence of a lady." Agnes flopped into the chair in front of the chief's desk, set her shopping bags on the floor and glared.

"What issue of national security are you here to report this morning? I'm pretty busy, you know. There's a war on." He reached tobacco stained fingers toward his cigar.

"Don't you think I know that? Why else would I be here? As I was saying before I was so rudely interrupted… I came to report a Black Market ring right here in Newbury regarding our Ration Stamp books and I—"

"Black Market, is it? Not a Nazi spy ring or a mad cyanide poisoner running amuck? Well, this *is* different." Chief Waddlemucker chuckled and tapped the ash off his cigar. He stood and stepped to the end of the desk, put his hands on his hips and leaned his protuberant gut toward Agnes. "Look here, Mrs. Odboddy. I've been more than patient with you, but you can't keep coming in here, disrupting my work, yammering about some foolish conspiracy theory. I don't have time for such nonsense."

Agnes's cheeks burned. The roots of her hennaed hair tingled. Her stomach flip-flopped. She heaved out of her chair. "You're no gentleman, and I won't sit here and be insulted. If you won't listen to me, then I'll just deal with this myself." She gathered her shopping bags and started across the room. *Control yourself, Agnes. He's just a foolish man.* She turned at the door. "Perhaps the FBI will be more interested in this matter. Perhaps they'll wonder why you failed in your duty to listen to a citizen reporting a crime. Good day, Chief Waddlemucker." Up went her nose in the air.

"Good day, Mrs. Odboddy. Don't be a stranger." His guffaws followed her to the door.

The glass in the window rattled as Agnes slammed the Chief's door. Typewriters stopped clacking. Telephones stopped jangling. All heads turned as Agnes stalked through the precinct, the click of her heels across the tiles like firecrackers on the Fourth of July. She could feel the clerks' eyes boring into the back of her head. Her vision blurred as her eyes filled with tears. *I will not cry!* She struggled to keep them at bay, determined not to let the scoffers see her break down. Wasn't she a hometown warrior?

A giggle broke out from the back of the room.

Never in my life have I been so embarrassed. She tromped down the hall toward the elevator. This was the last time she'd come to the police station. Good for nothings, that's what they were. She would uncover the culprits stealing the ration books herself, and turn them over to the FBI. But why stop there? She would investigate anyone she thought might be a German agent. After that…who knew?

Like Ellery Queen, the inimitable movie detective, she'd bring war criminals to justice. But, unlike Mr. Queen, she would do it all in secret. No one would suspect her—an outspoken old lady by day and a secret scourge of the underworld by night. After the war was over, she'd go after the white slavers. Perhaps she'd get a mask…

With her head held high, Agnes stomped past the elevator.

"Mrs. Odboddy?" Jackson's voice barely penetrated her thoughts. "You're not gonna take the elevator, ma'am?"

She waved him off. No time for small talk. As a warrior fighting the war from the home front, she was on a mission. She had to get home and make plans. Not only that, but her margarine was melting and in this heat, her milk was likely to curdle.

She paused at the top of the stairs. Wait! *Jackson Jackson! He might come in handy, after all.* She turned. "Jackson?"

"Yes, ma'am?"

"Can you drive?"

"Yes, ma'am. I don't got a car, but I can drive and I gets them gas ration coupons every month, but I—"

Agnes pulled the hem of her suit jacket firmly over her hips. "You available for a little night work from time to time? It's for the war effort. You could accompany me around town and perhaps you'd let me use your gas ration coupons... Of course, I'd pay for the gas. Is your phone number in the book?"

Jackson grinned. "Yes, ma'am. I'd be most pleased to assist you, Mrs. Odboddy. Anything for the war effort, ma'am."

Agnes glanced back over her shoulder. "We need to talk, but not here. I'll give you a call tonight after you get off work." She pushed open the outer door and walked down the steps, a smile on her face so wide it made her ears hurt.

Chapter Eight

Agnes pedaled away from the courthouse, shoulders hunched, and knuckles white from gripping the handlebars so tight, blood pounded across her forehead with each heartbeat. Her stomach rocked and the back of her head tingled. *I'll show that Chief Waddlemucker. I'll find the Black Marketers and bring them to justice or my name isn't Agnes Odboddy!*

At the center of town, Agnes turned her bicycle into the park, stopped by the pond and sat on the bench near the fountain. She closed her eyes, took three deep breaths, and forced her body to relax. A mockingbird chittered, first with one call and then another, as he went through his repertoire. The fountain burbled in the nearby pond. Her heartbeat slowed as she concentrated on the sounds of the bird and the fountain. The stress wrinkles in her forehead smoothed away. A gentle breeze rustled the leaves overhead and she breathed in the scent of cherry blossoms. *Ahh…that's more like it.*

No way would she let that foolish man add one more wrinkle to her face or drive up her blood pressure. No sense starting her first mission without a plan. She needed to be calm to figure out just exactly how she and Jackson should accomplish their goal.

Within ten minutes, Agnes regained her composure and left the park bench with a plan. Following the example in Ellery Queen's mystery books, first she must understand the lay of the land. The first order of business was a reconnaissance mission.

She turned her bicycle toward home, but by an indirect route. From Main Street, she turned down Berghame Boulevard, recently renamed to honor Mayor Leonard Berghame's son, who died at Pearl Harbor. Agnes pedaled past bungalow styled houses, most of which had Victory gardens in the front yard. Near the end of the block, she stopped her bicycle in front of a brown clapboard house with a tiled roof, the absence of a garden and a yard full of dry weeds. 445 Berghame Boulevard. *My first objective. But, how am I going to remember these addresses?*

A search through her handbag revealed a fountain pen, but not a scrap of paper to write on. *My stars! I must remember to carry a notebook in my purse.* Wait! The coffee beans! She could write on the plain brown paper bag.

She dug through her shopping bag and retrieved the beans. Agnes jotted tiny letters on the side. 445 Berghame—tile roof.

On she traveled, up and down the blocks, stopping near each deserted house, writing each address on her ground coffee beans, until she came to Gem Crest Circle where the house at 21018 had triggered the original mission. Agnes added the address to her wrinkled bag, her fingers now covered with ink blotches that would likely take days to wear off. It was worth it. What she and Jackson would accomplish when the black marketers were apprehended was worth any price, even ink-stained fingers.

Eventually, Agnes turned down Trumble Lane, past The First Church of the Evening Star and Everlasting Light and Pastor Lickleiter's parsonage next door.

Agnes pulled up beside the mailbox where Pastor's wife stood thumbing through her mail. "Morning, Mrs. Lickleiter. Beautiful day, isn't it?"

"Indeed. I was just telling Mr. Lickleiter this morning, that I thought it was unseasonably—"

"Would you happen to know if any of the houses on this street are empty? I'm doing a survey for the Chamber of Commerce about how many houses in Newbury are vacant and/or for sale." *Now I've lied to the pastor's wife. Good going, Agnes. Another punch on your ticket to H.E. double toothpicks…*

Mrs. Lickleiter gazed up and down the street. "I believe the Goodall house has been empty ever since Charlie Goodall enlisted and his wife went to live with her parents." She pointed down the street. "It's the pink house over there, three houses down on the left."

"Thanks. Well, *ta-ta*. Busy day, you know." Agnes shoved off on her bike and then stopped in front of the Goodall house. *107 Trumble—pink.* More letters on the bottom of the coffee bag as both sides were covered with her notes. Agnes pedaled on. Over the next hour, she traversed a ten-block radius surrounding her neighborhood. When she got home, the carton of milk was warm and her margarine was soft, but her ground coffee bag contained the scrawled addresses of fourteen houses. *Now we have our targets. All that's left is the coup de grace.*

Agnes scrubbed at the ink stains on her fingers in vain. It didn't matter. The ink was a badge of honor, the price one must pay as a self-appointed scourge of the underworld.

Agnes slid a batch of oatmeal raisin cookies into the oven. She checked the temperature and ran water into the bowl in the sink.

Ling-Ling sauntered into the kitchen, her dark paws brushing soundlessly across the maroon linoleum floor. She crouched by her water bowl. Drops of water moved in a constant stream over the bowl as her little pink tongue rose up and down with the speed of a tattoo needle.

Agnes stroked Ling-Ling sleek tan back. She thought of Lilly, somewhere in a Japanese Internment Camp. She whispered a little prayer that Lilly would be safe and could return home soon. What would Lilly have said about her plans for the evening? "Just think, Ling-Ling. The ration books should be delivered today or tomorrow at the latest. As soon as they arrive, Jackson and I will execute *Operation Ration Book.*"

Agnes could picture herself flitting through the pending *night-ops*, the scourge of the underworld, fast on the heels of the black marketers.

She stepped onto the back porch where she had hung one of her husband's old hats and his black raincoat on a hook, still smelling of mothballs from the garage trunk. She lifted the flashlight from the shelf over the washing machine and carried it back to the kitchen table, flicking it on and off, checking the new batteries. *Good. It's ready to grab as soon as the game is afoot.*

Ling-Ling twisted, beads of water sparkling on her chin. She licked her left shoulder and then cruised past Agnes's ankle.

Agnes opened the ice box. "I know. You want to know whether I bought milk this morning. Well, I did, on my way to the police station. I wonder if I should bring Katherine in on the caper."

The cat sat, her gaze fixed on the milk carton in Agnes's hand.

"You think I should tell her, don't you. But, I've decided not to worry her. She has enough on her mind, dealing with her own demons. She has to go to the mortuary tonight and work on her first client.

"No. It's not anyone you know. At least I don't think you knew him. Poor old Clyde Hoffelmeister fell off his roof, trying to rescue Mrs. Turnbull's cat. You might have known the cat… Mitzie?"

Ling-Ling blinked. Apparently, she didn't know her.

"Yes, it was sad. Don't worry. Mitzie survived the fall."

Ling-Ling blinked again.

"Clyde didn't."

Agnes smiled and then wiped her hand over her mouth. *It's not funny. The poor man is dead.* She poured a dollop of milk into a cereal bowl and set it on the floor. "Here you go, Lamb Chop!"

Katherine had her work cut out for her, alright, making old Clyde, with his stringy hair and shaggy grey beard, presentable enough to meet his Maker. "Gossip is that Mrs. Turnbull hasn't left the mortuary since the old gentleman came into *Eternity's Staging Room.* She feels responsible for Clyde's death, since he was trying to rescue Mitzie.

"Mr. Whistlemeyer can't convince her to leave. He's about at his wit's end with her wailing. He even called Mrs. Turnbull's daughter and asked if she'd drive up from Sacramento and deal with her mother."

Ling-Ling lost interest in Mr. Whistlemeyer's predicament or Mitzie's apparent close call with death and turned her attention back to the bowl of milk.

Agnes glanced up at the sound of the mailbox lid snapping shut. *The mail is here!* With heart a-flutter, she hurried down the sidewalk and jerked open the mailbox. *Yes!* There was the Saturday Evening Post featuring Willie Gillis on the cover. There lay the large brown envelope, her ration book, addressed in her own recognizable handwriting with the large open *O*. She'd read somewhere that your handwriting was supposed to say things about your personality. Apparently, her handwriting claimed she was talkative and social. *What nonsense! Social, yes, but I'm not the least bit talkative.*

Agnes hurried back into the house with the mail, pulled the cookies from the oven and scooped them onto a rack. Only a bit on the scorched side, the aroma of the cookies made her mouth water. "I was going to take these to the bake sale, but now that the ration books are delivered, I can't go to the Veteran's Hall tonight." She pried a cookie off the tin sheet and took a bite. A raisin tumbled onto the floor.

"What do you think, Ling-Ling? Should I run over to Mildred's house and take her some cookies? She always liked my oatmeal raisin cookies."

Ling-Ling lapped from the milk bowl. She stopped in mid-lick and lifted her head. Milk dripped from her black-rimmed mouth. Her turquoise eyes narrowed. She arched her back and danced sideways toward the raisin, gave it a swipe and attacked it as it skidded under the kitchen table.

"Yes. My thoughts exactly."

Later that Afternoon

Agnes dumped the cookies from a paper bag onto Mildred's orange Fiesta platter and arranged them in a neat circle. She picked one up and took a bite. "So, Jackson and I will park in front of the green house on Gem Crest and wait until—"

"Agnes. You can't be serious. You're not actually going to sneak around town tonight, with *that man*, are you? Have you lost your mind, dear?" Mildred slid a cookie to the side of the plate, pinched it in half, and popped it in her mouth. "I can't *beweave Kaferine* isn't doing *anyfing to stomp you*." She glared at Agnes, swallowed hard and took a sip of lemonade. "...to stop you."

Agnes crossed her arms across her ample bosom. "I most certainly do intend to get to the bottom of this, and Jackson's not a *man*, he's... Well, of course, he's a man, but not like you mean. He's the elevator boy at the courthouse." The fingers on her left hand fluttered in midair.

"Running an elevator at the courthouse doesn't make him any less of a man. And, he's...you know...he's not white! There. I've said it. What will people say if they see you two out at night, alone?"

"Nothing worse than they already say about me on any given week with a Tuesday. Your suggestion is ridiculous. I'm old enough to be his mo...*um*...his older sister. Besides, we don't intend for anyone to see us. We're going to park near one of the houses on my list and watch. If anyone comes to steal the ration book, I've got my Brownie camera. We'll be back before midnight. No one is going to recognize me. I'm wearing a disguise."

"Your Brownie camera can't take pictures in the dark. And, wearing Douglas's old raincoat won't keep someone from recognizing your yellow and brown 1930 Model A Ford parked on the street. Agnes. Agnes. What am I going to do with you?"

Mildred shoved another cookie in her mouth and chomped. She stood and paced the kitchen, poured another glass of lemonade and sat down. "Why don't you just pack up the rest of these cookies and take them over to the Veteran's Hall like you planned? Forget all this cloak and dagger nonsense. If you really think someone is stealing ration books, then go to the authorities—"

"I told you. I already went to Chief Waddlemucker's office and he laughed me right out the door. I'm not going back! When I figure out who's behind this, I'll call the FBI and they can follow up. Until then, mum's the word." Agnes's fingers zipped across her mouth.

"You're sure about this? Absolutely sure? There's nothing I can say to change your mind?"

"Yes, yes and no!"

"Then, at least tell me where you're going, and call me in the morning. I don't want to call Chief Waddlemucker and have him start searching for your body!"

"Mildred! Have a little faith. Remember, during WWI, it was not unusual for us to—"

"Yes dear. I'm quite aware of what we did during WWI. We worked together, remember? And, even if we hadn't, you've certainly told me umpteen times."

Agnes lifted the kickstand and jumped onto her bicycle, rolled down Mildred's driveway and turned left, her head full of plans for the night-ops she and Jackson planned. *We might actually catch a black marketer in the act. Should I turn in the crook anonymously, or take credit for his capture when he's brought to justice, more in the Ellery Queen fashion?*

Agnes pedaled toward the corner of Brush and Humboldt Street. Right up ahead, one of those new-fangled traffic lights swung on a pole over the intersection. She glanced up at the red light overhead and slowed the bicycle. *Wonder if that stoplight applies to bicycles, or just cars?* The traffic light switched to green just as Agnes's bike approached the crosswalk. She pedaled into the intersection.

An engine roared as a large black Packard coming from the opposite direction leaped across the crosswalk, swerved into the intersection, headed straight for Agnes's bicycle.

Agnes yanked the handlebars to the right. *My stars! Has the driver lost his mind?* Blood rushed through her head. No time to move from the car's path. Her stomach churned. Images of Douglas, John and Katherine collided as the possibility of imminent death loomed. Was this the end? Right here on Main Street, on a sunny spring morning?

Agnes flung out her arms and leaped off the bicycle. She landed hard, as her hip hit the pavement. *Oww!*

Screech! Crunch! The Packard's left front tire struck the bike, twisting the wheel sideways as it slid beneath the front bumper.

Agnes lay on the pavement, stunned. One minute she was pedaling down the street and the next nearly squished beneath the wheels of the giant Packard. *Praise the Lord! I'm still alive!*

Pedestrians clustered around. "Are you hurt, lady?" A man in a dark suit leaned over Agnes's head.

"Should we call an ambulance?" A woman with a curly white dog on a leash hovered nearby. Agnes's head whirled as she stared at the dog's red-checkered leash. *Is that the way our mind works when we've barely escaped death?* Maybe, at that critical moment in time, we notice unimportant things we wouldn't ordinarily notice, like red-checkered leashes. Wouldn't it have made more sense to notice whether it was a man or a woman driving the car?

Agnes put her hand to her forehead as images of red-checkered leashes paraded by, one after the other. The images faded and the faces of the Good Samaritans came into focus. Her dizziness passed. "I...I think I'm alright." She flexed her legs and arms.

The man in the dark suit helped her rise to a sitting position.

"I'm okay. Perhaps you'll give me a hand up?" Agnes clutched the man's arm as he helped her to her feet. She moved her limbs and twisted her neck. "Nothing's broken. I think I'm just a bit shaken up. And, my self-esteem is a little battered." She rubbed her hip and smiled. There would be a bruise the size of New Jersey there tomorrow. Count on it.

"Oh, Agnes. I don't know what to say."

Who? A familiar voice. "What?" Agnes turned toward the woman climbing out of the Packard. *Sophia Rashmuller!* Agnes took a step to retrieve her handbag, apparently flung from the side basket when the bicycle hit the street. She turned back to Sophia. "You were driving? What were you thinking? You about killed me!"

Sophia nodded, wide-eyed. "I'm so sorry. I didn't see you."

"I'm wearing a pink and purple sweater! How could you miss me?"

"Well, it appears I almost didn't. My goodness! I only looked away for a moment to reach for my sunglasses." Sophia pointed toward the Packard parked in the middle of the road. The smashed bicycle stuck out from under the front wheel. "I'm so sorry. Are you hurt? Imagine how upset I'd be if I'd hit you."

"Not half as upset as *I'd* be if you hit me!" Agnes brushed dirt from her skirt. "Don't worry about it. I'm fine." *Fool woman. Needs her eyes checked.*

Whoop! Whoop!

Heads turned as a patrol car pulled to a stop. Chief Waddlemucker stepped out. "What's going on here? Was anyone hurt?"

The man in the suit explained the situation. An accident. Momentary lapse on the driver's part concluding with Agnes's near escape from being flattened like a fritter in the crosswalk.

"I'm to blame, officer. I'd never forgive myself if I'd hit my dear friend." Sophia pulled a monogrammed hankie from her pocket and dabbed her eyes.

Agnes blinked, feeling slightly guilty for her angry thoughts. *Poor woman. She obviously feels terrible. And, I've been less than kind to her lately.* "There, there! It's quite alright, Sophia. Accidents happen. Don't carry on so. I'm not hurt."

"I'll replace your bicycle, Agnes. Now, if one of you gentleman would help me get this thing out from under my wheel, I'll be on my way." Sophia moved toward her car.

Chief Waddlemucker stepped between Agnes and Sophia. "Perhaps you'd best let me drive you home, Mrs. Rashmuller. I'll call for an officer to come and pick up my vehicle." The Chief reached into his car and pulled out his radio. "Mrs. Odboddy, it wouldn't hurt if you stopped by the Emergency Room and got checked out." A second patrol car pulled up to the curb.

"Fiddlesticks. I'm fine. It takes more than falling off my bike to hurt these tough old bones. I'd appreciate it if someone could give me a lift home, though."

The Chief waved to his officer. "Crimshaw. Pull that bike out from under the car and drive Mrs. Odboddy home. I'm taking Mrs. Rashmuller home. We'll write up the accident report when we get back to the station."

Agnes's gaze followed the big black Packard until it turned the corner. Something niggled at the back of her mind; not quite clear. The bruise on her hip began to throb and the disturbing thought disappeared from her head.

Chapter Nine

K atherine sucked in her breath as Mr. Whistlemeyer unlocked the pink door and stood aside. The desire to turn around and race away was overwhelming. She clutched her purse tighter, shrugged and stepped into the room.

Mr. Whistlemeyer pulled off his round horn-rimmed glasses and tucked them into a pocket protector protruding from his front coat pocket. "Here we are. We call this the *Journey's Beautiful Beginnings* room. Mr. Hoffelmeister, the recently dearly departed, is just finishing up in the *Serenity Room*. He's all dressed and ready for you. Oh, the wonders of makeup! All you have to do is give him a haircut, trim his beard and put a little *life* back in his cheeks. *Heh, heh.* See how I made a little joke there? I'm very jocular, you know, much to the surprise of folks."

"I'll do the best I can, sir." Katherine gulped and glanced around the room.

Mr. Whistlemeyer's smile wavered. "My dear wife had such a way with making our dearly departed look so...so...peaceful and lifelike. She had a gift; indeed she did. I do hope you can do as well. Our departed loved ones deserve to look their best, don't you agree?"

Katherine's face tingled like she'd walked into a spider web. She brushed her cheek with a shaking hand, and then shoved her purse under her arm. She nodded. Saying something comforting regarding his unfaithful wife was probably in order here, but her lips wouldn't form the platitudes that clashed around in her head.

She licked her lips and swallowed the sawdust feeling in her throat. "About your wife… I'm so sorry for your loss." Her voice cracked as the words eked out. *How's that?*

"Really, Katherine. She's not dead. She just left me!" A pained expression crossed Mr. Whistlemeyer's face. "After thirty-nine years of wedded bliss, she left me for another man." He reached into his inside jacket pocket, dragged out a handkerchief, dabbed his eyes and then honked into it.

"I'm so sorry, Mr. Whistlemeyer. That didn't come out right. I'm very nervous being here. I hope you'll forgive my blunder."

"It takes a little getting used to, for sure. I'll show you where my… my…Ethel kept the makeup and supplies. Right this way." He opened a door into another room.

—In the Sweet Bye and Bye—

Music piped in over the loud speakers drowned out the street sounds. A breeze wafted across the room as the electric fans hummed, stirring the tall palms beside the door leading into the work area. The smell of alcohol, formaldehyde and a sickly sweet odor she couldn't identify struck Katherine's nostrils. She stopped in her tracks, wrinkled her nose and turned to Mr. Whistlemeyer, her eyes wide.

"Yes. I know. It's a bit overwhelming for the first time visitor. This is where I do my…*um*… It won't be so bad in the room where you'll be working. Come along, Katherine."

Myrtle, I'm going to kill you for sticking me with this job. Katherine grit her teeth and followed Mr. Whistlemeyer into an adjoining room full of more familiar items. To the right stood a large sink with a spray nozzle attachment, shampoo bottles and stacks of towels. To the left, an odd looking hair dryer on wheels, and a tray covered with razors and scissors awaiting the touch of a master's hand. It almost looked like a beauty shop, but with no client chairs. Mr. Whistlemeyer's clients didn't need chairs. *How exactly does one style hair on a dead client lying on his back?*

Mr. Whistlemeyer turned at the door. He pointed toward a cupboard. "You can put your sweater and purse here, Katherine. Go ahead and check over the supplies. If you need anything at all, make a note of it and I'll have it here next time. *Uh*...there will be a next time, right? You're not going to quit on me after one night, are you?" His hand gripped the doorknob. His expression made her think of a little boy at the pet shop, begging for a puppy.

"Let's see how this goes, Mr. Whistlemeyer. No promises."

"That's fair. I'll be right back with...Clyde." Mr. Whistlemeyer scurried out.

—We shall meet on that beautiful shore... In the sweet—

The door snapped shut, drowning out the music. Katherine walked around the quiet room, touching the familiar, yet unfamiliar equipment.

Before her heart had settled down to a steady beat, Mr. Whistlemeyer returned, pushing a body on a gurney covered by a sheet. He whipped off the sheet. "His funeral is scheduled day after tomorrow. Think you can make him presentable in time?"

Katherine's heart smashed against her breast bone. She sucked in her breath.

Bright angry abrasions were visible on Clyde's cheeks, likely results of his fall off the roof. A large scab had formed on his forehead, pre-existing, no doubt, and not related to the mechanics of his demise. Deep grooved blue lips sunk into his oral cavity. Shaggy grey hair covered his head and chin. Deathly pale skin and bristly cheeks completed the context of the miracle Katherine was supposed to perform before Clyde's permanent departure from this earthly plane.

"Oh, my goodness gracious!" Was she up to this? Extra money or not, what was Myrtle thinking, asking her to take on such an impossible mission?

"I have a picture of Clyde, taken some years ago, of course. Maybe it will help some. His face will look better when we put his dentures back in and he's shaved." Mr. Whistlemeyer pulled down the sheet, revealing a photograph and a box holding Clyde's dentures lying on his chest.

Katherine picked up the picture. She squinted at the black and white photograph. "Can't really see his face that well." She glanced at Clyde. "Can you at least put his teeth back in? I'm a beautician, not God."

"Sorry. I should have done that before I brought him to you. We always remove the client's dentures while performing the...*er*... preparing the body, for fear they'll get lost or broken during the...*er*... proceedings." He pried Clyde's mouth open, shoved in the dentures and gave Clyde's jaw a hefty slap. Clyde's mouth snapped shut with a click as his teeth came together. The dentures filled out his lips and cheeks into a more natural shape. "There. See? Much better."

Katherine shivered and sighed. "Considerably. Thank you. I think it would have made more sense to do his hair and makeup before you dressed him. I hope I don't mess up his clothes."

"Ordinarily, we would have, Katherine, but when my wife left...I didn't have anyone... Can't you wrap an apron around his neck?" He opened a cupboard and pulled out a plastic apron.

Katherine nodded. "At this point, I guess I'll have to do my best."

"Well, if you'll excuse me, I have to deal with Clyde's neighbor lady. I never knew a woman's head could hold so much liquid. I hope her daughter gets here pretty soon. We've all been on edge, listening to her wail. I could only convince her to sleep for a couple hours last night in the chapel. She refuses to leave. Shame, what guilt does to a person.

"I'll let you get on with your work. If you have any questions, don't hesitate to call me." He reached for the doorknob.

—how sweet the sound, that saved a wretch like me—

Katherine was alone with Clyde. She shivered. Nothing for it but to assess the situation and get to work. Katherine glanced at her watch. She should be home listening to The Green Hornet on the radio, not standing over a dead body that looked like...

"Well, Clyde. I didn't know you well, but we're going to get better acquainted over the next several hours. Now, where exactly should I begin?"

Clyde's shaggy hair was matted with blood and dirt and what looked like weeks of neglect culminating in his fatal injury. *I have to wash your hair before I do anything.* Why didn't she ask Mr. Whistlemeyer how that was done before he left? *You're a bright girl, Katherine. Figure it out.*

Katherine glanced toward the large sink where a circle of damp tiles on the floor indicated a leaky pipe or a careless attendant. She should mention it to Mr. Whistlemeyer.

Clyde's gurney was the same height. The sink had a groove about where Clyde's head would fit if she could fold the gurney down to the level of his shoulders. A crease in the gurney and a lever beneath suggested this was its purpose. She laid the plastic apron across Clyde's neck, dropped the ledge beneath his shoulders, and supported his head and neck as she slid the gurney up to the sink. His neck rested on the edge of the sink at just the right angle. How clever.

Over the next hour and a half, Katherine shampooed and cut Clyde's hair and trimmed his beard. She cringed just a little at first as her fingers spread makeup over the abrasions and the forehead scab. Once used to the feel of his unyielding cold flesh, she added a bit of color to his lips and cheeks, but not enough to make him look *made up.* Next, she smoothed out the lines beneath his eyes, scrubbed her hands in the sink and checked the photograph. "Why, Clyde. You don't look half bad, if I do say so myself. You probably haven't looked this good for twenty years."

On a hill...far away...stood—

"How are things going, Katherine? Do you need any...?" Mr. Whistlemeyer stepped through the doorway. "Well, I'll be a greased pig on Founder's Day. Look at old Clyde. I'm downright impressed, Katherine. That's a fine job of work you've done here."

Katherine beamed. *And the Academy Award goes to Katherine Odboddy...for the best hair and makeup on a stiff...uh...dearly departed.* "It wasn't as bad as I thought, once I got used to it. He does look pretty good, doesn't he, considering he's dead?"

"Now, tell me you'll come back again, the next time we need you. God forbid it should mean someone's died, but on the other hand, if a Newbury citizen's got to die in order for me to make a living, then so be it."

Katherine smiled. "I'll come back if you need me. Give us a call at the salon."

Mr. Whistlemeyer turned. "Oh, there's the telephone. Thanks again. I'll let you know…"

—hill far away, stood an old— And, he was through the door and gone.

"Well, Clyde, bon voyage, wherever you're going." Katherine pulled her sweater and handbag from the cupboard. As she turned, her lipstick tumbled from her purse and rolled across the wet floor toward Clyde's gurney. Katherine stepped toward the sink, stooped and made a grab for her lipstick. Her foot slipped on the wet tiles; she lost her balance and began to fall.

In the split-second that it took to visualize herself lying on the floor in a heap, a torrent of worries raced through her mind. *I'm falling and I'm going to break my ankle, just as sure as there are kittens in springtime. With a broken ankle, I won't be able to work.* She threw out her hands to break her fall. She was supposed to be helping Myrtle earn extra money for the shop, but with a broken ankle, Myrtle would be down one beautician and earning less money than before. And, Grandma would have to wait on her hand and foot. *Oh dear, oh dear!*

She stumbled and flailed, reaching for the nearest thing to break her fall. Her hand touched the edge of the gurney. The gurney swayed. "Oh, no!" She fell against the teetering gurney, throwing it even more off balance. *Is Clyde going to fall?* What would Mr. Whistlemeyer say? She twisted and tried to support it, but the gurney jounced forward, smacked into the sink and tipped. Over it went, toppling Clyde.

Katherine jerked back, landing on the floor. *God help me.*

Clyde's body plunged down, down, his arms outstretched toward Katherine's face.

Oh my God! He's falling, right on top of me! Katherine twisted, trying to escape Clyde's hands, reaching for her. She lurched back and screamed. "Help! Mr. Whis—"

Clyde plopped face down in the puddle, his hand jutting across Katherine's face and his leg astride her torso.

Katherine wrenched back. Frantic to get away from the body, her head whacked against the corner of the sink.

And I love that old cross... "Katherine?"

Everything turned black.

Wednesday Evening—Somewhere across town

"There it is! There it is!" Agnes jiggled a finger toward the street. "I'll pull over right here, Jackson. See? 21018. Right across the street. Run on over there and check the mailbox. See if the ration book is in there. I'd do it myself if it wasn't for my sore hip." Agnes scrunched down and shoved Douglas's hat lower over her eyes.

Jackson opened the passenger door and closed it gently without engaging the latch. He stooped and ran across the dark street, ducking behind the shrubs, then running to the tree next to the pathway.

Good grief. If anyone looked out the window, Jackson's behavior looked so suspicious trying not to look suspicious, they'd call the cops for sure. She pulled the collar of Douglas's overcoat tighter around her neck.

Jackson scurried back to the car and slipped open the door. "It's there, Mrs. Odboddy. Just like ya said. Right in the mailbox." His chest heaved with each breath.

"Wonderful. Then we just sit and wait until someone comes to pick it up." Agnes's heart thumped in her chest.

"Is this what Ellery Queen calls a stakeout, ma'am? It that what we's doing?" Jackson's teeth gleamed.

"It's been so long since I've had a steak, I'm not sure I'd recognize one if I saw it." She chuckled. "But, I guess this is as close to a *stakeout* as we're likely to see until this blasted war is over." Agnes's bruised hip throbbed as she leaned forward and reached for the thermos of hot coffee at Jackson's feet, just beyond her fingers. "Would you hand me that thermos?"

Jackson retrieved the bottle and spun the lid as he turned to hand it to her. "Here, let me help."

The thermos collided in midair with Agnes's outstretched hand. Hot coffee spilled out, down onto her raincoat, splashed the steering wheel and splattered onto the floor. "Oh, dear God! Look at this mess." She grabbed the thermos and spun the lid back on, then set it on the seat between them.

"I'm sorry, ma'am. How did that happen? I just loosed the lid—" Jackson sputtered.

"It's my fault. I couldn't find the cork. I just screwed on the lid. Not to worry." She wiped at the raincoat with her bare hand. "There's no harm done. Look in the glove box. There should be a rag in there."

Jackson popped the lid and shook his head.

"Better yet, hop out and check in the rumble seat. I know I have some old rags out there."

Jackson jumped out and within a minute, returned with a ragged red-checkered flannel shirt. "Will this do? It looks pretty clean."

"Thanks." Agnes took the shirt, wiped the coffee off the steering wheel and dabbed at her coffee spattered coat.

An engine rumbled. Agnes looked up. A pickup truck peeled away from the curb across the street and tore away, its engine roaring.

"What on earth?" The dark pickup turned the corner. The sound of its engine faded into the distance. "Was that… Did you see who…? Dag-nab it! Did that guy in the truck grab that ration book when we weren't looking?"

"I'm afeared so, Mrs. Odboddy, but I'll run acrost the street and check it out."

"Yes, do that. Hurry, but I don't think there's much point." Agnes's gaze followed Jackson across the street.

He shook his head as he hurried back and slid into the passenger seat. "It's gone, ma'am. Just like you *disca-membered*."

Agnes started the car and rattled down the block to the next house on her list. Just as she turned onto Diamond Circle, the pickup truck zoomed around the corner and sped away. "There's that truck again. He's getting to the houses before us." Her foot pressed the throttle and the Model A zoomed around the corner. She cruised the blocks listed on her paper, but the pickup truck was long gone. "It's no use. We've lost him. He must be onto us. He'll probably wait until the wee hours of the morning and then come back. I don't suppose you want to sit up all night waiting for him."

"I don't think we's got enough gas to drive around all night and if we parks somewhere to wait, he'll see the car soon as he comes near. There's not much point in stayin' out any longer tonight, ma'am."

"Exactly. We have to come up with a better plan." Agnes stared down the street for a moment. "I've got it. We'll abandon the car and hide somewhere. It's the only way we'll catch this guy red-handed. Let's find a house he hasn't come to yet. Over there." She checked her list. "That one on the corner. Run and check that mailbox. See if he's been here yet." She pulled the car to the curb.

Jackson sprang out the door and ran up the driveway, flipped open the mailbox on the porch and zipped back to the car. "It's still there, ma'am. What does you want ta do?"

Agnes scanned the rundown yard and the overgrown driveway. "We'll park at the end of the driveway behind the house, and then hide in the bushes by the front porch. When he comes, I'll take his picture with my Brownie camera. Then…"

Whoo whoo!

Jackson grabbed Agnes's sleeve. "What was that? Is there a haunt out there?" The whites of his eyes gleamed large in the dark.

"Don't be silly. Don't you know a mourning dove when you hear one?" She backed the car down the long dark driveway, opened the door and started walking toward the front of the house.

Jackson followed at her heels. "How does we know a haunt didn't make itself sound like a dove?" His hand plucked at her sleeve.

Agnes shook her arm away. "I can't believe that a grown man—"

"Get down, ma'am. That pickup's coming down the road!" Jackson dragged her into the bushes.

The truck slowed and crept toward the house, the rumble of its motor sounding loud in the stillness. "I don't believe I can jump the fellow. He looks like a pretty big un'…" Jackson's hand shook on Agnes arm.

Golly darn! Mildred was right. It was too dark to take a picture with her Brownie and it wasn't likely the thief would stop under a streetlight for her benefit. At least they'd get a good look at the fellow. Thank goodness tonight wasn't a *practice* black-out drill like the one scheduled next week.

On black-out drills, all the window shades had to be drawn. Street lights were extinguished and citizens were encouraged to stay home. Any light showing from a front window warranted a visit from the black-out warden. So far, black-out drills in Newbury were just that… drills.

There was a greater risk of a Japanese submarine attack along the West Coast, than an air attack. The folks in New York had black-out protocol every night and Japanese submarines *had* attacked multiple ships along their coastline.

"I have a better idea, Jackson. Try and see his license number and report it to Chief Waddlemucker. I'll get into the back of his truck and find out where—"

"What? I can't let you do that, ma'am. An old lady like you? It wouldn't be safe. Maybe I oughta—"

The truck pulled up to the curb and a man in dark clothes jumped out, headed for the porch. He walked down the pathway and climbed the steps where the mailbox was nailed on the post.

"There's no time to argue. Do as I say," Agnes whispered. While the thief's back was turned, she stooped and scurried along the bushes toward the truck. She stepped onto the bumper and threw her leg over the tailgate, flung herself down with a plop, crawled under a pile of blankets and lay as still as death. She held her breath and willed her heart to stop pounding, lest the man hear it when he returned to the truck.

The truck swayed. A door slammed. Her grin faded as the engine purred and the truck moved slowly down the street. *Uh-oh, Agnes, what have you gone and done now?* She hadn't exactly thought this through. What if the driver found her when he stopped the truck? If he had no problem stealing ration books from his friends and neighbors, how far would he go to protect his black market secrets? She tried to think of a comforting Bible verse that might cover this situation. *Lo, I am with you always, even to the end of the world.*

Would that include in the back of a pickup truck headed—God knows where?

Chapter Ten

Late Wednesday Night—Tracking a Thief

Agnes held her breath against the smell of sweaty, moldy blankets covering her head. The wind whistled past the truck as it bounced down the weather-rutted street. She shivered, drew up her legs into the fetal position and wrapped her arms around her chest. "What have you done, you fool? How could you be so stupid? Please, God, if you get me out of this, I promise to never again do something so dumb." How many times had God heard her utter these same words?

Was there something wrong in her head that made her do such ridiculous things? If she got out of this alive, she'd think twice before… "Honest, God, I mean it this time," she whispered as she clutched the little gold cross around her neck.

Agnes's heart plunged when the pickup slowed. The man would see her for sure when he climbed out of the truck. Then what? She hadn't thought past climbing over the tailgate back on Emerald Circle, much less what would happen when the truck stopped.

Agnes stretched out flat on her back, sucked in her belly and tried to *become one* with the pickup bed. Was the blanket covering all of her or were her feet sticking out? She expected the blanket to be whipped off her body at any second and to be dragged forcibly from the truck. She gulped. *Our Father, who art in Heaven…*

The truck bounced through town, and then into the outskirts. It jounced over ruts in the road, across a railroad track, past the high school where the kids were playing football and out of town, past the fairgrounds where she heard a band playing Big Band tunes. They were heading north from the sounds she had identified, probably on Route 99. As a warrior on the home front, it was important that she take note of these things, else how could she find her way back if she managed to escape the jaws of death?

After what seemed hours, the truck stopped. The door squeaked. The man was getting out! She held her breath. *Hallowed be thy name. Thy kingdom...* Her mouth felt dry. She blinked back tears.

She jerked when the truck door thumped shut. Footsteps! Then, a metal sliding door slammed to the floor. *Bang! Clunk!* A padlock?

Oh, great! I'm locked in somewhere.

Then all was quiet except for the sound of her heart pounding in her ears. She lifted her head and pulled the blanket slowly down to her nose. It appeared she was inside a large warehouse.

Agnes peeked over the side rail. The hair on her arms stood up and prickled. Other than the bit of moonlight streaming from high windows near the ceiling, illuminating several rows of rectangular crates stacked two and three high, the darkness obliterated the corners of the warehouse.

She pulled Douglas's flashlight from his raincoat pocket and flipped the switch, casting shards of light across the cartons and along the roll-down door. She was still alive, thank God, but now that she was apparently locked in a warehouse in an unknown location, what was her chances of remaining so?

Agnes crawled over the back of the tailgate. She stomped her feet to get the circulation into her stiff limbs, and then moved along a row of crates. A scratching sound off to the right sent her crouching behind the nearest stack of crates. Probably a rat. She focused on her heart, trying to stop its pummeling in her chest.

An address tag protruding from the end of the crate tickled her cheek. She pushed it away and the paper tag came loose from it's fastener and fluttered to the floor. She flicked the light over the paper and picked it up. Her stomach lurched. *Whistlemeyer Mortuary— Newbury, CA.*

The label crinkled in her hand. *Whistlemeyer? What on earth?* She shined the light down the length of the six-foot-long crates. Coffins? The warehouse was full of coffins?

Another skittering sound nearby! Agnes drew a quick breath. She scrambled to her feet and shined the light toward the sound. A rat scuttled behind the stack of boxes. *Great.* The place was overrun with vermin! Where was a good cat when you needed one? She stuffed the address label back into a crack in the top crate and pulled the cinch of Douglas's raincoat tighter around her waist.

Using the torch, she explored from one end of the warehouse to the other. On the far side, a crack of light seeped out from under a door. An office. She flicked off the flashlight, tiptoed closer and put her ear to the door.

Voices mumbled inside, one male, the other female. Footsteps! Coming toward the office door!

Agnes ducked behind the nearest crate. What if they found her? How could she explain her presence? *Oh, it's quite simple. I accidentally found myself in the back of a pickup truck while the driver was stealing ration books and then he locked the truck in the warehouse. So I crouched behind this box, so I wouldn't be a bother to y'all while you're plotting your nefarious and treasonous deeds. If you'll excuse me, I'll be on my way...*

The door creaked open and a man and woman stepped out of the office. A light switch clicked. The warehouse lit up like a roman candle in mid-July.

Agnes crouched lower, crossed her arms over her head and closed her eyes. Her heartbeat sounded louder than an Indianapolis 500 raceway. Surely they'd hear the thumping and—

"Agnes Odboddy! What on earth are you doing down there?"

She yelped as the hand she had envisioned on her shoulder for the past few minutes became a reality. She opened her eyes and looked up. The outline of a man hovered over her, his silhouette dark against the floodlight directly overhead. She put up her hand to shield her eyes.

"Who is—"

"It's me, Albert Finklebaum—from the Ration Stamp Office? Whatever are you doing, crouched behind this box?" Albert pulled Agnes to her feet.

The woman beside him leaned forward, her arms crossed, her head tilted, her eyebrows raised. "Who is it? What the Sam Hill is she doing here?"

"Agnes? You'd better come into the office and explain yourself." Albert propelled her through the door and gave her a gentle shove toward a chair.

Agnes stepped back. The edge of the chair grazed the back of her legs. She flopped down. Her heart thudded. Buzzing in her ears nearly drowned out Albert's voice. The room seemed to darken. *Not now! I can't faint now! Control, Agnes!* Her brain seemed locked in neutral as she tried to come up with some plausible excuse for being in a casket warehouse, crouched behind a crate. Obviously, there was none. No one knew where she was. She didn't even know. As so often quoted on the Ellery Queen radio show every Monday through Friday at 9:00 P.M., 'I'm afraid the jig is up.'

Poor Katherine. She'd been through so much. Now, never to know what happened to her grandmother. Hopefully, Jackson got the license number on the truck and had sense enough to call Chief Waddlemucker, for all the good it would do her now.

She glanced through the doorway toward several bright green round containers nearby. They'd probably find her skeleton sometime about 1985, wrapped in Douglas's raincoat, stuffed in one of these round containers. They'd bury her in Potter's Field in a grave marked, Jane Doe.

Get a grip Agnes. You've talked your way out of tougher spots before. You can do this.

"Agnes? I'm waiting for an explanation. What are you doing here? How did you get in here?" Albert sat on the edge of the desk, his knee cocked, one foot still on the floor.

"I...I..." Agnes's chin went up. "You might as well come clean, Albert. We've been watching you. We know all about your little ration book charade." Agnes's mouth twisted in what she hoped was a confident sneer, while her stomach did the *cucaracha*.

"You mean these ration books?" Albert pointed toward a cardboard box full of addressed envelopes next to the desk.

Agnes recognized her own handwriting on the book nearest the top. Her eyes opened wide. She nodded. "I know what you're up to. Stealing the books, selling them on the Black Market. The FBI is right outside." Agnes stood and took a step toward the office door. "You better let me go out and talk to them, before they come in here with guns blazing."

Albert put up his hand.

Agnes stopped, glancing from Albert to the woman beside him.

"You're not going anywhere until we get to the bottom of this." Albert tipped his chin and glared over the top of his glasses. He crossed his arms and nodded toward the chair. "Sit!"

Agnes backed up and sat.

"You think I've been stealing ration books? Is that what this is about? I still don't understand how you got in here."

Agnes laughed. A laugh full of confidence, meant to terrify and disarm an opponent. Perhaps. Sadly, it failed, having no effect on Albert. "I'm part of an FBI undercover unit. You've been under surveillance. I got into the back of your truck at Emerald Circle. The FBI is following. They'll burst through that door any second." Agnes jerked her head toward the roll-down door, her mouth clamped in a firm line. *How am I doing? Is it working?* She gulped and the corner of her mouth quivered. Unbidden tears stung the corner of her eyes. She would not cry. Her only chance was to fake him into thinking the cops were right outside and capture was imminent. Maybe they wouldn't kill her before they made a run for it. On the other hand...

Katherine's sweet face drifted into her mind again. How would she survive another death of a loved one so soon after losing Stephen?

Would she have to curl Agnes's hair and put make up on her, now that she worked at the mortuary? *Don't be ridiculous. Of course they wouldn't make Katherine do—*

Peals of laughter snapped her back to the situation at hand. Agnes glanced between Albert and his gun moll again. "What!"

Albert was bent in half, his arms folded across his pudgy middle. Peals of laughter shook his paunchy belly, while tears rolled down his cheeks. "Did you hear that, honey? Have you ever heard anything…?" He reached for his mistress's arm, gasping for breath, and then burst into loud guffaws again. "Agnes… My dear, Agnes. Please let me explain."

"What are you talking about? You don't seem the least bit worried about the FBI right outside the door." She just wished someone was right outside the door. Someone who would burst in with a machine gun. Fat chance of that. She turned toward the door and raised her voice, hoping Albert would think she was trying to make her voice heard outside. "What's so all-fired funny, Albert Finklebaum? You're going to Leavenworth, that's where you're going!"

Albert wiped his eyes with a handkerchief, walked behind the desk and sat. He put his feet up on the desk. Another cackle burbled out. "Now, let me tell you what's going on and then you can tell me why you thought I was stealing ration books."

"Nothing you can say will change the facts, Albert." Agnes's hand swept over the box of ration books. "But, go ahead. Give it your best shot." She crossed her arms across her chest and squinched her face into as severe an expression as she could muster, considering the fact that her head was about to burst and her life expectancy could most likely be measured in minutes.

"Then let me explain." Albert ran his hand over his face, wiping away his grin. "I realized the other day that the government list of addresses included every house in town, even all the abandoned houses. By the time I noticed, the books were already mailed. I went around town tonight to retrieve the books at the empty houses so I could return them to Washington with a revised list. I brought them here for safe keeping until tomorrow."

Agnes's mouth dropped open. *Oh, my good gosh and little fishes. Don't tell me I did it again!*

"This is my business—Finklebaum Casket Distributors," Albert continued. "Here's my card. As a reputable local business owner, Washington asked me to oversee the Ration Stamp Office a couple days a week. I'm a volunteer there too, just like you. Now, tell me, what's all this about the FBI right outside?" He nodded toward the roll-down metal door at the front of the building.

Agnes's mouth snapped shut. She glanced at Albert's business card. *A Tisket, A Casket—Finklebaum Casket Distributor.* Wasn't that just too cute? She gulped. Albert's explanation made sense. Getting in the back of his truck and accusing him of black marketeering just didn't. Her cheeks burned. Another of her hair-brained notions gone hay-wire.

Embarrassment surged through her belly. Agnes buried her face in her hands. Her shoulders slumped. She shook her head. "There isn't any FBI outside. I made it up." *Once again, a prize fool. Worse than ever before, this time.* "I realized we were sending books to empty houses when I addressed the envelopes. I should have come to you, Albert. *But I didn't because I'm so gol-darned full of myself.* "I thought we had a black marketer thief, so I waited outside the house on Emerald Circle and…and…I jumped into the back of your truck. That's how I got here. I didn't know it was you. How will you ever forgive me?"

Humiliation scorched her cheeks. Oh, Lord above, when would she ever learn? How could she face him again at the ration office? She laid her head on the corner of the desk and wept.

"There, there, Agnes." Albert chuckled. "I can see how you'd think…" He coughed and cleared his throat, clearly trying to stifle another chuckle. "Don't cry. No harm done. In fact, it's pretty funny when you think about it. We'll not say another word about it." He reached across the desk and patted her hand.

She raised her head and wiped her eyes. "You mean, you don't hate me? I'd be furious if someone thought—"

Albert grinned. "I'm not mad. Let's just keep this our secret." He glanced at his companion. "It's funny, right, honey?"

The woman's cheeks flushed. Her mouth pulled down in a grimace. Apparently, she didn't see the humor in Agnes's actions. "I don't know. I—"

Albert shot out of his chair and barked, "Sweetheart? We all see the humor in this, don't we?" He walked around the desk and took her arm. "Now, why don't you go out and bring the car around back. We'll run Agnes home and then we'll put all this behind us, as if it never happened." He gave her a shove toward the door.

She glared at him, and then opened the door into the warehouse.

Agnes stood and pulled the sash of her raincoat tighter. "Really, Albert? You're not going to tell anyone? It's our secret?"

"Of course, Agnes. No one else knows, do they?"

"*Umm*… No. Not a soul. Scout's honor. She raised her fingers like a good Girl Scout. *God forgive me. I asked for help and He rescued me from the pits of Hades. Not five minutes later, I'm telling lies.* Surely, He'd understand that she didn't want to involve Jackson and Mildred in her mess.

"Come along, then. I hear the car. Let's just pop right out the back door and I'll run you home. I won't tell a soul how you acted like a fool and embarrassed yourself, if you won't."

"Oh, I won't. I promise. I'm just so relieved that I was wrong and you're not involved in anything… I mean…" She stepped out the door. "Oh, you have one of those new-fangled convertibles? Pretty fancy, *huh*?" She climbed into Albert's Hudson, reached up and touched the canvas top. "The casket business must be booming." She gulped. Thank goodness it was too dark in the car to see what must be her crimson face. *Of course, it's booming, idiot. There's a war on.*

Albert's lady friend moved over and Albert slid into the driver's seat and slammed the door. "Let's just say, people die every day, don't they, Agnes? We'll leave it at that, if you get my drift."

Agnes's heart skipped a beat. *Yikes! He could have talked all night without saying that.* People die every day? Did that mean that the casket business was good or… A shiver crept up her spine. Albert was innocent, right? He'd just explained everything, right?

Albert pulled away from the warehouse and back onto the highway.

Agnes recognized the flying red horse logo on the Mobile gas station on the outskirts of town. Just past the railroad tracks next to the high school, she saw her Model A coupe stopped at a stoplight with Jackson at the wheel. He must be worried sick, driving around, looking for her.

Agnes knocked on the window and waved, but the light changed and Jackson and her coupe chugged past, headed the opposite direction. Like a child, when his balloon floats off into the sky, she watched as her car disappeared down the street. Anger and helplessness welled up in her chest. "Stop. There goes my—"

Albert twisted in the seat. "Tell me, Agnes, where do you live so we can drop you off?"

She could see his grin in the moonlight. Where did she live? Did she really want him to know where she lived? *Don't be silly. What harm could come from that?*

"*Umm.* I'm on Minton Street. Turn left three blocks up. Mine is the yellow house on the corner. I live with my granddaughter, Katherine. She should be home by now."

Albert pulled his Hudson to a stop in front of her house. "What a pretty house, Agnes. How fortunate you are to have such a lovely home." He got out and opened the rear car door.

Agnes climbed out. "Thanks for the ride, Albert. Sorry about everything."

"Not a problem. It's our little secret, right?"

"I'll keep the secret if you will. You will, won't you?" Agnes's breath caught in her throat as she peered into Albert's face.

He smiled. For an instant, the harsh glow of the streetlight caused the lines in his face to take on a ghostly appearance like Bela Lugosi in the King of the Zombies. "You bet your life…" He turned, waved and climbed back in his car.

Agnes swallowed the lump in her throat and hurried up the pathway and into the house, snapped the lock and leaned back against the front door. She took a deep breath and blew it out. How good it was to be home and put all this nonsense behind her. "Katherine! I'm home."

No answer. The house was still as death. Ling-Ling hopped off the sofa and circled her ankle. "Lingy! Baby! Mama's home. Did you miss—"

Ring! Ring!

She hurried to the kitchen. "Hello?" She flung off Douglas's raincoat and draped it over a kitchen chair.

"Mrs. Odboddy? This is Michael Farthingale, from the Newbury County Hospital. I'm calling about your granddaughter, Katherine. She's here in the Emergency Room. She's been hurt. Can you come down right away?"

Chapter Eleven

K atherine? In the emergency room? What happened?" Agnes paced toward the icebox, until the phone cord snapped tight and jerked the phone from her ear. She turned and paced back.

"She had a fall, you see. We've admitted her to the hospital for observation. Could you bring a few things to make her more comfortable? There are papers to sign and we'll also need to know who is financially responsible." The voice on the phone dripped with boredom, as though he'd already made dozens of similar calls and couldn't wait for his coffee break.

"I...I...of course. I'll be there as soon as I can." Agnes hung up the phone and collapsed into a kitchen chair. *Why didn't I ask more questions?* She should have asked him for details. Katherine! What could have happened? Hadn't she gone to the mortuary tonight?

All this time, while she was running around on a fool's errand, poor Katherine was laying in the hospital. *Now, what shall I do?* Jackson had her car, driving around looking for the black pickup truck, probably thinking the worst. She jumped up and paced the kitchen.

Had Jackson notified Chief Waddlemucker? She'd never hear the end of it if Chief Waddlemucker's officers were out scouring the countryside, looking for a black pickup truck, thinking she was kidnapped...or dead.

Should she call the station and tell them she was home and it was... what exactly would she say? A prank? A false alarm? Another one of her crazy conspiracy theories run a-muck? Agnes's face warmed. How would she ever live down accusing poor Albert of stealing ration books? Such a fine upstanding man. How could she ever—?

The bell on the front porch jangled. Agnes hurried to the door, her heart in her mouth. *Please, let it be Jackson.* Or Chief Waddlemucker come to arrest her for defaming Albert's reputation, or falsely reporting a crime or maybe just to haul her away to the looney-bin for a psychiatric evaluation. She couldn't think of a defense. She was pretty much guilty of all three.

Agnes flung open the door.

Jackson stood on the dark porch. The whites of his eyes glinted in the light, spilling out from the living room. "Thank you, Jesus. You're home. I've been drivin' up and down for the past two hours, tryin' ta spot that 'eir pickup truck."

Agnes grabbed his arm and pulled him inside. "Did you call Chief Waddlemucker? Please tell me you didn't call him." She sucked in a breath and held it.

Jackson shuffled his feet on the entryway tile. "Well, ma'am, it's like this. I didn't rightly know what to do—whether I shoulda' called him or not. I thought I could catch up with the truck and see where it went. I had it in sight for a while, and then lost you right outside of town. I drove around, hoping to spot it parked somewhere. After bit, I was getting low on gas, so I thought I'd better come back here and ask Miss Katherine's advice. But, here you are safe and—"

"You made the right decision. It was all a mistake, you see. Oh, I don't have time to explain now. The hospital just called. Katherine's in the emergency room. I must get some things together and go down there. If you want to wait a few minutes, I'll drop you off on the way to the hospital. Thank you for going with me tonight."

She rushed into Katherine's room and stuffed her nightgown, comb, toothbrush and the small teddy bear her fiancé bought her on their first and only Christmas together, into a small blue train case. "I'm so glad you didn't call the Chief," she called down the hall. "That would have been so embarrassing." She scurried back, gripped Jackson by the arm and hustled him out the door.

"But, that's just it, Mrs. Odboddy," Jackson pulled away from her and stood on the bottom step. "On the way back ta' your house, I decided I oughta report what happened. I stopped at the drug store and called the station. The officer in charge was mighty upset when I told him what you done. He notified Chief Waddlemucker and they sent out a patrol car. They's lookin' all over town for that 'eir black pickup truck."

Agnes's hand was on the key, ready to lock the front door. She pulled her hand away and rubbed her eye. What else could go wrong? If they didn't arrest her and Jackson for calling in a false report, at the very least, she'd be the laughing stock of the police department—again! "You wait in the car, Jackson. I better go back and call the station and tell them it was a false alarm."

Agnes opened the door and dashed into the kitchen. Her heart felt like *The Little Engine that Could* in the nursery rhyme she used to read to John. She opened the phone book to the dog-eared page for the police department, dialed and held her breath. If they were busy, maybe she could just leave a message with the receptionist.

"Newbury Police Department. Can I help you?" The deep masculine voice on the other end of the phone was a sure sign there'd be no message-leaving tonight.

"*Umm*... This is Mrs. Odboddy. I'm calling to let you know..." What exactly could she say? That she saw conspiracies everywhere and this was the second time in less than a week she'd chased after...? No. Don't go there. They didn't need to know about the Packard on the beach and the Japanese submarine she had imagined out to sea.

Just tell them it was all a mistake and she wasn't kidnapped. They should call back the troops. Yes. Tell the truth. Be humble and apologetic for any inconvenience she might have caused. No more lies.

Promise never to report a crime again.

Honesty is always the best policy.

Definitely…the only sensible thing.

"Hello? Hello?" *Click. Click. Click.* "Are you there, ma'am? Can I help you?"

"*Umm*… Yes. I'm calling to tell you that…that…" Agnes gulped. "This is Mrs. Odboddy. I was able to outsmart the kidnappers and loosen my bonds, picked the lock on the door where they held me prisoner and escaped. I hitchhiked home and I'm fine…so…so you can let Chief Waddlemucker know I'm safe and he can stop looking for me. Please tell him I'm sorry to have caused a bother, but everything is okay now. Okay? Thank you. Goodbye!"

She slammed down the phone. Her fingertips tingled and beads of perspiration formed on her upper lip. She pulled a hankie from the neck of her dress and dabbed her face. *Great job, Agnes. Now you've told another bald-faced whopper.* Did she really think Chief Waddlemucker would buy that hunk of bologna? More likely, he'd be here tomorrow with handcuffs.

Agnes shook her head. "Can't worry about that, now. Katherine needs me."

She huffed out to the Model A and roared down Minton Avenue. Last time she drove this block, she thought she was closing in on a ration book black marketer! *Don't think about that now.*

"You can drop me off near the courthouse, Mrs. Odboddy. I know you're in a hurry. I can walk home from there. It's not far."

"Don't be silly, Jackson. After all you've done tonight, I'll take you home. Just tell me which way to go." Agnes turned a grateful smile toward her companion. Jackson had been a champ all evening, helping her track the truck, as misguided as that was, and then trying to come to her rescue. *I'm such an idiot.*

"Just up there, ma'am. Turn left on Charles Street and then right on Brighton Circle. Third house on the left."

They drove in silence for a few blocks. Agnes turned the corner and pulled to a stop at the curb. Jackson's porch light cast a warm glow across the neat rows of tomato vines and cabbages where a trimmed green lawn had been just last summer. She shivered at the sight of the homemade scarecrow wearing a raincoat that looked too much like Douglas's for comfort. She closed her eyes and turned her head. "Here you go. Thanks a lot, Jackson. Sorry to get you mixed up in this mess. Turns out, I was wrong about someone stealing ration books."

Jackson's mouth dropped. His eyebrows flew into his forehead. "Wrong, ma'am? I don't understand. We saw—"

"I'll explain it all to you tomorrow, but right now, I've got to get to the hospital. I'm sorry." She nodded toward the door and waved her hand. "Nice garden."

"Yes, ma'am. Give my best to Miss Katherine. Me and the Missus will pray for her." Jackson closed the door and gave it a slap.

Agnes gunned the motor and tore off toward Newbury County Hospital. *What will I do if Katherine is seriously hurt?*

Chapter Twelve

Agnes pulled her car into the closest parking space near the emergency room door. She yanked on the brake and rushed toward the entrance. *Hurry, Agnes, Hurry.*

Constructed just months before the attack on Pearl Harbor, the Newbury County Hospital glowed bright under the night sky. Light from the sleek metal fixtures overhead bounced off the bright square glass blocks surrounding the entrance doors of the emergency room.

A bronze plaque beside the door read—

> Have not I commanded thee?
> Be not afraid, neither be thou dismayed,
> for the LORD thy God is with thee
> whithersoever thou goest.
> Joshua 1:9
> Donated by Whistlemeyer Mortuary

Wasn't that just like old man Whistlemeyer? He wanted to make sure people remembered his name, even during their darkest hour—just in case the hospitalization was not successful and his services were required.

Agnes hurried through the door and up to the reception desk, stepping in front of the couple with a baby, standing near the counter. "My granddaughter's here. Katherine Odboddy?"

"Please step back, ma'am." The white-haired clerk held up her hand. "I'll be with you just as soon as I finish registering this baby."

As if on cue, a wail emanated from the infant swathed in blankets in its father's arms. The mother, her haggard face suggestive of too many sleepless nights and work-worn days, pursed her lips and turned away.

Agnes's face burned. "I'm so sorry. I was so worried about my… I guess I didn't even see you there." She lowered her head and stepped back. *Good one, Agnes. Shove aside a sick baby. You're really batting a thousand today.* She gulped down the giant coal-sized lump in her throat and batted back the tears stinging her eyes, threatening to spill down her hot cheeks. "I'll just wait over here, ma'am. If you'll call me when you get a moment?"

The clerk nodded and returned to the couple who had moved closer to the window.

Agnes sat in one of those new-fangled Eames chrome and plastic chairs. If only she could crawl back into bed and start this day over. What would she do different? She sure wouldn't drag poor Jackson all over town on a wild goose chase. She wouldn't feed the police department a *whopper* when her escapade took a nosedive. And, she wouldn't shove a sick baby aside in the emergency room. *What is wrong with you, Agnes?*

She dabbed her eyes with her hankie. Just relax for a minute. Nothing she could do until the clerk called. She gazed at the people sitting in the waiting room. Not too many folks out this time of night. Thank goodness. Mostly older men and a few younger women with children. A baby wheezed on the opposite side of the room. Probably had the croup—plenty of that going around these days.

A young woman with a coughing toddler moved from the far wall to the row of seats directly behind Agnes. She turned and smiled.

Agnes nodded. "Sick baby?" Would being nice to the young woman make up for her indiscretions today? Probably had a husband overseas. Maybe she was a widow. Almost as many of those these days as there were croupy babies.

The young woman twisted in her seat. "Little Chuckie has asthma. The damp night air always makes him worse. When his temperature reached 100 degrees, I thought I should bring him in to be checked."

"Good idea. One of these days, they'll perfect that new wonder drug I've read about. *Pemicillum?* Heard they're using it on some of the troops overseas with a good deal of success. Poor baby. Have you tried a mustard plaster on his chest?"

The young mother shook her head. "I don't know how to make one."

"I used it on my boy years ago." Agnes stood and walked around the end of the chairs and sat down next to the woman. "First, you make a paste with dry mustard and warm water, and then apply the paste to a clean linen cloth."

The young woman nodded. "I can do that."

"Fold the cloth over and place the plaster on the baby's chest over his lungs. Make sure the mustard paste doesn't touch his skin or it can cause a rash."

The young woman dug in her purse and found a piece of paper. "Clean cloth. Dry mustard paste. Got it. How long should I leave it on?"

"For about ten minutes, then take it off. You can repeat the treatment every few hours to loosen the chest congestion." Agnes smiled at the toddler. "He's a cutie."

"And, it really works?" The mother glanced at the boy sitting at her feet, running a toy truck across her shoe.

"Like a charm. Maybe someday that *pemicillum* will be available to the rest of us, but until then, a simple mustard plaster has worked on asthma for centuries. Colds and flu, too. You should—"

"Ma'am? I can see you now." The receptionist leaned through her window and waved her pen. "You had a question?"

Agnes stood. "Good luck with your boy." She grinned at the young woman and hurried to the receptionist. "I got a call that my granddaughter, Katherine Odboddy, is here. They said you had some forms?"

Agnes reached into her purse and pulled out her wallet. She gazed behind the clerk, where a row of beds lined the back wall. Several had bright blue curtains pulled around. Katherine must be behind one of those curtains just across the room…

The receptionist shuffled through a stack of papers. "Yes. Odboddy. She's in bed three, over there." She pointed over her shoulder. "If you like, you can visit for a few minutes. Please come back here before you leave and we'll take care of the paperwork."

Agnes rushed to the row of beds and threw back the curtain around the third bed. Empty! Tight hospital corners held the top blanket snug and wrinkle-free. A fluffed pillow lay full and fat, as though waiting to comfort a suffering head. The bare nightstand showed no evidence of a patient utilizing the space.

Agnes's heart missed a beat. Was she too late? Had Katherine died and already been moved to the morgue? Her chest convulsed in a sob. *Katherine! Not even a chance to say good-bye.* The blue curtains blurred into a grey blob as her eyes filled with tears.

"Excuse me, Mrs. Odboddy?" The white-haired receptionist's face blurred. She touched Agnes's arm. "My mistake. They moved Katherine over to the far end, closer to the attending doctor's desk. If you'll step this way?"

Katherine wasn't dead! For a moment, the room swam in front of Agnes's eyes. The blue curtains looked dim and far away. Had she forgotten to breathe since the moment she pulled back the curtain? *For a moment there…* Air surged back into her lungs and the waffle-weave on the blue curtain snapped back into view as clear and sharp as when she first walked up to the bed.

She followed the woman toward the far end of the row of beds. With each step, the objects in the room sharpened into focus. A tray of instruments here. A gurney with pink sheets there. A machine with hoses extending and round dials. The clerk pulled back the curtain surrounding the last bed. "Here she is. Doctor? This is Katherine's grandmother."

"Katherine! My dear!" Agnes's heart seized with love at the sight of her.

Katherine lay on the bed, her face as pale as death. A bandage circled her bright red hair, spread across the pillow like a summer sunset. *Please, God, let her be alright. I cannot bear to lose her. She's the most important thing in the world to me.*

Agnes glanced up at the young doctor. Her heart throbbed. "What happened? Wasn't she working at Whistlemeyer's Mortuary this evening?" Agnes took Katherine's hand and pulled it to her cheek in a caress. A tear dripped onto Katherine's bright red fingernails.

The young doctor stood beside the bed, his hand on Katherine's other wrist, counting her pulse. His finely chiseled features and blue eyes reminded her of Jimmy Stewart.

He laid Katherine's hand on the covers and reached across the bed. "I'm Dr. Donald Dew-Wright." He grinned. "I know. Stupid name, *huh*? Folks call me Dr. Don."

Agnes extended her hand. "How is she? She looks so pale."

"She's doing as well as can be expected. Her pulse is strong, but she's been *out* since the accident. That's a bit worrisome. We stitched the gash on her head, but the area is still swollen. We'll know more when she wakes. She's young and healthy. I'm hoping for the best."

"How did it happen?" Agnes wiped her tears off Katherine's fingers with her thumb.

"According to Mr. Whistlemeyer, Katherine had just finished working on a client. Apparently the gurney fell and Katherine must have gone down with it. It appears she struck her head when she fell. He called an ambulance."

Agnes laid her head on Katherine's bed. "Poor Katherine. She didn't want to go down there, and I talked her into going. This is my fault."

"No, it's not. Accidents happen every day, Mrs. Odboddy. We see this kind of thing all the time." He picked up a clipboard and made a few notations. "Please excuse me. I have to tend to other patients. Will you be alright?" He hung the clipboard on the end of her bed. "Shall I call someone to come and wait with you?"

Agnes lifted her head. "No, thanks. I'll just sit here for a moment and gather my thoughts."

Dr. Don slid back the curtain and turned. "The chapel is on the second floor. Pastor Lickleiter may be on duty tonight."

"Oh? Thank you. That's my pastor from the First Church of the Evening Star and Everlasting Light. I'll go up and speak with him."

"If there's anything I can do, ask the nurses to ring for me." Dr. Don waved and jerked the curtain closed behind him.

"If you have a miracle in your pocket, I could use one of those," Agnes whispered.

She moved to the chair, laid her head back against the headrest, and closed her eyes. "Lord, I'm a wicked old woman. I haven't done anything lately to warrant any special favors, especially tonight, but Katherine is good and I love her. She doesn't deserve this. If you could see your way clear to—"

A sound from the bed. Agnes opened her eyes. "Katherine?"

Katherine moaned and touched her face. She turned toward Agnes's voice.

"Katherine?" *Thank you, Jesus!*

Katherine's eyes fluttered. She ran her fingers over her mouth. "Water…" Her voice was barely a whisper.

"Here. I'll call the nurse." Agnes scurried to the door and shrieked, "Nurse! Come quickly! She's awake."

The nurse on duty strode into Katherine's room. She placed her fingers on Katherine's wrist and checked her pulse. "Welcome back, young lady."

Katherine's eyes roamed toward Agnes. "Grandmother? What… what are you doing here?" She glanced around the room. "Where am I?" She jerked her arm away from the nurse. "What are you doing?" Her eyes opened wider. She looked back at Agnes. "Oh. I remember now. Clyde…Clyde fell. Oh!" Her cheeks flushed pink and tears gathered in her eyes. "Mr. Whistlemeyer must be furious. How is Clyde?"

Agnes raised an eyebrow as she took Katherine's hand. "You're in the hospital, *punkin'*. Who is Clyde?" *Is she hallucinating? Oh dear. I hope this isn't permanent.*

"Clyde is the…was the…client at the mortuary. I had just finished with him and the gurney fell. I hope he's alright."

Agnes chuckled. "I see. He's probably still just as dead, but other than that, I expect he's fine." She giggled. "I'm sorry. I shouldn't make such crude jokes. It's really terrible, isn't it? The poor man. It's just that I'm so glad you're okay. We didn't know… That is, Dr. Don wasn't sure if you…" She shook her head. "That's not important now. You're going to be fine." She patted Katherine's hand. "You know what? I'm going to run upstairs for a minute. There's something I need to do. Now, don't go away, okay?" She grinned at her joke and plunged through the curtain and out the door before Katherine could see the thankful tears that leapt to her eyes. *I must go to the chapel and thank God for Katherine's recovery.*

A man and a woman approached as Agnes pushed the elevator button. Not wanting questions or an embarrassing moment, she turned and climbed the stairs, whisking the tears from her eyes and brushing the back of her hand across her hip.

A large sign over the door indicated the chapel on the second floor. She shoved open the door. Dim lights overhead and floor lamps placed strategically around the room created a soft, comforting glow. Soft music flowed from hidden speakers in the corner. Six rows of purple padded benches stood in front of an altar adorned with candles and a tall vase of lilies and carnations. Agnes heaved her body into the last bench and closed her eyes.

The fragrance of the lilies and carnations took her back to the day of Douglas's memorial service so long ago. On that day, the cloying scent of lilies was almost enough to take her breath away. There must have been a hundred friends and neighbors at his service. Her son, John, had managed to call her long distance, but was unable to come home for his father's funeral.

Not six weeks later, the men in dark suits were at her door again, telling her that John's plane was blown to smithereens somewhere out to sea, and not a scrap of it was ever located. They held his memorial service at Arlington, where a plaque with his name was laid in the grass while his body lay somewhere under the ocean. A twenty-one gun salute acknowledged his sacrifice, and they placed a bouquet of lilies and carnations in her arms along with the American flag. The scent and sight of lilies and carnations had made her sick to her stomach ever since.

Agnes couldn't breathe through the lump in her throat. The tears she'd choked back in the hallway careened down her cheeks. Sobs shook her body, a combination of relief and thankfulness for Katherine's recovery mingled with memories of Douglas and John…and the other man. Forcing thoughts of him from her mind, she concentrated on her prayer, thanking God for Katherine's recovery.

A deluge of tears flowed unchecked for several minutes until the pressure of a hand on her shoulder startled her. She jerked up her head. *Leave me alone.* Between the dim light and her tears, the face of the intruder was sheathed in shadow. *Pastor Lickleiter?*

"Agnes. Take my handkerchief. You never have a handkerchief when you need one."

The scent of Old Spice overshadowed the lilies. A chill tore up her spine and chill bumps careened down her arms. Even after too many years to count, she would never forget the man who wore that scent or the insouciance of that voice!

Chapter Thirteen

Good Grief! Godfrey!

gnes shaded her eyes. The years zipped away as the flickering light played across the man's face. How long had it been? She took his handkerchief, dabbed her eyes and blew her nose. She stumbled to her feet and stared at the tall, distinguished man with a touch of grey at his temples. He grinned down at her with the same rakish smile she remembered too well. Her hand moved to her cheek, trying to brush away the feel of spider webs. Her stomach clinched. "You! What on earth are you doing here?"

"I might ask you the same." He gestured toward the altar. "I don't remember you being religious back in the day."

"How would you know what's in my heart? It's been over twenty years."

"Correction. *Twenty-four* years, if memory serves." He reached for her hand.

She jerked it away. *Godfrey Baumgarten!* "And nothing's changed between us, Godfrey. Like I said, what are you doing here?" She crossed her arms and glared, making a conscious effort to still her shaking hands and her pounding heart. It took all her willpower to blink back the tears clinging to her eyelashes.

He held her gaze. "I thought maybe I could help." His voice gentled. "Like that day in Paris. Don't tell me you've forgotten. Do you want me to stay or not?"

Agnes's mouth turned down. "I don't need your kind of help. I didn't need it twenty-four years ago in Paris, and I certainly don't need it now." Her fingers tingled. Her cheeks warmed at the memories and emotions his presence revived. She swiped her thumb against her index finger, trying to rub away the irritation that still lingered.

Godfrey's blue eyes, so like cornflowers in springtime, sparkled in the dim light. "Agnes..."

She turned her head and closed her eyes. After all these years, surely she couldn't still have feelings for him. *Don't look at me like that.*

He turned toward the altar and then back to face her. "You're thinking of Douglas, aren't you? You know, I loved him too. I lost both of you when he died and you went away. It didn't have to be that way."

He was much too close for comfort. His aftershave triggered memories of moonlight, bonfires at the beach, marshmallows on a stick, too many stolen kisses and gentle hands... As pleasant as the memories, all were a betrayal to Douglas and to her marriage vows. Agnes sighed, sat back on the bench and scooted away. "I had to leave you if I was ever to regain my self-respect. We both knew it was wrong."

"How can you forget what we had together? I thought when he died—"

"How could you think that? When he died, how could that suddenly make it right?"

"Surely, you don't think I'm responsible for what happened between us." He sank down beside her, his eyebrows raised. "Was it all my fault?"

"I counted on you to keep me strong, to control the situation. Yes. I blame you. You knew how I felt. How the guilt tortured me when we..." Agnes put her hands over her eyes. "I'm sorry if I hurt you. I had to make a fresh start." She shook her head. "None of it is important, now. I'd forgotten about it years ago. I can't remember the last time I even thought of you." *Liar! Liar! Pants on fire...*

In truth, over the years, Godfrey crept into her thoughts all too often. And, just a moment ago, she was thinking of him and the next minute, he was sitting right beside her. It was uncanny. It was...well, it was downright spooky.

She pursed her lips. He was grinning again, the rascal! The grin that had won her heart and changed her from a dutiful wife and mother into a...into a...what? A fallen woman? A harlot? That's what they were called in 1918.

How many times had she planned what she would say, should they ever meet again, face to face? How many nights had she imagined the conversation and scripted the dialogue? Now that he was close enough to touch, she couldn't remember one sentence, one comment so carefully rehearsed. Twenty-four years since they'd laid eyes on each other, not to mention other body parts, and she couldn't recall one single well-rehearsed phrase. *I suppose my face is all puffy from crying.*

Her lips curved in a smile, in spite of herself. Now that the opportunity was at hand, her tongue was tied in knots and the only thing that popped into her head was whether her eyes were puffy. She swallowed hard and sighed.

"Agnes?"

"How did you know I was here?"

"I spoke to Chief Waddlemucker and he—"

"What?" Agnes's head jerked toward him. "Chief Waddlemucker knows I'm here? I don't understand. What does that have to do with you?"

Her thoughts raced. The pickup truck—the warehouse—Jackson calling the station—Katherine lying still as death in a hospital bed...

As troubling as the events were, none of it compared to an old lover from nearly a quarter of a century ago appearing out of nowhere, smelling of Old Spice and peppermints. He still looked the same as back in the day when they had spread a blanket on the beach, and... and...

Don't go there, Agnes. Perspiration beaded between her breasts.

Her attention snapped back to Godfrey's voice. *What did he say? I wasn't paying attention.*

"...in Hawaii for the last few months, right after the bombing of

Pearl Harbor. They reassigned me to California to investigate reports of black market ration books all over the state. When Chief Waddlemucker called the FBI and reported the possibility of stolen books here in Newbury, I caught a transport flight and—"

"The Chief contacted the FBI? Oh, my goodness gracious!" Her hand flew to her mouth. So, Chief Waddlemucker believed her story, after all, at least enough to report it. Now, what? She was caught in her own fabrication—like a gnat in a giant flypaper. She touched her cheek and ran her tongue over her bottom lip.

"What's wrong? Didn't you want the chief to follow up on your concerns?"

"*Um*…well. I guess at the time I did. But, now, everything has changed. I mean—"

Godfrey's eyes narrowed. His smile faded. He looked so official, it made Agnes's stomach hurt. The cat was out of the bag. She had to tell him the truth. It was bad enough that the Newbury police had wasted taxpayer dollars running all over town looking for her tonight when she should have been home in her bed. She certainly couldn't allow the FBI to get involved, searching for a thief that didn't exist. It was time to 'fess up.

Agnes's stomach did another flip-flop. "Godfrey. I can't let this go on any longer. Especially, here in the chapel. It's all a lie, well, not exactly a *lie*, but…" She lowered her chin and folded her hands in her lap. Now, he'd think she was a nut farmer, just like everybody else.

"Agnes, dear. Whatever is troubling you can't be all that bad." He lifted her chin with one finger. Their eyes met.

The touch of his finger took Agnes back twenty-four years to the day she learned of Douglas's death. Godfrey had rushed to her house, burst through the front door and pulled her into his arms. She crumpled against his chest, sobbing, and then turned away. With conflicted feeling of guilt mixed with overwhelming sorrow, she couldn't look him in the eyes. "It's over. We can't do this anymore." Tears streamed down her face. She pushed him out the door and out of her life. Shortly thereafter, John died, and she had moved to Newbury, hoping to forget her indiscretions and the man that had captured her heart.

Godfrey's name was never spoken in her house again.

Agnes sighed. *That's ancient history.* So much time had passed, and still the touch of his finger made her toes curl and her heart race. *What's wrong with me? I'm an old woman. I'm not supposed to have such feelings.* She jerked her head away. "You might as well know the truth. There never was any ration book theft. It was all a mistake. Just me, thinking there was a conspiracy when there was none."

Godfrey's blue eyes looked darker in the dim light of the chapel. "Go on. Details?"

"It was my boss, Albert, collecting the books. He was going to return them to Washington." Agnes closed her eyes. "Go ahead and say it. I'm an old fool. That's what everybody thinks. Just an old fool." She glanced up through her lashes.

Godfrey slowly shook his head. He looked her up and down. "I don't think you're an old fool. But, tell me everything, right from the beginning. Don't leave anything out, and then we'll see what's to be done." He patted her hand and flashed the grin that still turned her legs to Jell-O.

Over the next fifteen minutes, Agnes gave him all the gory details from the moment she solicited Jackson's help, to hopping in the back of Albert's truck, to Katherine being in the hospital. "So, that's what happened. Albert wasn't stealing anything. I just jumped to conclusions, as usual, and made a big idiot of myself."

Godfrey raised an eyebrow. "I didn't catch this Albert's last name."

"Albert Finklebaum, the manager at the Newbury Ration Stamp Office."

"Finklebaum... You don't say. Name rings a bell, but I can't quite..." Godfrey ran his hand over his chin. "*Humm...* Agnes, dear. Why don't you run on back and check on your granddaughter. I have some things to sort out."

"You never explained how you knew I was here."

"I was in Sacramento, looking into the matter of missing ration books there. Seems there were other reports of similar goings-on in little towns all over California. We thought there might be a state-wide operation, maybe some sort of underground connection. When the FBI got Chief Waddlemucker's call and mentioned Newbury, I asked for the assignment because…well, you know. I knew you were here."

"You knew I lived here?" Warmth crept up the back of her neck clear into the roots of her henna-freshened hair.

"I've always kept track of you over the years, Agnes." Godfrey stood. "That's about it. Now, if you'll excuse me, I have some business to attend to. Maybe I'll give you a call tomorrow and we—"

The chapel door squeaked open. "Is Agnes Odboddy here?" A nurse in a tall starched hat stood at the doorway, one hand still on the swinging door.

Agnes turned. "Yes?" She rose from the bench. "I'm Agnes. Is it Katherine? Has something happened?"

"Katherine's fine. Dr. Don asked me to find you. She's asking for you."

"Oh, Godfrey. I have to go!" Agnes grabbed her purse and dashed to the door.

She hurried down the hall toward the elevator, her thoughts a-jumble. *Did he say he'd call tomorrow?* She turned, torn between wanting to go back and clarify Godfrey's intentions and the need to rush to Katherine's side. She stood in the hall looking back and forth between the chapel and the elevator. Her cheeks tingled, cold as ice.

A nurse stopped beside her. "Are you alright, ma'am? You look pale. Is there something I can help you with?"

"No. No. I'm fine." Agnes pushed the elevator button. "My granddaughter's in the emergency room. I know the way." She rushed into the elevator. Just a glimpse of Godfrey appeared outside the chapel as the elevator door snapped shut.

In the emergency room, she walked past the empty bed that had given her such a fright, and on to the last one in the row. She pulled back the blue curtain.

Dr. Don leaned over Katherine again, his hand on her wrist. The wistful look in his eyes suggested he didn't want to let go, even though he'd completed the task several times over.

What's this? Katherine and Dr. Don? Now, there's a thought.

A smile twitched Agnes's lips. "My! Looks like I got here just in time. What's going on?"

Dr. Don dropped Katherine's hand like it was a hot skillet. "*Umm... er...she's doing just fine.*"

Katherine's face flushed.

So, she's interested, too. Good. It's time Katherine found a young man to make her happy. And a doctor to boot! Agnes sat in the chair next to the bed. She took Katherine's hand, the one that Dr. Don had caressed only moments before, warmer now than when she first came to the emergency room. *Probably the result of the good doctor's attention.*

"So, when can I take this young lady home?" Agnes's gaze turned to Dr. Don, noting the pink tinge also clinging to his cheeks, behind the scattering of light blond whiskers he'd missed shaving.

"We'd like to keep her overnight. It's best to keep a close eye on a head injury." He turned toward Katherine. "And, I'm not quite ready to let her go yet, if you don't mind." A smile lit up his eyes. It was the admiring smile of a young man toward a pretty woman, and not at all like any doctor Agnes had ever seen looking at his patient.

"Oh, I don't mind," Agnes said. "As you think best. I can come by anytime tomorrow and drive her home. First, I have to stop at the feed store and check on the price of hens. Did I tell you, dear? We're going to have chickens. Now, we'll have fresh eggs every day. Think of the money we'll save.

"My friend, Jackson, is building us a coop this Saturday. Isn't that wonderful?" Agnes beamed, glancing between Katherine and Dr. Don. *Why, look at them. Neither one is even listening to me.*

"And, I thought the chickens could roost on the head of your bed and lay eggs in your bloomers drawer. I didn't think you'd mind. You don't mind, do you, Katherine?"

Katherine and the good doctor's eyes were locked on each other, again. They were somewhere together, perhaps on a sunny beach with a picnic basket spread out on a checkered tablecloth, and a half-empty bottle of imported Chianti, but they were definitely not in a hospital emergency room listening to Agnes talk about chickens.

"Katherine, did you hear what I said? Hello. Chickens?" Agnes slapped the bedcovers.

"What?" Katherine's head slowly moved from Dr. Don toward Agnes's face. "Chickens? What about chickens?"

Before Agnes could open her mouth to chide Katherine, the blue curtain jerked back and a nurse appeared. "Did I hear someone say something about chickens? Isn't this just your lucky day?"

She moved to the side of the bed and straightened Katherine's sheet. "It just so happens that I have six wonderful half-grown chickens that need a new home. My landlord says I have to get rid...*umm*...I mean, find another place for them." Her cheeks flushed. She ducked her head, her hands busy fluffing Katherine's pillow and picking imaginary lint off the bedspread. "If you're interested, you can have those chickens for free, but they have to be gone by tomorrow evening. What do you say?" She looked up into Agnes's face, a wavering smile clinging to her lips.

"Free, you say. Well, isn't that just a fine idea?" *She looks desperate. It must be hard for her to give up her pets.* "Of course we want them, but I couldn't possibly pick them up by tomorrow night. Perhaps by the weekend—"

"Oh! Sorry. That's the deal. My landlord has given us a deadline of tomorrow night. Otherwise, he says he'll confiscate them and cut off their heads and fry—"

"No. No. You can't do that." Agnes stood and put up her hands. "I'll take them. I'll figure out something. Leave your address at the reception counter. I'll come by tomorrow afternoon and pick them up." How much trouble would it be to take care of a couple of chickens until

Saturday when Jackson could build the coop?

Dr. Don reached over and took Katherine's hand again.

She needs her pulse checked again, so soon?

"Well, I must get on about my duties, Katherine, er...Miss Odboddy," Dr. Don said. "The orderly will move you upstairs to room 221 on the second floor. Good day, Mrs. Odboddy." He scurried out the door, his cheeks flushed again.

The nurse shuffled items around on Katherine's nightstand. "I'll ask you to leave, ma'am. I need to get Katherine ready to move. Good. I see you brought her some night things. We'll give you a call about picking her up tomorrow."

Agnes nodded, kissed Katherine's forehead and picked up her purse. "I'll see you tomorrow, dear. It looks like Dr. Don is taking good care of you." She winked and backed toward the curtain.

"Don't be silly, Grandmother." Katherine's face flushed as pink as a baby's behind.

Agnes blew her a kiss and stepped through the curtain, her mind already on what kind of cake to bake to welcome Katherine home, confirming Jackson's plans for the chicken yard and...Godfrey. He said he'd call. Wasn't he always lingering somewhere in the back of her mind? How incredible, that an old flame she hadn't seen in years should appear out of the blue.

Chapter Fourteen

*A*gnes backed the car into the single garage and pulled down the wooden door, her head near bursting with the evening's events. All's well tonight, but what about tomorrow and the next day, and the next? Sooner or later, she'd have to face Albert at the ration office. Not to mention Chief Waddlemucker. What would he have to say about her latest caper? Not likely she'd heard the last from either of them. Thank goodness, at least Katherine was going to be alright.

She pulled the belt on Douglas's raincoat tighter around her ample middle and stopped half-way up the steps. *Good grief!* Was she still wearing that stupid raincoat? She had it on in the chapel when she saw…

Godfrey! What to do about Godfrey?

Agnes walked slowly through the front door, rubbing her hand over her forehead. It was a bit chilly in the house, but not enough to turn on the thermostat and waste the gas. She took off Douglas's raincoat and tossed it onto a pile of boxes on the back porch. *I really must get rid of that thing. It reminds me how stupid I am. I'll send it to Goodwill.*

Agnes struck a match and lit the burner on the top of the kitchen range. The gas ignited and flames circled the prongs beneath the tea kettle. *A cup of tea would be nice. Might help me figure out what to do about…* She held the match to the hole inside the oven. The gas *whooshed* as the flame caught. The heat from the oven would warm the kitchen. She left the oven door open and dropped the match into the can beside the salt shaker.

Hunger pangs gurgled through her stomach. *That's right. I skipped dinner.* Was it only a few hours since she left the house with Jackson? It seemed like days ago. *Will Albert keep my secret?*

Ling-Ling sauntered in from the living room and wound around her ankles.

Agnes opened the breadbox beside the kitchen sink. "I don't remember Katherine baking bread. When did she find the time?" The bread must be several days old. No problem. It would be fine toasted.

Ling-Ling turned and circled her ankles the opposite direction.

She must be hungry, too. Agnes took a kitchen knife from the drawer and cut off two pieces from the half loaf. She opened the cupboard and removed Katherine's birthday gift from last year—her new pop-up toaster. She leaned down and grinned at her reflection in the shiny chrome-plated finish. It was almost too pretty to use. She unplugged the electric mixer and plugged the toaster into the wall socket, popped the bread into the toaster slots and pushed down the handle. The margarine plate and fig jam came out of the icebox.

The kitchen was warming nicely. "I think I can turn down the oven." She smiled at Ling-Ling and thoughts of Lilly popped into her head. *I hope she's okay.*

Pop! Up came the bread, now a toasty golden brown. How many pieces of toast had she burned over the old bread rack that used to straddle the stove burner? These new-fangled appliances were a godsend. Hopefully, Katherine's toaster would outlast the war years. There would be no more toasters produced this year. Every scrap of metal went into ships and airplanes.

Still holding the knife, she lifted off the margarine saucer lid. "Oh, fudge!" Only the tiniest smear of margarine clung to the edge of the dish. "We used the last of it this morning. I forgot. I was going to mix up more." *No. I didn't forget. I was too busy chasing imaginary ration book smugglers around town. No time to tend to my own household affairs. When Chief Waddlemucker gets hold of me, I may never see the inside of my kitchen again.*

Ling-Ling sat at her feet, staring up at her, one blue eye looking toward the icebox and the other toward Agnes's face.

"You're right. I forgot to feed you, too, didn't I, my lovely?" Agnes patted Ling-Ling's head. "I'll get you some milk." She opened the icebox and pulled out the milk carton and a new package of Oleo margarine-mix and set them on the table. *What I'd give for a slab of real butter. We haven't had any since before the war.*

She poured a bit of milk into a bowl and set it in front of Ling-Ling. "If you give me a minute, I'll get you some bread," she said, slicing off another hunk. She broke it into tiny pieces and dropped it into Ling-Ling's milk. "There you go, sweetheart."

Now. The margarine.

Agnes dumped the white lump of Oleo margarine into a large bowl. She bit off the end of the dye package and squeezed it over the top. She squished the yellow liquid into the chunk of white margarine with a fork until the margarine softened and began to take on a yellowish hue. Now, thoroughly blended, she spooned some into the butter bowl on the table. She snapped a plastic bonnet over the remaining glob of *make-believe butter* and slid it back in the icebox. At least it *looked* like butter. With a glob of jam and lots of imagination, you could hardly tell the difference. She smeared her toast with the concoction and added a generous dollop of fig jam. The teakettle whistled.

Between sips of tea and bites of toast, she flipped through the telephone book. "Here it is. Jackson Jackson." She took another bite, swallowed, and picked up the phone to dial.

"Hello?" A sleepy male voice gurgled. "Jackson residence."

"Jackson? Is that you? It's me, Mrs. Odboddy." She glanced at the clock over the stove. *Good heavens. It's after midnight. I should have waited until tomorrow to call.* "I'm sorry to bother you so late—"

"Is sumpin' wrong? Did them smugglers come back? Is Miss Katherine okay?" Jackson's voice cracked. He coughed and cleared his throat.

"No. No. Katherine's fine. I just got home from the hospital. I don't want to talk about the ration books tonight. It's something else. I was wondering if you could come by tomorrow afternoon and build that chicken coop we talked about. I've got a chance to bring—"

"Missus Odboddy. You waked me up this time a night to talk about chickens? My wife, she don't feel so good and... Why does you need such a chicken yard tomorrow? I gotta' work till 5:00 o'clock tomorrow. I can't take off work to build you no chicken yard. I even got my friend to take my Boys and Girls Club shift on Sattidy just so's I could help you. You know I works every day a' the week. I ain't no lay-about like some—"

"Oh, I never thought..." Agnes's heart tumbled. "Of course, you work every day. What was I thinking? I'm sorry to bother you. I guess with all this going on tonight, I'm so wrought up, I didn't think. You go back to sleep, Jackson. Can you come over early Saturday morning? You can take my car to the lumber yard and pick up the material. I'll give you some money. How does that sound?"

"Sure thing, Missus Odboddy. I'll see you 'bout 8:00 A.M. Sattiday morning. You sure that's all that's troublin' you?"

"Yes, Jackson. Thanks. See you later."

"Good night, ma'am."

Agnes hung up the phone. She popped the last bite of cold toast in her mouth and sat back down at the table, chewing. "Ling-Ling, what am I going to do with six half-grown hens until Saturday?" *That is, if I'm still here Saturday. If Chief Waddlemucker decides to press charges...maybe Godfrey will intercede on my behalf.* Godfrey!

She shook her head, sighed and ran her fingers around her mouth, wiping away bread crumbs.

Ling-Ling's pink tongue slurped across her front paw. She pulled it over her ear. Several drops of milk clung to her white whiskers.

"You're right. Nothing I can do about that, now, is there? But, I must decide what to do with those hens." Agnes drummed her fingers on the red and white checkered tablecloth. "I know. We'll just put them in the bathroom. How much trouble could they be for a couple days?"

Ling-Ling trailed her to the bedroom and then jumped onto the end of the bed. She turned her body into a letter *C* and flopped down on the feather duvet and licked her shoulder.

That cat! Not a care in the world. I should have so few worries. Wonder what she'll think about sharing the house with six chickens in the bathroom?

Faith! Weren't half a dozen hens the least of her worries? Tomorrow, with the ring of the doorbell, it could be Chief Waddlemucker coming to arrest her or Godfrey, coming to declare his undying love. Either way, tomorrow promised to alter the course of her life forever.

Chapter Fifteen

Thursday Morning, 6:45 A.M.—Rolling Bandages for the Troops

At the sound of the ringing phone, Agnes opened her eyes. Exhausted from her harrowing night's adventure and restless hours tossing and turning, she lay sprawled across the bed, her head buried under the pillow and one foot outside the covers. She pulled the pillow off her head, climbed out of bed and stumbled to the kitchen. "Hello?"

"Agnes? Did I wake you? It's Godfrey."

"Oh!" Agnes's stomach did a jig. She yanked her nightgown down over her hips from where it had crept up and clung to her bloomers. *Ahem!* "Godfrey?" She glanced at the clock over the stove. 6:45 A.M.? What was he thinking, calling this time of morning? *I've only been asleep for four hours.* "I'm awake. So nice to hear from you…so early this morning…" She yawned and ran her hand over her flyaway hair. *If he could see me now…*

"Sorry if I woke you. I guess I'm still on Hawaii Time. I'd like to come over this morning. How about 9:30 A.M? We need to talk."

Hawaii time? That doesn't make sense. It's only 3:45 A.M. in Hawaii.

"That's not good for me. I have to be at the hospital at 10:00 A.M. I'm scheduled to roll bandages for the troops this morning. Katherine's coming home today and this afternoon, I'm fetching my chickens. Perhaps this evening?" Agnes clutched the neck of her nightgown, pulled out a kitchen chair and sat. The cold chair chilled her bare thighs.

"Tonight, then. I'll come by about 6:00 o'clock. Shall we go out for dinner?"

"*Umm*. I don't think so. I'd rather not leave Katherine home alone so soon. Why don't you join us for supper? I'll just whip up some oxtail stew this afternoon."

"Sounds wonderful. I haven't had oxtail stew for ages!"

"Then, that's settled. About 6:00 P.M.?" *Do I have time to have my hair done today? Oh dear!*

"Good. See you then...*dear*."

Agnes had just lowered her posterior into a steaming bathtub when the phone rang again. She heaved out of the tub, wrapped a towel around her middle and hurried to the kitchen phone, leaving a trail of water across the kitchen tile. "Hello? Who's calling? This better be important. You got me out of the tub."

"Mrs. Odboddy? Sorry about that. This is Chief Waddlemucker."

Mother of God. Retribution was on her doorstep before she'd even taken a bath.

"I see that you're home, safe and sound. After Jackson called last night, I guess you know we had a patrol car out for an hour looking for a black pickup truck."

Alcatraz, here I come. "Yes...*umm*...well, about that—"

"Tell me how you escaped from the kidnappers."

"*Um... Uhh...* Yes, well, perhaps I exaggerated a bit. But, I do appreciate your concern. Thanks for call—"

"Not so gol-darned fast, Mrs. Odboddy. What does that mean, you exaggerated? Just as I thought. Were you kidnapped, or weren't you? Perhaps I should come over there and arrest you for reporting a false crime, *humm*?"

"Well, *uhh*...That is..." Agnes pulled the towel tighter around her bosom. Arrest? That sounded bad. Right when Katherine needed her. "Please, Chief Waddlemucker. It was all a big mistake. You know how I get carried away sometimes. I don't mean any harm."

"Like when you accused Sophia Rashmuller of being a Nazi spy and poisoning Mildred? I want to tell you, Sophia and I had a good laugh about that when I mentioned it to her. But, seriously, Mrs. Odboddy, I'm not going to put up with this much longer. These shenanigans have got to stop. Do I make myself clear?"

"Yes, Chief. No more tall tales. I promise. I really mean it this time. I'm truly sorry for all the trouble I caused." A cool breeze from the back porch swept under her towel, chilling her bare legs and backside. The puddle of water circling her feet felt as if it had turned to ice.

"Good. I don't want to shave this constellation with you again, do you hear?"

"What does that mean? Shave what constellation?"

"What? I didn't say anything about shaving…whatever… I said I don't what to have this conversation with you again. Your hearing, Agnes. I've told you before, and I'm telling you again. You need a hearing aid. Now, you have a nice day, okay? Good-bye."

"Yes, sir. Thank you, sir. Good-bye, sir." Droplets of perspiration trickled down Agnes's forehead. She hung up the phone and wiped her brow. This time, she'd learned her lesson—no more whoppers. That was *waaay* too close for comfort.

Why was Chief Waddlemucker so keen on her getting a hearing aid? She didn't need a hearing aid. He just mumbled too much.

Agnes shivered. Getting chewed out by the chief of police while standing practically naked, no matter how well-deserved, was not a good way to start the day. Agnes adjusted the towel around her middle again and turned back toward the bathroom.

She threw one leg over the bathtub and dropped her towel. Gripping the edge, she started to lower her body…and the phone rang again. "What the heck!" She climbed out of the tub, grabbed her towel and raced to the phone. More water pooled on the linoleum beneath the wall phone. "Hello? Who is it this time?"

"Abigail Ratchet, here. Sorry if I woke you. Just checking to see if you're still planning to come for those chickens."

"Oh, it's you. Indeed. When can I come for them?" *Nurse Rachet must have had to think long and hard before she married a man with that last name!*

"I'm pulling a double shift at the hospital." She yawned. "They scheduled me back to back today. Could you come about 3:00 o'clock?"

Agnes glanced at the clock. 7:15 A.M. "Do I need to bring a box or something?"

"I think they'll be fine riding home in a gunny sack, if you don't have far to go." A baby wailed in the background. "How far do you have to go?"

Chill bumps raced up Agnes's backside. *If I don't get off this blasted phone pretty soon, I'm going to catch my death of pneumonia.* She tightened the towel around her middle. "I'm on Minton Street, near the high school. I'll be there at 3:00 P.M." Agnes glanced at the clock.

"Don't be late or they're going into the stewpot." Nurse Rachet slammed down the phone.

"Well, I swan! How rude. And I'm doing her a favor taking the hens off her hands." Agnes finished her bath and gathered clean undergarments from her dresser. Bloomers, a pink corset, and last year's nylon stockings. She stepped into her undergarments and laced up the front of her corset, tying a neat bow beneath her bosom. She sat on the bed and pulled on the right stocking; the one with only one hole just below the knee. *Couldn't get a new pair of nylon stockings this year if my life depended on it.* Score another vital unintended consequence of war.

Agnes glanced into the mirror. "You'll wear patriotic holes in your stockings, Agnes, before you resort to painting a line up the back of your legs with that wretched lotion Katherine uses when she goes out." She grinned at her reflection as she reached for the garter hook at the back of her corset.

Ring-ring! "Not that blasted telephone again!"

Agnes stumbled into the hall with the left nylon hanging half-way down her leg. On the way to the kitchen, the stocking crawled the rest of the way down and bunched around her ankle. "Hello!" More of a snarl than a greeting.

"This is the discharge planner from Newbury County Hospital. Mrs. Odboddy? I'm calling about Katherine."

Agnes reached down and yanked her stocking up to her thigh. She tried to hook the garter snap with one hand. The snap slipped away and the stocking crept back down her leg. "Oh! Horse feathers!" She made a grab for it and pulled it back up.

"Excuse me? I thought you were expecting a call about Katherine's discharge time."

"Yes, of course. I wasn't talking to you. Is Katherine ready to come home?" Agnes clutched the errant stocking and plopped into a kitchen chair.

"She'll be ready after lunch. Could you come about noon?"

Agnes held the receiver against her shoulder and fastened the garter snap to the top of her stocking in the front, stood and fastened the back hook. "That's fine. Thank you for calling. I didn't mean to bark at you. I was talking to my stockings."

"Beg pardon? Are you sure you're alright, ma'am? Should I send somebody?"

"Don't be impertinent, young woman. I said I wasn't talking to you. My stocking kept falling down."

"I see. Well, you have a good day, hear?" The phone went dead.

"*Humph!* There you go. Can't even have a normal conversation but someone rushes to the wrong conclusion."

Meow! The shriek came from the living room.

What on earth? Agnes rushed out of the kitchen.

Ling-Ling hung on the drapes, half-way to the top, one paw swiping at a moth fluttering just beyond her reach. "Ling Ling! Get down from there this instant. That's a no-no! Mama's drapes!"

Bing-Bong.

Agnes peeled Ling-Ling off the drapes and stuffed her under one arm "Oh, rats. Probably the Fuller Brush man. One of these days…" She yanked open the door. *Mrs. Rashmuller?* Had she come to gripe about her gossip with Chief Waddlemucker?

Ling-Ling squirmed from under Agnes's arm, dropped to the floor and raced into the kitchen.

"Agnes, dear. I just stopped by to tell you how much we missed you at knitting circle this week. Will we see you next week?" Sophia's hennaed hair glinted in the bright morning light.

"Sophia. What a nice surprise." Agnes batted her eyelashes and grinned like a Jack-o-lantern. "Unfortunately, you've caught me just rushing out the door on my way to the hospital. My day to roll bandages." *I'd like to roll the old battle-ax right out of town.*

"Oh, so sorry. I should have called." Sophia held up a plate covered with a linen cloth. "I've brought you a sample of my lemon tarts. I noticed you didn't get a chance to taste them at knitting circle last week." She shoved the plate toward Agnes.

Would these be the lemon tarts that poisoned Mildred? Shame, Agnes. You know that was just your imagination. "Wasn't that nice of you? What a pity I can't ask you in, but I really must go. Perhaps another time? Thanks again." Agnes took the plate. "Good bye." She eased the door closed and leaned against it.

Ling-Ling sauntered in, one eye on Agnes's face, the other angled toward the moth still beating itself to death against the window.

"Well, aren't we starting the day off with a bang? Now, I've been rude to someone bringing goodies. At the rate I'm going, I'm headed for H-E-double toothpicks, for sure." She sighed. "I always have such good intentions. I just don't know where I go wrong."

She carried Sophia's dessert to the kitchen and set it on the counter next to the sink. "At least Godfrey will be pleased. Now, we'll have something for dessert after dinner tonight. I won't need to bake a cake, after all."

Katherine laid her head back on the pillow and closed her eyes. She'd really done it this time, passing out and whacking her head on the mortuary sink. Who would Mr. Whistlemeyer get to fix up Clyde in time for his funeral? Maybe she could go over tomorrow and put on some last minute touches before his services. Poor Clyde.

She glanced at her watch. 10:00 A.M. Grandmother was probably already rolling bandages downstairs with the other volunteers. Wasn't she something? The woman never stopped. Knitting circle, USO, Ration Stamp Office, rolling bandages, coast watch. *I hope I have half her energy when I'm her age.*

The blue curtain snapped back and Dr. Don stepped through. "Good morning, Miss Odboddy. How are we this morning?" His eyes twinkled.

Katherine's cheeks prickled. She pulled the bedspread closer to her neck. "Good-morning, Dr. Don. I don't know how *we* are this morning, but I'm just fine." She giggled. "Can I go home today?"

He took her wrist and glanced at his watch. "Nurse Rachet says you ate all your breakfast this morning." His face lit up like a little boy with a new paper airplane.

Katherine's heart squinched. She sucked in her breath. *Where did that come from?*

Dr. Don checked the clipboard at the end of the bed. "Temperature—normal, pulse—normal. Your lab results are fine. I can't think of a reason to keep you any longer. Wish I could." His smile would have melted ice cubes, as Grandma would say.

At the very least, his smile was melting her hardened heart. Katherine's heart already felt like oatmeal. "You probably say that to all the girls." She ended in another uncontrolled giggle. *Now, I sound like a foolish school girl. What's wrong with me?* Had the room brightened since Dr. Don came in? It was certainly warmer than a few minutes ago. She pulled the blanket down and readjusted the sheet at her neck. "Can you crank that window open a bit?"

Dr. Don looked toward the window overlooking the parking lot. "It does seem a bit warm in here, now that you mention it. *Umm.* Miss Odboddy… May I call you Katherine?"

"Might as well. All my friends do."

"Katherine. We're releasing you after lunch, but you should take it easy for a few days. I still have some concerns…*umm*…with a head injury, you see. I'd like to drop by your home in a day or so…just to make sure you're alright."

Katherine nodded. Her tongue felt dry. She licked her lips. *My, it is stifling in here.* She fanned her face with her hand. "Of course." *What other reason would he have? Probably stops by all his patients after discharge.* "When can I go back to work at the salon and Mr. Whistlemeyer's mortuary? I have responsibilities."

"You must promise to rest this afternoon and go to bed early tonight. Your grandmother can keep an eye on you. If your temperature is normal in the morning, I think you can go to work for a few hours. But, take it easy. No heavy lifting and no collapsing on the floor. I'll not have it. Do you hear?" He patted her hand.

Katherine's heart pattered and her stomach lurched at the touch of his hand. What could be wrong with her? She hadn't reacted to a man like this since Stephen died. Probably the whack on her head had affected her judgment. She'd be back to normal in a few days.

Edith Braithwaite shoved a wad of gauze into Agnes's hand. "You can start with this. Our goal is to roll 800 bandages this morning, between the three of us."

Agnes sighed. To think that so many young men would need so many bandages was heartbreaking. But, at least she'd do her part to see they had a bandage if they needed one. She looked up as Mildred came through the door. "Hello. Glad to see you're feeling better. I've missed you."

Mildred smiled and pulled a stack of gauze toward her. "Glad to be here."

Agnes didn't mind rolling bandages. While Edith cut large rolls of cotton gauze to size, Mildred and Agnes sat together, winding the bandages into tight rolls. They could chat or contemplate their private thoughts, depending on their mood.

It was a sight better than working in the influenza prep room. Down there, one had to wear a mask, gloves and a smock, in a germ-free environment, sterilizing items. Breathing through the blasted mask was hard enough. Carrying on a conversation with another volunteer was nearly impossible. But, willing to assist in any way possible, Agnes would go where the lead nurse felt the need was greatest on any particular day.

Two hundred and fifty seven rolled bandages later, she finished her shift shortly after noon. Agnes hurried to the cafeteria, choked down a sandwich and then dropped by Katherine's room.

She arrived just as Nurse Rachet snapped the lid on Katherine's overnight bag. "There you go. Here's your grandmother now, right on time. We'll get a wheelchair and take you down to the Discharge desk. Just a few papers to sign and you'll be on your way."

Agnes glanced at her watch. 12:45 P.M. Enough time to get Katherine home and settled, start the oxtail stew and race back across town to pick up her Victory hens. She should have told Nurse Rachet 4:00 P.M. Why did everything happen at the same time?

Oh, bother. We'll work it out. We always do.

Forty-five minutes later, they left the Discharge Planner's office. Agnes wheeled Katherine out the door. "I'll leave you here and run get the car." She hurried down the ramp to the parking lot where she'd left the Model A.

"Thanks for driving me home, Grandmother. I'm sorry to be so much trouble. I can't tell you how embarrassing all this is." Katherine's mouth pulled into a pout.

"Don't be silly. It's no bother." Agnes glanced at her wristwatch. 1:35 P.M. "I have to be across town at 3:00 to pick up our chickens. I'll start an oxtail stew, and you can tend it while I'm gone. Just keep an eye on it so that it doesn't boil dry."

"I think I can manage that." Katherine pulled her overnight bag closer to her feet.

"I…uh…I'm having a guest for dinner tonight. An old friend of your grandfather's. Well, actually, both of us. I haven't seen him for years. He's in town for a few days and I asked him to dinner." Agnes glanced at Katherine, gripped the steering wheel, leaned forward and focused on the road straight ahead.

Katherine turned toward her. "Why, Grandma, you're blushing. Is there something you'd like to share? I think maybe there's more about this gentleman then you've mentioned. Don't be keeping secrets from me. I won't tell."

"Don't be ridiculous. He's just an old friend. Nothing more. But, what about you? Seemed to me you were mighty chummy with Dr. Don. Something you'd like to share? You can tell me. I won't tell." Agnes grinned at Katherine. "Now, who's blushing?"

Agnes carried Katherine's overnight case into her bedroom. "Now, you lie down on the sofa and spread that afghan over your legs. I'll make you a nice hot cup of tea before I go. Are you hungry?"

Katherine waved her hand. "I had lunch at the hospital. Go get your stew started. It's almost 2:15 P.M. Didn't you say you had an appointment pretty soon?"

Agnes nodded and dashed into the kitchen, pulled her recipe box down from the cupboard and thumbed through the cards. "Here it is. Oxtail stew." She grabbed a large kettle from the cupboard and lit the stove burner. "Let's see now. What do I need?"

She scanned the recipe and read aloud. "Dredge three large oxtails in flour and brown with an onion in butter or shortening." She brought out a frying pan, scooped out two tablespoons of lard from the bowl on the back of the stove. She tossed the floured meat into the frying pan with a diced onion. While these browned on all sides, she poured two cups of beef broth from her canning shelves, two cups of water and two cups of diced tomatoes from her garden into the large kettle. Finally, a bay leaf, a teaspoon of salt and a dash of pepper.

When the meat and onion were nicely browned, she scraped them into the kettle and turned down the burner. She stepped to the kitchen door and called to Katherine, "It's simmering on the back of the stove. I really don't think you'll need to add anything before I get back."

"Yes, Grandma. I'll take care of it. Don't worry."

"It needs to cook for three hours. I'll be home long before that and add the rest of the ingredients."

"What else goes in it? You know, for future reference, in case I want to make it myself someday."

"Just some vegetables during the last hour. Half a cup of carrots, half a cup of chopped celery, a tablespoon of parsley and six potatoes. I'll thicken the gravy just before we eat. Our bread is several days old, but if we pop it in the toaster, it should be just fine."

Agnes grabbed her purse and hurried past Katherine. "Do you need anything before I go? I won't be long."

"Wait. Before you go... What are you going to do with the chick—?"

Agnes slammed the front door. She wasn't ready to discuss the chicken issue with Katherine just yet. Truth to tell, she hadn't exactly figured out how they'd manage between now and Saturday, getting six free hens was preferable to buying them come Saturday. Why, they'd cost good money at the Farm Bureau. How would you save money on eggs if you had to pay a whole dollar for each hen to start with?

Agnes pulled up at Nurse Rachet's house at exactly 3:00 P.M. *Right on time.* Sounds of babies shrieking emanated from inside the house. She knocked.

With a sweaty face, hair tumbling over her forehead and a squalling baby in her arms, Nurse Rachet yanked open the door. "Yes? Oh, it's you. Come on in." She jounced the baby and shoved a strand of hair behind her ear. "Sorry I can't offer you a cold drink. Little Arnie has colic and keeps waking up the other baby." She nodded toward the squalling infant lying on a blanket on the floor. "My mother watches them while I'm at work, but the minute I get home, she shoots out of here like a German rocket. If you don't mind, can you just take the chickens? Maybe we can chat another day." It sounded more like a command than a request.

"Twins! I see you have your hands full. I'll just get *my* babies and go. And thank you." Agnes turned back at the door. "Where are they?"

"They're in a gunny sack out in front of the garage. You can't miss them. You passed right by them." Nurse Rachet slammed the door. The crescendo of infant screeching reduced to a dull screech.

Well, isn't she a ray of sunshine on a cloudy day! At least the hens are free. Agnes spotted the wiggling gunnysack on the pavement in front of the garage. "Now, how did I miss that when I came in? Okay, girls. Mama's come to rescue you from the mean old lady in the crazy baby asylum. I'm sure you'll be much happier at our house." She picked up the sack and lugged it to her car. "My, you girls are a hefty lot, aren't you? A wee bit on the portly side? We'll take care of that, by jingo. Have you nice and svelte in a jiffy. Once you start laying eggs, you'll have your waistlines back in no time."

Within minutes, Agnes was back across town, hauling the sack through the front door. "I'm home with the babies, Katherine." She set the wiggling sack on the living room floor amidst a variety of squawks, and untied the string holding it closed. She peeked inside.

The six captives flopped around the bottom of the bag. Spying freedom overhead, one of the colorful birds scrabbled to the top of the sack and onto Agnes's shoulder. "Oh, my! Isn't she pretty? Look at her colors. All red and brown. And, so friendly. See? She knows her mama already. Won't this be fun?"

A plop of gooey grey-white substance dribbled down the front of Agnes's blouse. "Oh, dear!" Her hand flew to her cheek. Wasn't this a fine how-do-you-do? Not the best way to make a first impression.

Katherine sat up and folded the afghan. "Grandmother. Now that they're here, what do you plan to do with them?"

"Jackson is building us a coop on Saturday." Agnes wiped at the stain with her handkerchief.

"That's fine. What about between now and then? It's Thursday afternoon. You can't keep them in a sack until Saturday. Where—"

"I'll just pop them into the bathroom until I figure it out. Maybe Godfrey has a suggestion. He'll be here in a few hours."

"That's your friend who's coming to dinner? The one that made you blush?"

Agnes lifted the sack and carried it to the bathroom. "Not now, dear. Come and help me figure this out. Oh, do you want to use the facilities before I turn them loose?"

Katherine hurried into the bathroom. "Perhaps I'd better. Sharing a bathroom with six chickens isn't exactly my idea of privacy."

"You go first and then come and hold the sack while I go. Here's a thought. Perhaps we can set up the clothes-drying rack in the bathtub. They can roost on that. On Saturday, we can wash out the tub and clean up after them." She grinned as the image of three cooperative hens lined up on the top row of the drying rack and three across the bottom, like pigeons on a telephone wire, popped into her head.

Katherine retrieved the wooden drying rack from the garage and unfolded it in the bathtub. "Actually, that's not a bad idea, Grandmother. It looks like a chicken roost. I'll bet they'll love it."

Their hygiene needs completed, Agnes closed the bathroom door and opened the gunny sack. The chickens flapped out in a mass of squawks and feathers. One hopped on the back of the toilet, one into the sink. Two downy feathers drifted down, as the third flapped up to the top of the shower curtain rod. The fourth chicken flew to the top of the window curtain. The fifth perched on the tub faucets and the sixth sat on the edge of the towel bar. All six avoided the clothes-drying rack like it was a charcoal spit covered with barbecue sauce.

Agnes sighed. *It's going to be a tough slog around here until Saturday.* Now that she knew they could fly, what would keep them from flying out of the coop once it was built? *Uh-oh, Agnes, Have you gone and done it again?* She gulped.

"Think of it, Katherine. Fresh eggs for breakfast any time we want. Isn't this a great idea?" A cold chill wormed its way up her spine.

Chapter Sixteen

Thursday Evening—Chicken Chaos

Agnes hurried to the front door at the sound of the bell, and then paused, her hand on the knob. *Okay, here we go. Time to put on the full armor of the Lord and gird my loins with...* She shook her head. *Stop thinking about loins, Agnes. You're only stirring up... Just open the door, already.*

She grabbed the handle, pasted a smile on her face and pulled. "Come on in, Godfrey." She stepped aside as Godfrey came through the door, a bouquet of violets in his hand.

"For you, m'lady."

Agnes took the bouquet and nodded. "How thoughtful. This is my granddaughter, Katherine." Agnes pointed toward the sofa. "Have a seat. Dinner will be ready soon." *And the sooner we eat, the sooner you'll be gone.* She laid the flowers on the coffee table.

Godfrey nodded and sat. "Nice to meet you, Katherine."

"Nice to meet—"

Squawk! Er er erer er!

Godfrey leaped off the sofa. "Zounds! What was that?" He scanned the room, his hand on a bulge under his coat that could only be a pistol.

Gracious! Is he going to shoot my chickens?

"Calm down!" Agnes shooed him back. "That's Mildred, Sophia, Abigail, Clara, Myrtle and Mrs. Whistlemeyer—my new hens. They're in the bathroom."

"Grandmother! You named the hens after your friends? Isn't that a bit cheeky? What made you think to do that?" Katherine stood, picked up the violets and headed for the kitchen, shaking her head. "If you'll excuse me, Godfrey, I'll put these in water and see about dinner. Can I get you something to drink? We have a bit of coffee, but it's left over from breakfast."

Godfrey raised an eyebrow and glanced at Agnes. "*Uh…* Sure. That would be splendid. Thank you. I drink it black."

"I'll just be a minute." Katherine disappeared into the kitchen.

"Okay, Agnes. What gives? Chickens? I remember you were always up to something. I'd believe almost anything, but chickens in the bathroom? That's a bit half-baked, even for you."

"It's just temporary. My friend is building a coop on Saturday, but until then, it's a teeny inconvenience, to be sure, but we'll share the facilities until Saturday and clean up the bathroom later."

Agnes nodded toward the hallway. "Let's not talk about the chickens. What have you been doing all these years, Godfrey?"

"My life is too boring to talk about. I spent twenty years in the service and the FBI. I haven't done anything noteworthy since I last saw you." He reached for Agnes's hand. "And, that's been far too long. Tell me, did you ever remarry?"

Leave it to Godfrey to go straight for the gullet. After all this time, does he think I'm going to fall into his arms like a swooning debutante? "I never remarried, nor do I have any intention of doing so at this late date." She yanked back her hand and glared at his snarky grin. *He's playing with me! How impudent.* She drew her eyebrows together and crossed her arms. "What is it you're after, Godfrey? Showing up out of the blue like this and acting like a blithering schoolboy." Could he tell that her heart was flying around in her chest like a ping-pong ball?

"Why Agnes, don't be that way. Actually, I've already told you, I'm on an assignment here in Newbury. How inconsiderate would I be if I came to town and didn't look you up? Some things never change, Agnes, even after so long apart." He reached for her hand again.

Agnes stood and moved to the sofa chair across the room. Putting a little distance between them might calm her pounding heart. "Exactly.

And nothing's changed since I last saw you, either."

"Here's your coffee, Godfrey. I hope it's hot enough. I didn't want to boil it again. It's already twelve hours old." Katherine set the steaming mug on the coffee table with a blue and white linen napkin.

"I'm sure it's fine. Thank you. I'm pretty used to twelve hour old coffee."

Scratch, scratch, scratch.

Agnes cocked her head toward the bathroom. "That's not…Ling-Ling?" She jumped up and dashed toward the hallway.

Ling-Ling lay on her side, attacking the bathroom door with all four chocolate-brown paws. There was no question about her plans for the feathered delicacies that lay just beyond the safety of the bathroom door.

"Ling-Ling! For shame. That's a *no-no!*" Agnes scooped up the blue-eyed killing machine, and pitched her down the hall toward the open garage door. "Mama's chickens! No! No!" She shook her finger at the furious feline, ears pulled down, one eye glaring in her general direction, and the other pointed toward the desired quarries behind the bathroom door.

Now, that could be a problem she hadn't thought of, if Ling-Ling was determined to have *poultry tartare* either now or in the near future.

Agnes stood for a minute, trying to calm her rapidly beating heart before returning to the living room and Godfrey's sultry blue eyes. Was she really up to this? Maybe she shouldn't have asked him over tonight. She had not considered her reaction to learning that he still had feelings for her. Her blasted body was in total rebellion to her intentions to send him back to wherever the heck he'd been for the last twenty-four years.

As a recently un-retired undercover agent for good, rooting out Nazi-Jap spies and righting social wrongs, she had no time to take up with an old flame. Ellery Queen wouldn't keep a girlfriend around any longer than it took to film a two-hour movie. Having Godfrey underfoot would definitely cramp her style, as much as he might stimulate a Saturday night or a leisurely Sunday morning.

Maybe after the war, she could look him up. No. That wouldn't do either. After the war, she intended to deal with the white slavers.

Agnes shook her head. *For heaven's sake, get dinner over with and send him packing.*

She straightened her dress, put a smile on her face and hastened back to the living room.

"Just the cat. No problem. Where were we? You were saying you were so busy, you only came by to say hello, right?"

"No. I wasn't saying that—"

"My! Look at the time. Katherine, isn't dinner ready yet? I'm so hungry, I could eat a camel." Agnes fluffed her hair and readjusted the silver chopsticks on the back of her head.

Katherine jumped up. "Oh! I thought you wanted to visit. I'll dish up the stew. The table's already set. Give me five minutes." She fled into the kitchen.

Godfrey stood. "It smells wonderful. May I use your restroom before dinner?"

"*Uh!* If you're sure you can handle it. You know…" Agnes raised her eyebrow and nodded toward the bathroom.

"I've dealt with a chicken or two in my day, Agnes. Remember, I was in the military for the past twenty-odd years." He stood and looked toward the kitchen, apparently feeling confident he could handle the poultry challenge.

Agnes walked with him into the hallway. "Second door on the left."

Godfrey turned the knob.

Meow! A beige streak raced by Agnes and slipped past Godfrey's feet as he shoved open the door.

Agnes gasped and dashed toward the bathroom. Godfrey might have dealt with a chicken or two during his exhilarating career in the military, but he wasn't equipped to deal with a cross-eyed cat on a Black-Ops Death Raid.

If a hand grenade had detonated in the bathroom, there couldn't have been greater chaos. Ling-Ling sprang from the floor to the back of the toilet, and then to the top of the shower curtain. Within the close confines of the bathroom, feathers flew as the six chickens exploded in six different directions. The frightened fowl squawked. Ling-Ling yowled. For a little cat, she was making a grand effort to annihilate the six-pack.

Godfrey flung up his hands as a chicken—was it Sophia—flapped into his face, and then to the shoulder pad of his jacket, and onto the top of his head.

Agnes screamed.

Chicken Mildred escaped, raced down the hall and turned at the first doorway. Myrtle and Mrs. Whistlemeyer sprinted toward the living room. Clara flapped into the kitchen. *Crash!* Was that the kettle of oxtail stew hitting the linoleum? *So much for dinner!*

Belly to the floor, Ling-Ling had Abigail by the throat, dragging her kill out the bathroom door, down the hall and into the garage.

"Godfrey! Run, catch Ling-Ling. She's got Abigail!"

Godfrey shoved Sophia off his head and raced after Ling-Ling, toward the garage.

Katherine followed a trail of pinfeathers into her bedroom.

Agnes streaked toward the living room behind Mrs. Whistlemeyer. This had turned into the dinner party from *H.E.L.L* She burst into giggles. Yes. This ought to dampen Godfrey's amorous intentions. She should write a piece for Luella Parson's advice column.

Six Ways to Utilize your Victory Chicken to Dis-Ignite Unwanted Ardent Advances Number One: Turn your Victory chickens loose in the bathroom

Number Two: Open the door and toss in the cat

"Everybody! Just hold it!" Agnes reached the living room where Myrtle and Mrs. Whistlemeyer had taken refuge on the top of the front window drapes. "Katherine? Have you cornered Mildred?"

"She's here in the bedroom," Katherine called from down the hall. "Shall I try to catch her?"

Agnes scratched her head. "Clara's in the kitchen. The other two are here in the living room. I don't know where Sophia is. Godfrey? What is the status of your detainee?"

Receiving no answer, Agnes stared at the feathered fowl on the drapes. "Katherine. Just leave Mildred in the bedroom. Find Godfrey and bring him back in here. We have to reconnoiter."

She collapsed onto the sofa, her chest heaving. She covered her mouth with her hand and giggled again. Two chickens sat on the drapes over her head, their feathers fluffed, as happy as a pair of moths in a blanket factory.

Katherine and Godfrey returned to the living room.

Godfrey looked like he'd been sucking lemons. He shuffled in, his head down. "Sorry, Agnes. I got the chicken away from the cat, but I'm afraid it's dead. I put it out in the garbage can. Didn't think you wanted the cat to have it."

Maybe we should have plucked the thing and cooked it for dinner. Apparently our supper is ruined.

Katherine glanced toward the bedroom. "The one in the bedroom is perched on my headboard. Sophia is back in the bathroom on top of the shower curtain."

Agnes sighed and looked up at the two chickens overhead. "Since we know where all the culprits are, perhaps we should all use the facilities before we make any further attempt to corral them."

"Me, first." Katherine scurried into the hallway. The bathroom door closed. Her muffled squeal carried into the living room.

"Are you alright?" Agnes called.

"I'm fine. Just sat in something. There's chicken...*mumble, mumble*...on the toilet seat."

"Oh, dear! Godfrey. What am I going to do with...?" She glanced up toward the drapes. "Myrtle and Mrs. Whistlemeyer?"

"Agnes, dear. You must stop calling them Myrtle and *Mrs.* Whistlemeyer. That's hardly appropriate names for a couple of roosters. I wonder if you know, there's not a hen in the lot."

"Roosters? Sophia? Clara? Poor dead Abigail? These two?"

Godfrey lowered his eyes, his mouth set in a scowl. "*Uh-huh.* If that was your intention when you got them, you've been snookered." The corners of his mouth twitched as he tried his best not to laugh.

Agnes felt the blood drain from her cheeks. "Why, that sneaky nurse, Abigail Rachet. No wonder she had them tied up in a sack and was in such a hurry to get rid of me. Now, I don't feel so bad about Ling-Ling killing the one I named Abigail! Katherine! Did you hear what Godfrey said?"

"What? I'm in the kitchen cleaning stew off the linoleum. Clara knocked the stew pot off the stove. She's up on the top of the cupboard now."

Agnes threw up her hands. "What else can go wrong? Excuse me, Godfrey. I must help Katherine clean up the mess in the kitchen. She shouldn't even be out of bed. If you want to leave, I'll understand." She stood, glancing between Godfrey and the kitchen door. *Will he take the hint and go?*

"I'm not leaving. I've dealt with worse in my life. Let me help you clean up the stew and then we'll decide what to do with your little miscreants." He pulled off his coat and laid it across the back of the sofa.

The impish grin on his face melted Agnes's heart. *Okay, stay. Stay forever. Hang your coat in my closet. Put your knickers in my drawers. Crawl in my bed and warm my toes for the rest of my life! Stop it, Agnes. Get a grip.* She backed toward the kitchen. "As you like. But, I'm afraid if you want supper, it's going to be liverwurst sandwiches with day-old toast. However, we do have the lemon tarts my…*er*… friend, Sophia, brought over."

"Sounds great." Godfrey pushed past her into the kitchen. "Hand me a towel and a bucket, Katherine. We'll have this mess cleaned up in three shakes of a lamb's tail."

Look at Katherine's face. She's as captivated by the old fool as I am.

After a supper of canned tomato soup and liverwurst sandwiches, a serious chicken discussion ensued. Keeping the chickens corralled in the bathroom was nigh impossible. The advantages of uninterrupted bathroom privileges weighed heavily against the disadvantages of a chicken-free house. Thus, a unanimous decision was made. Better to give them free run of the house until Saturday, to be followed by a massive spring cleaning once they were safely in their chicken yard.

"Would you like a lemon tart, Godfrey?" Agnes pushed back her chair and turned.

Clara had jumped from the top of the cupboard into the middle of the lemon tart plate. She stood with both feet completely buried by the yellow goo, joyously picking away at the frosted crust.

Agnes yelped. "You monster! Get away from there." She stomped her foot and waved both arms. Little feathers drifted down onto the counter as Clara fluffed his wings and flew onto the tea towel rack beside the sink. His sticky claws grasped the metal rod.

"Well. So much for lemon tarts." She glanced at Godfrey. *And I thought this day couldn't get more embarrassing.*

"Don't worry about it. I'm not much on sweets, anyway." Godfrey chuckled and gave her a heart-melting smile.

Once the remains of the lemon tarts were tossed out and the last crumb swept from the kitchen table, Katherine stood in the doorway beside the icebox. "I'm going to bed and read for a while, Grandmother. You and Godfrey, have a nice talk."

"Good night, dear. Call me if you need anything."

"I will. Good night."

Agnes led Godfrey back into the living room where he settled on the sofa. She moved across the room to the over-stuffed chair. "Could you drink another cup of coffee before you go, Godfrey? Hopefully Clara hasn't contaminated that. Yet." She glanced toward the kitchen.

"If I didn't know better, I'd think you were trying to get rid of me, dear." Godfrey leaned back on the sofa and winked. "I don't believe I'll have coffee, but I wish you'd come and sit beside me." He glanced up at the chickens and scooted over to protect his head from a direct line of fire.

"I'll just sit over here, if you don't mind." Agnes wiggled her bottom in the sofa chair next to the fireplace. She pulled a sofa pillow into her lap. "Tell me what you were working on in Hawaii before they sent you to investigate the ration books. I didn't quite follow how that all transpired."

"I'm not really supposed to talk about the Hawaii project, but I'm sure you'll keep it to yourself." Godfrey glanced around the room.

"You can talk in here. We don't have any spies lurking behind the Philodendron plant."

Godfrey shrugged. "After the attack on Pearl Harbor last December, the government was fearful of a Japanese invasion. In such an event, to prevent the loss of millions of U.S. dollars that might be taken off the island, the government replaced all the citizen's legal tender with specially marked currency with a big bold HAWAII printed on each bill. It would be easy to demonetize such currency and made it worthless if there was a Japanese invasion."

"My! Wasn't that clever? But, how did that all work? Did the citizens cooperate without a fuss?"

"They directed everyone living in Hawaii to turn in cash and securities in a dollar for dollar exchange for the new Hawaii notes. Citizens were allowed to hold only $200 each in cash. Stores were allowed $500 cash. The amount turned in came to over $200 million dollars."

Agnes's eyes popped open. "Really! So, what happened next? As if I couldn't guess."

"The old money was supposed to be shipped to the Nuuanu Mortuary in Oahu to be burned, but the crematory was unable to dispose of such an extraordinary amount of paper, so the overflow currency was sent to the Aiea Sugar Plantation mill with instructions to destroy it."

"*Uh-Oh!* I can see several flaws in that plan." Agnes grinned.

"You're right. Rumor is that before all the money was burned, much of it went missing. We suspect that it was smuggled back to the mainland. I was assigned to a task force to find the culprits and bring them to justice."

"You and a gypsy with a crystal ball, right?"

Godfrey nodded. "Problem is, everything was so chaotic after the attack and so many people were involved in the process, we couldn't narrow down who was responsible for the theft. We think much of the money was hidden on the island, but we can't figure out exactly how they're getting it to the mainland."

"So, that's what brought you to Newbury? You think some of it is here?" *Think of it! All that money might be right here in Newbury.*

Godfrey shrugged. "Not particularly. The money could be anywhere. Actually, that's not what brought me here. They pulled me off the Hawaii money fiasco and sent me back to the states to investigate reports of black market ration books. When I heard the name Agnes Odboddy connected with missing ration books, I knew it had to be you, so I drove over from Sacramento to look you up."

"So, people *are* stealing ration books? Maybe I wasn't so wrong, after all. Hunting ration book thieves isn't nearly as exciting as tracking down several millions of dollars, though. You must be bored."

Godfrey chuckled. "We weren't making much headway on the missing Hawaii money, anyway. I could care less either way. A thief is a thief, whether it's money or ration books. It's all part of control over government programs." He shrugged. "Agnes. Let's not talk about thieves anymore. Seeing you again… It's like all the years between us never happened. Can't we—?"

"My! Look at the time. 9:00 o'clock! I'm due out at the coast watch tomorrow morning at 8:00 A.M. I really must get to bed." She stood and snatched Godfrey's coat off the sofa. "It was so nice to see you again, Godfrey. Sorry dinner was such a flop."

He reached for her hand.

She took a step toward the front door, fighting the urge to fling herself into his arms.

"But, I…" Godfrey glanced up at the chickens over his head. "I hate to leave you like this, with the chickens still running loose. I—"

"Thanks for helping us clean up the kitchen." She had to get him out of the house before she lost her ability to resist. "Katherine and I can handle things from here. Please do give me a call before you leave town." *You can do it, Agnes. Only another minute and he'll be gone.*

Godfrey took his coat from her. "Will you have dinner with me tomorrow night? I'll call you. Maybe we could—"

"We'll see. I'll be out at the coast until noon. Good night." She was weakening. She could feel her resistance swirling, like water going down the drain.

Godfrey stepped through the door. "Well, okay. I'll call you tomorrow. I'm staying at the Sleepy Time Motel if you need me. Thanks for dinner."

Agnes smiled. "A dinner we'll not soon forget, to be sure. Good night." She closed the door, leaned against it and closed her eyes. The old attraction was still there, but common sense had won the day. She'd sent him away…again! Just in time. Even twenty-four years later, the man turned her knees to butter.

The last time Godfrey caused her to lose her senses, she'd blamed it on the stress of war, loneliness, and a weak will. What was her excuse this time?

Godfrey was gone. Now, if she could just keep him away. If he called in the morning, she'd decline a dinner date. Once Godfrey realized that she didn't want to see him again, maybe he'd leave town.

Satisfied with her new strength and determination, Agnes returned to the kitchen to turn out the lights.

Checking the table and countertops for anything left unattended, her gaze moved to the kitchen sink where chicken Clara lay, his red eyes glazed over, his sticky little pointed feet straight up, dead as a rock.

"Oh, dear God! What's happened?" Agnes touched his feathered back. *Still warm. Probably had a heart attack. Poor Clara.* No doubt it was the sugar from the lemon tarts. Sugar couldn't be good for chickens.

The poor things had only been under her care for a few hours, and already two of them were dead. What kind of a caretaker was she? Her eyes prickled. *Go to bed, Agnes, before the roof falls in over your head.*

Chapter Seventeen

Friday Morning—Coast Watch Calamity

Agnes lifted the binoculars and scanned the horizon. What a beautiful day at the ocean. Almost pretty enough to erase last night's dinner fiasco with Godfrey and the blasted chickens—but not quite.

Seagulls squawked and swooped around the watch tower. Waves crashed against the shore, dribbled across the sand, and bubbles chased themselves back into the sea. Serving as a coast watch spotter was, by far, her favorite way to fight the war from the home front. Today, it was an opportunity to steady her heart, quiet her mind and put aside the increasing stresses in her life.

The hum of a plane buzzed in the distance. She adjusted the headphones and flipped the switch to tune the roof amplifiers.

The expanse of ocean melted into a clear blue sky. Not a plane in sight. She followed the hum with her binoculars as the military trainer had instructed. As the sound receded, it appeared the plane was further to the west. Another coast watcher would report it from their location.

Left to right, up and back, right to left, 180 degrees across the sky from north to south. She pulled off her scarf and laid it across the two-way radio. Thank goodness the balmy mornings, now an average of 72 degrees, were quite pleasant compared to the mornings last December when she'd first volunteered for a weekly coast watch shift.

Right after the attack on Pearl Harbor, each three-hour shift involved shivering in the cold wooden watch tower, huddled in her raincoat next to a kerosene heater, twenty feet off the ground, staring at a foggy, drizzling sky. Often, rain sluiced sideways into the tower, soaking her clothing from head to foot. Some days, the fog was so dense, she couldn't have seen a seagull fifty feet away, much less spot an enemy plane intent on bombing the coastline. Granted, an enemy plane couldn't have seen the coastline through the fog, either.

Her binoculars moved across the horizon in the instructed manner. *Left to right, up and back, right to left.*

She turned her face to the sun, closed her eyes and took a deep breath. Godfrey's face popped into her mind. *God forgives. It's harder to forgive myself.*

Now that he was back, did he assume they would pick up where they left off twenty-four years ago? It wasn't that easy. Maybe for him. *Not for me.*

Left to right, up and back, right to the left. Something there to the northwest! Her heart jumped, and then settled as the *something* came closer and became a trio of seagulls flying in a tight formation.

She glanced at the papers tacked on the wall, outlining the various shapes of airplanes. Several weeks ago, she had spotted a shiny silver aircraft with two pilots clearly visible through a glassed-in cover resembling a ribcage. The unfamiliar shape and design about gave her heart failure, thinking it was some new-fangled Japanese bomber.

The air base commander assured her that it was *one of ours*, a Fleetwing BT-12, the Army's first all stainless steel plane. The plane had left San Francisco with a new pilot and his trainer, headed for the Boyles Springs Air Field. She smiled. Paying attention and reporting an unfamiliar plane that day really paid off. Following her report, the commanders updated the sketch packet of planes sent to each watch tower along the coastline. Thanks to her, no one else would worry about a new airplane that strongly resembled Katherine's toaster.

Left to right… A cloudless sky.

A seagull landed on the wooden half-wall surrounding the tower. He danced toward Agnes, pecking at an ant crawling across the wood. "*Shoo*, bird. Don't expect me to share my lunch with you. I barely have enough stamps in my ration book to feed myself and Katherine, much less the killer-in-training cat, and four death-defying roosters."

Ration books! Now why did she have to think of that now? How was she supposed to return to the ration office and face Albert Finklebaum after…? She would die of embarrassment if the office staff got word of her shenanigans. "Maybe I should stop volunteering there and make a more determined effort to take cookies to the USO every week."

Apparently, having no opinion on the matter, the seagull squawked and flapped off across the water.

Too many things had gotten in the way of her USO visits recently. Realistically, it was of small consequence, as the young men came to meet girls, not to eat her brown sugar cookies. She wished Katherine would come and meet some nice young man, but she had made her feelings about that quite clear.

Then again, Katherine's interactions with Dr. Dew-Wright showed promise and contradicted her alleged vow of spinsterhood. Agnes smiled. Despite a desire to avoid a romantic entanglement, such intentions are often thrown to the four winds when one meets one's soul mate. Time would tell.

…*right to left.* Wait!

A blob of white against the blue sky! Her heart beat faster. She trained the binoculars on the object. Approximately 90 degrees over the ocean at about 1000 feet elevation, and approximately a mile off shore, the thing appeared to be descending. Agnes swallowed the lump in her throat. The buzzing in her ears drowned out the sound of the waves. This was no trainer aircraft! Nor was it a trio of seagulls! It was a giant round, white ball with something hanging from below.

Agnes scanned the papers on the wall. Nothing like it. She put the binoculars to her eyes again and adjusted the focus. The blob moved closer, still descending. An air balloon? Round and white, not brightly colored and egg-shaped like the popular passenger air balloons she'd seen at the county fair last summer. Maybe a weather balloon, blown off course? There wasn't a cloud in the sky or a hint of a storm.

Closer now.

Long ropes connected a conglomeration of tangled *thing-a-ma-bobs* hanging from a wheel-shaped device beneath the balloon. Her heart thumped when two small sandbags dislodged from the device and plummeted into the ocean. With the release of the sandbags, the balloon made a sharp ascent, veered slightly north and then dipped again—its descent now on a direct trajectory with the watch tower.

This was not good. She grabbed the microphone and pushed the button. "Station thirty-two, coast watch, Agnes Odboddy here. Over." *Hurry, hurry! Answer, hang it!*

"Station thirty-two. Go ahead. Over."

"I've sighted what appears to be a giant white air balloon, 270 degrees, descending slowly, about 700 feet elevation, approximately one-quarter mile off shore. At the rate of descent, it will likely reach shore fairly close to my location within two or three minutes. *Umm...* over!"

"An air balloon? Are you sure? We don't have any...hold on." Excited voices and broken words crackled in the background. "Explosives...government...black-out...ocean..."

"Station thirty-two. Stay on the line and keep an eye on it. We're sending troops to investigate. Over."

"But, what is it? What—?"

"Sorry, ma'am. Top-secret. I'm not at liberty to disclose any information. If it lands, try to give us a—"

"What do you mean you can't discuss it? How can it be top secret? I'm staring at it with my two bald eyes. I called you, remember? It's less than a quarter of a mile away, headed directly toward the watch tower. What should I—"

"If it lands on the beach anywhere near you, get the heck out of there. It may explode on impact."

"Explode? Thanks a bunch." Agnes's mouth dropped open as the giant contraption still descended, clearly fifteen feet across the balloon and over seventy feet tall, including the ropes and the device below.

What appeared to be a bomb hung beneath the circular device alongside the small sandbags. Was it possible that a Nazi-Jap could be hanging on behind?

Agnes's heart pummeled her chest. Six miles from the nearest civilization, her only contact was a two-way radio. If she left the watch tower now, she had time to get to her car and drive away before the thing landed. Desert her post? *Not on your tin-type! I'm no quitter.* No way would she let some Nazi-Jap steal her car and sneak into town to raise havoc amongst her friends and neighbors. If there was a Japanese gunman on board, she'd just have to deal with him. But, how? She glanced around the tower. There was nothing that even resembled a weapon.

By gum! What would Ellery Queen do? She drew herself up to her full five foot, one and three-eighths inches and glared through the binoculars.

The air balloon was closer now, its outline and features clearly visible. It appeared unmanned. That didn't mean the thing wasn't dangerous. The radio technician said *explosive*—that it might explode on impact. The air current was blowing it directly toward the watch tower!

Agnes grabbed the microphone. "Station thirty-two. Abandoning post! Over and out!"

The enormous air balloon was less than fifty yards away. She snatched her purse and flung her leg over the rail. Skipping every second step, Agnes was down the ladder, hurrying toward her car as fast as jogging through sand in sensible shoes allowed.

A loud *whoosh* behind her nearly knocked her to the ground. She turned. The balloon had disappeared! One minute it was headed straight for the watch tower, and the next it was gone! *What on earth? Am I losing my mind?*

Agnes took a step back toward the ocean. Tiny dots of white material lay strewn across the sand, turning it completely white. A sudden breeze sent a flurry of the shreds spiraling up and scattered them across the beach and back into the ocean. The seagulls had stilled their cries. The only sound was the crashing waves.

Something crazy was going on. She clutched her purse to her chest and started back toward the watch tower. She'd get to the bottom of this or her name wasn't Agnes Agatha Odboddy!

Get off the beach, Agnes. Do it now!

The voice stopped her cold--had she heard it aloud or just in her head. "Who said that?" She turned in a circle. Wasn't she alone? Had someone from the military base arrived already? The white scraps flit across the empty sand and scampered around her ankles.

Get off the beach, Agnes. The commanding voice spoke again. Chill bumps erupted up and down Agnes's arms. Her cheeks prickled.

Go now!

She felt compelled to obey. "Okeydokey, Smokey! I'm out of here!" Agnes turned and raced for her car. At the edge of the parking area, she looked back toward the watch tower.

Kaboom!

A sheet of flames shot out from beneath the wooden tower, raged upwards, and licked at the front legs of the structure. The poles split like matchsticks. Shards of green wood splinters shot across the sand like miniature missiles. Agnes ducked and watched in horror as the structure leaned to the south, and then crumpled down, down until it was on the sand, engulfed in a roaring inferno.

A gush of heat rushed past, warming her face. Agnes threw up her arm to shield her head. Pieces of burning paper flew up, up, from the inferno, and then drifted down, sizzling when they struck the waves. Fiery shards wafted toward her and drifted to the ground near her feet. A siren wailed in the distance.

Agnes's knees trembled and threatened to buckle. She staggered to her car and collapsed onto the car seat. She laid her arms and head against the steering wheel, trying to steady her pounding heart. *What just happened?* Tears burned her eyes. Her nose prickled. *I heard God's voice, to be sure! If I had lingered even for a few seconds...*

Within minutes, two jeeps followed by a canvas-covered truck skidded to a stop beside Agnes's Model A. Five armed soldiers leaped through the canvas flap at the back of the truck, headed toward the flames and heap of ashes where the watch tower had once stood. They stopped at a safe distance. There was nothing they could do but watch.

There was no risk that the fire would cross the sand and extend into the grassy knoll beside the vehicles.

Through the rearview mirror, Agnes noticed an officer step from his jeep and walk toward her car. She swiped tears from her cheeks and pulled her face into what she hoped was that of a stoic warrior on the home front, unscathed by a near death experience. It wouldn't do to have a military man see her all weepy. She grappled with the clasp on her purse, pulled out a lace-edged hankie and gave her face a quick dab.

"You okay, ma'am? Are you hurt?" The officer stood beside her open door, his face pale, his lips taunt. Was he as shocked by the sight of the flaming watch tower as she was?

Agnes shook her head. "Let's just say, I'm mad as a scorched cat. My best silk scarf just went up in flames!" She stepped from the car, leaned down and picked up an eight-inch fragment of slick white paper. "What on earth was that thing? It looks like it was made of some kind of greased paper!" The odor of burning wood and accelerant hung in the air and stung her nose.

"What we have here is a devious invention from our Japanese friends. They've sent a number of these things across the air stream. Some have landed along the coastline and started a few forest fires."

"I haven't seen anything like this reported in the papers. Shouldn't we call—"

"Not so fast, ma'am. The government has a press black-out on the air balloons. There's no need to panic the public. So far, nobody has died. You need to keep quiet about this incident. Can you do that, ma'am? For your Country?"

"You mean to say, I came within a hair's breadth of being blown to smithereens and I'm supposed to keep quiet about it? Well, I never!" She clamped her mouth shut with a click.

"You do understand what *Top Security* means, don't you ma'am? What was your name, again? Ombiditty?"

"That would be Mrs. Odboddy, young man. You cannot give me orders about what I can and cannot say! I am a citizen-volunteer. I am not in the military."

The officer jerked his head toward one of the soldier. The soldier hurried over. "Private Bittlespear. Have one of the men drive Mrs. *Odboddy's* car home. Please escort her back to headquarters. Colonel Farthingworth will want to have a few words with her about what she can and cannot say regarding a *Top Secret* situation."

"What? I'm a loyal citizen. You can't take me—"

Private Bittlespear grasped her arm and propelled her toward his jeep. "Come along, ma'am. Don't give me any trouble. I don't want to handcuff you."

"Handcuff... You've got to be kidding. Do you realize who—?"

Another soldier jumped into her car, checked the address on the registration slip in a glassine and leather sleeve strapped to the steering column, and started the engine.

Private Bittlespear shoved her into the jeep. Her bottom hit the seat. He walked around to the driver's side as another soldier jumped into the back and put his hand on her shoulder.

Agnes looked back toward the beach. *Is this really happening? Or am I dreaming?*

The scent of burning wood faded as the jeep pulled away from the parking area, her Model A chugging along behind. Agnes clutched her handbag to her breast. The wind whistled past her head, snatching bobby-pins from her hair. She reached up and removed the silver chopsticks from her bun and dropped them in her purse. She couldn't risk losing them on this ridiculous ride.

We'll just see about this. When they got to the military base, wouldn't she just give this Colonel Farthingworth—whoever he was—a piece of her mind?

Chapter Eighteen

Early Friday Afternoon—Dr. Don Comes to Call

K atherine pulled the sheet, dotted with grey-white dribbles, off the back of the living room sofa. She wadded it up, tossed it on the floor, and replaced it with a clean one. She glanced up at Myrtle and Mrs. Whistlemeyer, still perched on the top of the curtain rod. They'd come down sooner or later when they got hungry. So far they seemed satisfied to fast and enjoy the view from their high vantage point.

Katherine swiped her cleaning rag across the coffee table, more for effect than necessity. Thank goodness, the sheet on the sofa caught all the rooster's transgressions. Tomorrow couldn't come soon enough to suit her. Jackson would be here early in the morning. By nightfall, their feathered-friends should be out of the bathroom, the kitchen, the bedroom and off the living room drapes and in their new coop.

Katherine carried the soiled sheet to the back porch and tossed it on top of the dirty towel she'd pulled from under Mildred in the bedroom and *what's-her-name* in the bathroom. Sophia? The names had stuck, though it was embarrassing that the roosters were named for Grandmother's friends.

Ring! Ring!

Myrtle, the human one, not the feathered one, was on the phone. "Katherine. Don't bother coming in to work today."

"You can't mean it. Because Clyde fell off the gurney? Really, Myrtle. It wasn't my fault. I—"

"No, silly. It doesn't have anything to do with Clyde." She chuckled. "Someone drove their car into the plate glass window in the front of the shop."

"Oh, my goodness! Was anyone hurt?"

"Just the window and the guy's self-esteem. I think he may have had a few too many snorts at Lucky's Bar and Grill. I've closed the shop today to have the window replaced. Thankfully, we have insurance to pay for the repairs and my loss of income."

"That's a shame, but if it had to happen, it couldn't come at a better time. It gives me another day to rest. That will make my doctor happy. *Dr. Don.* He wasn't too crazy about me going back to work full-time today, anyway."

"Okay, then. Take it easy. I'll see you tomorrow morning." Myrtle rang off the phone.

"Bye…" *Dr. Don!* She hung up the receiver. Katherine's heartbeat sped up. Was it likely she'd ever see the good doctor again? Did she even want to? She was probably the butt of his jokes around the hospital water cooler. Doubt he'd ever have another patient collapse under a dead body. A smile worked its way into the corners of her mouth in spite of herself.

Katherine brought the vacuum cleaner in from the back porch and plugged it in. This might get a rise out of Myrtle and Mrs. Whistlemeyer. The machine whirred as she pushed it back and forth across the rug collecting an errant feather here and there. She moved the coffee table and vacuumed under it.

The feathered rascals fluffed their wings and moved sideways on top of the drapes, putting as much distance as possible between them and the humming machine, and then settled down and ignored the noise.

Katherine cleaned under the chair and then pushed the sofa closer to the wall. *What's that?* Something white poked out from under the edge.

She pulled a piece of paper from under the sofa, laid it on the coffee table, finished vacuuming, pulled the sofa back into place, and returned the vacuum to the porch.

Bing-bong.

Who could that be? Grandmother should be home about now. Had she forgotten her key? Katherine opened the door. "Yes? Oh! Dr. Don! What are you doing here?" Her heartbeat surged from pattering into overdrive.

"Miss Odboddy? *Um…* I was in the neighborhood and thought I'd drop by and see how you're doing. *Um…* May I come in?"

Katherine opened the door wider. "Of course. I was just cleaning up. Sorry about the mess. You see, we have these chickens…" She glanced at the new flowered sheet she'd just laid across the sofa. Her stomach lurched. Several new blobs had already appeared since she'd last looked. Her gaze moved to the two roosters on the drape. *Oh, good grief!* She sucked in her breath.

Wait. He must have checked her medical record to know where she lived. He wasn't just in the neighborhood. He came specifically to see her.

Dr. Don shuffled his feet and fumbled with his hat. "I'm sorry. I should have called. I can see this is a bad time—"

Katherine grabbed his arm and dragged him over the threshold. "Let's go into the kitchen and I'll explain everything." She gestured toward the chickens. "It's my grandmother, you see."

Dr. Don followed her into the kitchen. He stopped at the door.

Mildred, the feathered one, not the human one, had moved from the bedroom into the kitchen and now clung precariously to the tea towel rod beside the sink where Clara had made his last stand.

"Another one? How many are there?"

Katherine's cheeks burned as she spotted the telltale grey-white blobs scattered across the counter directly under Mildred. "Oh!" She grabbed the dishrag, quickly wiped up the blobs and rinsed it out under the faucet. She tossed the dirty dishrag onto the piles of sheets on the porch, grabbed a fresh towel and laid it across the counter under the rooster's bum.

She turned, put up her hand, four fingers raised, her thumb across her palm. "Do you want to sit down? I can make you a cup of tea. This is so…embarrassing. I wouldn't blame you if you don't want to stay." She nodded toward Mildred.

Ere r err re. Mildred gurgled, fluffed his red tinged wings and settled back on the towel rod, a little mound of red and brown feathers.

Dr. Don sat at the kitchen table. He put his hand over his mouth and closed his eyes. His shoulders shook. He was laughing at her, "I'm sorry to laugh! I don't think I've ever seen anything quite as funny."

Katherine giggled and then burst into laughter. "If it wasn't so awful, it *would* be funny. You should try living in the middle of this chicken coop." She settled down to occasional giggles. "It was Grandmother's bright idea to get chickens to save money, but as usual, it sort of backfired. She brought them home before we had a chance to get a coop built. Then as fate would have it, they all turned out to be roosters." She wiped her eyes.

"Our friend, Jackson, is going to fix up a little yard for them tomorrow. Until then, I guess it's us against them. By the way, this is Mildred. You already met Myrtle and Mrs. Whistlemeyer in the living room."

"So you're sharing your living room and the kitchen with chickens?"

"And, Sophia's in the bathroom. Due to unexpected and tragic circumstances, we've already lost two, Clara and Abigail. The rest are doing their utmost to make sure we're as miserable as possible until the coop is built!"

"I see. Having an unannounced visitor doesn't help much, does it? I should have called."

"If you don't mind sharing tea with a chicken, then you're welcome. Anytime." She turned her head to hide her crimson cheeks, fiddled with the matches, lit the fire, and set the teakettle on to boil.

Dr. Don laughed. "I must admit, this is a first for me. But, honestly, I can't think of anyone I'd rather share tea with than you and Mildred, even if he is a chicken."

"In that case, do you take milk or lemon?"

"Neither. Thank you. I just take it straight."

"Oh, I hear Grandmother's car outside now. She'll be pleased to see you."

Katherine stood and walked to the living room, pulled back the curtain and peered out the window. "That's odd. Grandmother's car is in the driveway, but she's not in it. A military jeep just pulled away. What does that mean? Where could she be?"

Chapter Nineteen

A gnes squirmed in the chair in front of Colonel Farthingworth's desk. Her underarms itched. Perspiration beaded between her Double-D bosoms. *Here goes nothing!*

During WWI, her responsible take-charge approach as an undercover agent often brought her in contact with the military upper crust. They hadn't intimidated her then and she didn't intend for one to start now. Every man was a snap to handle when you treated him properly, like a puppy dog. A firm hand, plenty of flattery, and treats. She never met a man yet she couldn't handle with a soft word, a sweet smile and as a last resort, cookies, which she kept in ample supply in her handbag. This time, however, things felt just a shade different. Was it because this was a matter of national security? Or was she just a tad out of practice and less confident in her abilities to handle men these days?

Agnes drew in her breath in an effort to calm her pattering heart. She reached into her bag, pulled out her silver chopsticks and shoved them back into her bun. *There! That feels better.*

Having the comfort of Douglas's silver chopsticks firmly attached on the back of her head always made distressing situations easier to handle.

She glanced at the stout, grey-haired officer behind the desk, scratching his fountain pen across some nondescript document. A blob of blue ink had stained his index finger in a butterfly pattern. Was he ignoring her to make a point of how unimportant she was? *Well, we'll see about that!* "Excuse me, sir! I don't have all day to waste, you know. Why was I brought here in such a rude manner?"

The officer glanced up, and appeared surprised to see her parked in front of his desk. He returned to his paperwork.

Agnes huffed, her temper edging closer to the boiling point. "I said, excuse me! I'm a citizen and a volunteer. Somebody owes me an explanation!" She grabbed her purse and stood.

A young soldier put his hand on her shoulder and eased her back into the chair. "Sit down and keep quiet. Colonel Farthingworth will explain everything in his own good time."

"Well! I never!" Agnes jerked her shoulder and glared first at the young man and then at Colonel Farthingworth.

The Colonel laid down his pen and moved his fingers together in the shape of a tent. His head jerked toward the door. "Thank you, Bittlespear. If you'll step outside, I won't need you for a while. Close the door behind you, please."

The young man stopped by the office door. "Begging your pardon, sir, but I rode in the jeep with Mrs. Odboddy. She's a mean one. I'll be just outside the door if you need me."

"Oh, I think I can handle her. She doesn't look any meaner than some I've dealt with."

The young man touched his brow, shouldered his rifle and stepped out the door. It clicked behind him.

The Colonel turned to Agnes. "Now, why don't you tell me exactly what happened that brings you here today?"

"Apparently some Nazi-Jap balloon contraption nearly killed me on the beach. Then, your soldiers rudely shoved me into a jeep and hauled me here against my will. Never in my life have I ever—"

"And, hopefully, you never will again. Agnes…may I call you Agnes? What we have here is a national security situation. We brought you here today to respectfully request your silence. Unfortunately, we can't have you telling anyone what you saw out there."

"But, what on earth was that thing? It burst into flames when it crashed into the watch tower and burnt it to the ground. Was it some kind of bomb? A Nazi bomb?" The skin on the back of her neck tingled. Perspiration popped out on her chest and trickled under her arms, as icy as death's finger.

"Not Nazi. Our Japanese friends to the East launch the things, send them across the air stream hoping they'll reach the United States, start fires and create havoc amongst our citizens. I expect if many made it successfully, they would do just that, but so far, no one has been hurt. Most of them land along the California and Oregon coastlines. We've managed to put out the few fires they've started."

"But, if the wind was right, it might have blown clear into downtown Newbury. My neighbors need to be warned about—"

"That's exactly what we *don't* want to do. If people knew about these things, Agnes, imagine the panic and mayhem in the streets."

"Yes, but, I don't think—"

"The Japanese secret service intercepts our radio broadcasts and reads our newspapers. Such a reaction would fuel their resolve to send more balloon bombs. If we can keep a press black-out on them, the enemy may assume the balloons aren't reaching the states, as I expect many of them aren't. You can understand the need for secrecy. What do you say, Agnes. Can Uncle Sam count on your discretion?"

Agnes lowered her head and then looked up. "I see. But, how will you explain a pile of ashes where the watch tower used to be? That's bound to raise a few eyebrows."

"*Umm...* I'm afraid that's where you come in. Can we count on your patriotism again? In order to keep the balloon bombs secret, you'll need to take the blame for burning down the watch tower."

Agnes's hand flew to her mouth. She gasped, then coughed as her throat seized. They wanted her to take the blame for the fire? "You want me to say that I...? Just exactly how would I go about—?"

"I think you might say you knocked over the kerosene heater."

"I didn't turn on the heater. It was 72 degrees out there today. I—"

"Agnes. No one will even question the temperature. It really comes down to whether or not you're willing to help the war effort and keep a United States Top Secret situation."

"Couldn't I just say—"

"Your silence could save lives. If the balloons keep coming, one could land in downtown Seattle or San Francisco. Think of the possible loss of life if it exploded on a busy street, or in a school yard and killed a bunch of little kids. I know we're asking a lot, but are you willing to do it for God and Country?"

Agnes stared out the window. *Top Secret information.* She could take the blame. Her selfless act could save lives right here at home. Mrs. Roosevelt always said, 'watch for every opportunity to make a difference. Every citizen must be a hometown patriot. As wives and mothers, we must fight the war from the home front by every means necessary.' What better way to serve her country? Taking the blame for the fire would be a selfless and patriotic act.

Agnes's head shot up. "Of course, you can count on me, Colonel." She zipped her hand across her mouth. "Mum's the word. Not one syllable of what happened today will cross my lips. Loose lips sink ships!" She stood and threw back her shoulders. "If you ever need someone to assist you in any other way with the war effort, Agnes Odboddy is your man…woman!"

Colonel Farthingworth shook his head. "I'm not sure that will be necessary, but you'll be the first to know if something comes up. I felt sure I could count on you. My wife told me how dedicated you are to the war effort." He came around the end of his desk.

"Your wife?" *Who's his wife?* She didn't know anyone named Farthingworth.

"Edith prefers to go by her maiden name. Edith Braithwaite? I believe she's in your church knitting circle and rolls bandages with you at the hospital."

"Of course, Edith." *She's all chummy with Sophia Rashmuller. They've always got their heads together, whispering about something.*

Agnes plastered on a grin. "Edith is a dear friend. So, she's your wife? Who would have thought? I don't believe I've ever heard her mention you."

Colonel Farthingworth shoved his hands in his pocket and rocked back on his heels. "We prefer not to advertise our relationship. It wouldn't do to broadcast to the world that she's married to the Colonel in charge of national security in northern California—for security reasons, you understand." Colonel Farthingworth took Agnes's hand and squeezed it. "We appreciate your gallant sacrifice." He opened his office door. "Bittlespear? Would you drive Mrs. Odboddy home now?"

Agnes picked up her purse and stepped through the door. "I serve cookies at the USO here on the base several times a month. Perhaps we'll meet again, Colonel Farthingworth."

"Perhaps we will." The Colonel nodded and closed the door behind her.

Agnes followed Private Bittlespear to the jeep, a smug smile on her face. A matter of national security. Indeed, they had chosen the right hometown patriot for this Top Secret mission.

"Ma'am?" Bittlespear took her hand and helped her into the passenger seat.

Agnes looked back over her shoulder as they passed through the army base gate. As a home front warrior and a self-appointed scourge of the underworld, keeping a national security secret and explaining away a burned-down watch tower would be easy. Like Mother O'Leary's cow, no one would be surprised that ole lady Odboddy had kicked over a kerosene heater and destroyed the watch tower, even on a warm day in April.

How she could explain to Katherine why a soldier drove her car home and she came home with a military escort two hours later…that was something else again.

Chapter Twenty

Private Bittlespear pulled up in front of Agnes's house and killed the jeep's motor. "Do you want me to walk you to the door, ma'am?"

"I'm quite capable of walking up my own driveway, thank you very much!" *Well, that was rude, Agnes, after he was nice enough to drive you home.* "Thank you for the ride, Private. I'll look for you at the USO next week." Agnes gave him a big smile and hopped out of the vehicle. "I'll bring you some chocolate chip cookies." *That's more like it. I need to get my 'nice on.' I've been quite a sorehead lately.*

Agnes opened the front door and peeked inside. Katherine was home, but maybe, with luck, she hadn't seen the soldier bring the Model A back. *Maybe I'll have time to think up an explanation about what happened out at the—*

"Grandmother!" Katherine stepped into the living room, her hands on her hips. "Where have you been? We've been worried sick." Her eyes narrowed and her brows squinched together.

So much for luck...

Dr. Dew-Wright appeared in the doorway. "Mrs. Odboddy? Glad to see you're all right. Katherine has called all over town."

"Oh! My. I'm so sorry you were worried. I'm fine."

"But, where have you been? You were due back from the coast over an hour ago, and some soldiers brought your car home. They drove away before I could speak to them. We saw fire trucks heading out of town. Then I heard on the radio, there was some sort of structure fire on the beach." She wrung her hands. Her face paled and her lips trembled.

"I...I." Despite all her cogitation on the way home, Agnes had failed to come up with a plausible explanation about her car or her tardiness. There was no way around it. She'd have to follow Colonel Farthingworth's plan and take the blame for the watch tower fire. *Yes. That's the ticket. Just like I agreed, I'll do my civic duty and take the blame.* "Well, you see, it's like this..."

"I was doing my coast watch and some..." All her good intentions failed her. As though spilling from some foreign mouth, the words tumbled out. "...some soldiers off a Nazi-Jap submarine rowed onto the beach carrying machine guns. They opened fire on the tower. Bullets whizzed past my head. As I was trying to escape, my purse caught on the kerosene heater and knocked it over. As I climbed down the ladder, the machine gun fire must have struck the heater, igniting the kerosene. Everything went up in flames. I barely escaped with my life."

Katherine closed her eyes and shook her head. "Grandmother, really. You can't think that I'd—"

"Wait. That's not all. The military showed up about then and the Japs escaped. So, a soldier brought my car home while they took me to the Boyles Springs base for debriefing. Then, they swore me to secrecy, national security, and all, you know. One of the soldiers drove me home. So, I can't tell anyone except you, Katherine." She glanced toward the doctor. "You'll have to promise to keep quiet too, Dr. Don. That's about it." Agnes tossed her purse beside the door. "I'm starved. I think I'll make some waffles. Have you eaten lunch yet?"

She glanced from Katherine to Dr. Don. Her cheeks quivered with a forced smile. *That should do it!*

"Oh, Grandmother. You don't expect us to swallow that cockamamie story, do you?" Katherine put up her nose. "If you don't want to tell me the truth, then just don't. I'm going out. I need some air. Do you want to come with me, Dr. Don?" She took his hand and pulled him toward the front door. "Good-bye, Grandmother."

Dr. Don shrugged. "It was lovely to see you again, Mrs.—"

Katherine shoved him onto the porch and slammed the door.

Agnes sighed. She looked up at Myrtle and Mrs. Whistlemeyer. "So much for any good it did me to *make nice* with Private Bittlespear. I'm in trouble with Katherine and the *Big Guy* upstairs, again. As usual."

The phone jangled. *What now?* Agnes picked up the receiver. "Hello?"

"Agnes. It's me, Godfrey. I must see you. I've misplaced an important paper and I think I may have left it at your house last night. May I come over and look around?"

Godfrey! The man was tick on a fat dog's back. The harder she tried to shake him, the tighter he stuck. "*Umm*...sure. I haven't seen anything lying around." She twisted her head around the corner and glanced into the living room. A paper lay on the coffee table, half covered by a magazine. "Wait a minute. There's something... Let me look." She laid down the phone and stepped onto the flowered living room carpet.

Er er er ere er!

Myrtle had moved from the front window drapes to the lamp where he perched, casually picking at the fringe on the top of the lampshade. "Myrtle! Stop that! Shoo!" Agnes waved her hand.

Myrtle flapped back up to the top of the window. *Those curtains will certainly need washing when this is over.* Agnes sighed, noting the grey-white blobs that streaked down the front of the lampshade and spattered on the carpet. Only one more day of the chicken invasion and Jackson would be here to build the coop.

She picked up the paper from the coffee table. A list of names printed on a Pearl Harbor document. *This must be Godfrey's lost paper.* She hiked back to the phone, the paper in her hand. "It's something from the military base. Is that what you're looking for?"

"Thank goodness. May I come right over? Perhaps we could

go out somewhere for dinner later?" Godfrey's voice quivered with romantic fervor.

Agnes rolled her eyes. "Come on over. You can eat with us, if you're willing to take another chance. There's a pot of beans on the back of the stove and I can make some cornbread."

"I'll be there in six shakes of a lamb's tail."

She had so many things to worry about, and now Godfrey was adding to the list. Another evening with Godfrey. Were there enough beans in the pot for three people? Hopefully, tonight's dinner would go better than last night, if she could just keep the chickens out of the cornbread.

Agnes sighed. She could feel the worry lines etching irrevocably into her brow. It felt like everything was closing in on her.

At any moment, Chief Waddlemucker could be on her doorstep with an arrest warrant for falsely reporting a crime and wasting police time.

Sooner or later, the story about the watch tower fire would hit the newspapers. Everyone would blame her, rightfully so, and thanks to her agreement with Colonel Farthingworth, she couldn't even deny it.

She glanced up just as Mrs. Whistlemeyer let loose another blob that landed on the back of the couch. Weren't they the gift that kept on giving? The blasted chickens! Even the hope of several eggs every week had flown out the window. Too bad the roosters couldn't follow. Whatever could she do with four roosters now that they were her responsibility?

Now, Godfrey was turning up again, smelling of Old Spice and comfort. Every time he came within hailing distance, she went weak in the knees. Was she strong enough to resist round two? Maybe she should throw herself into his arms and let him take her away from all this. A life in Hawaii with the man of her dreams wasn't exactly hard time. Katherine was old enough to look after herself, and the thought of leaving behind a town full of people who thought she was a cornball was certainly appealing.

"Whatever should I do?" Agnes glanced back into her kitchen of twenty-four years.

The little white stove and ice box in the corner.

Katherine's new stainless steel toaster on the counter, beside the glass percolator and the Westinghouse electric mixer.

The little drop-leaf kitchen table covered with a bright white tablecloth Katherine embroidered for her last Christmas.

Mildred perched on the tea-towel rack beside the double porcelain sink. He fluffed his red and brown feathers, blinked his little red eye and gurgled. *Er er ere er.*

Agnes could just imagine what he might have said. *This is your home, Agnes, everything you love. You don't want to move to Hawaii. You hardly know that man, even if he does curl your toes and turn your knees to Oleo margarine every time he aims those baby-blue eyes your way.*

Besides, just because he acts all sweet and lovey, what makes you think he'd propose marriage? Get a grip, Agnes!

Agnes shook her head. "Now I'm getting advice from a Bantam rooster. And worse yet, I think he's right!" She reached into the cupboard for her large yellow Pyrex mixing bowl and began to gather the ingredients for cornbread.

Late Friday Afternoon

"Godfrey. Nice to see you, again. Won't you come in and sit down?" Katherine hung Godfrey's hat on the coat rack beside the front door. "Grandmother will be right in." *She's in the bathroom putting on lipstick, for Heaven's sake.* She hadn't done that for a while.

Godfrey sat. He pulled off his jacket and flung it over the back of the sofa, then moved it to the arm, out of the range of the chickens. He straightened his tie and pulled the paper out from under the edge of the magazine. "Here it is! Thank goodness. It must have fallen from my coat last night." He smoothed out the paper on the coffee table and leaned closer to read it.

"What is it? Something important?" Katherine sat beside him on the sofa and leaned over his shoulder.

"It's a list Headquarters gave me. I guess Agnes told you about the money that's gone missing in Hawaii?"

Katherine nodded. "She mentioned it in passing, but I wasn't sure if it was true. She tells a lot of tall tales." *Like this afternoon, for instance.*

"It's true, alright. This is a list of everyone involved in the process, from the first people who worked on exchanging the regular currency for Hawaii script, to the drivers who transported it to the mortuary, to the staff in charge of destroying it." Godfrey tapped the paper.

"It's quite a long list and we have no idea at which point the money went missing. I've interviewed just about everyone and done background checks. I'd be in the doghouse if I lost these names and had to ask for another list." Godfrey stood as Agnes entered the room. "Agnes, my dear. You look lovely. New hairdo?"

Agnes ran her hand over her hair, then smiled and spun in a circle. Douglas's silver chopsticks peeked through the Victory roll that circled the back of her neck and came up above her right ear. "Why, thank you, Godfrey. I saw the style in Katherine's movie magazine and thought I'd give it a try."

"Most becoming, to be sure."

"I didn't think you read my movie magazine, Grandma. I like it. You should wear it like that more often." Katherine waved the paper toward Agnes. "This is Godfrey's missing paper. I found it under the chair when I was running the vacuum this morning."

Agnes took the list from Katherine and perused the names. "Well, that's interesting. Oliver Finklebaum? I wonder if he's related to my manager, Albert, at the Ration Stamp Office. No, it's not possible. It's just another of my stupid conspiracy theories. I won't start that again."

Her face pinked up from her chin to her eyebrows.

Katherine pinched her lips together and turned away. *I won't even ask what she's talking about.* Things were already bad enough. She was still miffed about their quarrel earlier. Nazi-Japs, indeed.

"What were you thinking, dear? Let me see." Godfrey took the paper. "Oliver Finklebaum. That's right. Remember? I thought the name *Finklebaum* sounded familiar when you told me about the ration books and how you followed that guy around town the other night."

"What guy?" Katherine glared at Agnes. "Who did you follow? Grandmother? Is this another one of your monkeyshines? What have you been up to this time?" *If it's not one thing, it's another with her. Do I need to quit my job and stay home to watch her?*

Agnes hung her head, her cheeks flushed. "I had hoped you wouldn't find out how stupid—"

"Grandmother?" Katherine grasped Agnes's arm. "Tell me what you've done. Right now!"

"I...I... Oh, Godfrey, why did you have to bring that up? I wanted to forget about it." She shot daggers toward him with her eyes.

Godfrey put up his hands. "Honest, Agnes! I thought for sure she knew. I mean..." He gazed around the room. Was he looking for a hole to crawl into? "I'm sorry. Katherine, it's really nothing. Agnes told me something in confidence at the hospital before she knew...before you were... Well, I shouldn't have said anything. Why don't you just forget it? It was all a mistake, I'm sure, completely cleared up now."

"I don't think so." Katherine stood and began to pace. "If I'm going to share my life with you, Grandmother, you can't keep doing this to me. First you bring home a bunch of hens that turn out to be roosters. Then you tell me a whopper about Nazi-Japs burning down the watch tower when I have my suspicions you did it yourself. Now, you're hiding some secret shenanigan about ration books and stalking some man... Wait. I'll bet that was the night you took Grandpa's hat and raincoat from the garage. Was that supposed to be some kind of disguise?"

Katherine stopped beside the fireplace and spun on her heels. "You know what? This isn't working for me. I've had about all I can take from you today. I'm going to spend the night with Myrtle. That would be my boss, Myrtle, not the chicken!" She glanced up at the little brown and red bantam rooster perched on the curtain rod.

Ere r ere r ere!

Katherine jerked her thumb at the chickens. "My sentiments, exactly. I rest my case."

The roosters fluffed their feathers and shuffled across the top of the drapes.

Katherine stomped to the front door and yanked it open. "Let me know when you've resolved your chicken crisis, Grandmother. Then, maybe I'll think about coming home."

Agnes turned to Godfrey and burst into tears. "Now, see what you've done!"

Katherine slammed the door and dashed to her car. Hopefully, Myrtle had an extra nightgown and toothbrush. *It's bad enough trying to sleep in a strange bed when you're mad at someone. Even worse, if you have to sleep in your brassier and bloomers.*

Chapter Twenty-One

Missing Hawaiian Money

his is your fault. Now, see what you've done!" Agnes threw a
sofa pillow at Godfrey.

He caught the pillow and plunked it back on the sofa.
"What do you mean? Don't blame me for Katherine being mad at you."
He crossed to Agnes's chair, pulled her to her feet and settled her back
on the sofa, sat beside her and put his arm around her shoulder. "Seems
she was angry at you, my dear, not at me." He stroked her hair.

Agnes buried her face against his shoulder. Sobs wracked her body.
"Everything is just such a mess. I can't do anything right. No matter
how hard I try." She gulped, pulled her hankie from her neckline and
blew her nose. "What am I going to do, Godfrey?" She waved toward
the chickens overhead. "See? All I wanted was some eggs and…look
at us now. We're living in a chicken coop!"

Ling-Ling peeked around the corner, as if hearing the word *chicken*
has awakened another horde of inner demons.

Mrs. Whistlemeyer rose up on his little yellow legs, turned and let
loose with a blob that landed on Godfrey's shoulder.

"Oh, good grief. He just missed your head!" Agnes burst into
tears again.

Godfrey wiped off the offensive splotch with his handkerchief and
stuffed it back in his pocket. "Stand up. Help me pull the sofa out from
the wall. At least we'll be safe from the little bombardiers." Godfrey
heaved Agnes to her feet and pulled the sofa about fourteen inches
away from the window.

Agnes sniffed and dabbed her nose. "Why didn't I think of that several days ago? I could have laid a sheet on the floor under them. See? I can't do anything right."

"Now, Agnes, come sit beside me and let's think this through. Isn't Jackson coming tomorrow to build the chicken coop?"

She nodded.

"That will take care of your chicken problem. After you clean up things up, you'll have your house back in order."

"Jackson said he should have the coop finished by early afternoon."

"If he needs help, I'm pretty handy with a hammer."

"Oh, would you, Godfrey? That would be wonderful." Agnes lowered her eyes and looked up through her lashes with a smile. "Maybe that will smooth things over with Katherine, but she's mad at me. I told her that a Nazi-Jap submarine shot up the watch tower and burned it down."

Godfrey chuckled. "You're kidding. I heard the thing burned. What really happened out there?"

"*Umm...*" Hadn't she promised Colonel Farthingworth she would take responsibility for the fire to keep the public from knowing about the air balloons? On the other hand, as part of the FBI, wouldn't Godfrey already know about the balloon bombs? What would it hurt to share the real story with him? Or, Katherine, for that matter?

But, a promise was a promise and Colonel Farthingworth said it was a matter of national security. But, on the other, other hand, all the soldiers on the beach knew the truth, so where was the harm if she told Godfrey and Katherine? They wouldn't tell anyone. Wasn't the main concern not to panic the public?

"Buck Rogers to Earth! Hello, Agnes?" Godfrey snapped his fingers. "I asked what happened out there."

Decision time. Be honest, or in this case dishonest. Dishonesty seemed the best policy.

Agnes hung her head. She couldn't look Godfrey in the eye and lie. "I did it. I knocked over the kerosene heater. That's what started the fire." Perspiration prickled her neck beneath her Victory roll. She'd lied through her teeth to do the right thing. Now, wasn't that a paradox?

"I don't believe you. Why was the heater on? It was hot out there. Agnes? Why are you lying to me?" He put his finger under her chin and forced her to look him in the eye.

Agnes twisted away. "Please, Godfrey. It was my fault. Let's leave it at that. I don't want to discuss it anymore." For once, she would do the right thing, even if it meant lying to the man she... What was she thinking? The man she loved?

Her corset seemed to get about twenty percent tighter. Was that the truth? Did she love him? She turned back toward his questioning face. The same rakish smile she remembered from World War I days. The same unruly hair, falling onto his forehead, but grey now instead of steel black, like days gone by. She couldn't deal with those eyes that seemed to pierce her very soul. The same piercing blue eyes that made her heart skip a beat when he glanced at her across the room...even before she had used *loneliness* as an excuse. Before Douglas went off to war...

Another shiver of guilt raced up her spine. *God forgive me.* She'd loved Godfrey even before her husband died, and she loved him now. She would love him until her dying breath, but leaving her home was another thing entirely. Would he consider retiring in Newbury? For that matter, as she remembered her imaginary conversation with Chicken Mildred, was it even part of the equation? He hadn't exactly asked for her hand in marriage, had he?

"Okay, have it your way." Godfrey sat back on the sofa. "I won't ask any more questions, but you better come up with a better explanation about the watch tower fiasco if you want to make up with Katherine. I don't think saying, *I don't want to discuss it,* is going to butter that biscuit."

Godfrey reached for the document on the coffee table and glanced again at the list of names. "Another thing. You'd best come clean with Katherine about your little escapade at the casket warehouse, as well."

"I wasn't trying to keep it from her. I just didn't have a chance to tell her. She was in the hospital that night, and I was so worried about her when she came home, I guess it slipped my mind. I was embarrassed and wanted to forget about it. I just couldn't go into it again the next day."

"Makes sense to me, but now that she knows... Sorry about that—she's not going to let it rest until you tell her all the gory details."

Godfrey sat quietly for a moment, gazing at the sheet of paper. "This name you noticed—Oliver Finklebaum. It's such an unusual name. Maybe he *is* related to your friend, Albert."

"Oh, I don't think so. I don't believe Albert has any children. Besides, what different would it make?"

Godfrey leaned back on the sofa and closed his eyes. "I'm going to take a shorty nap. I need to cogitate on this for a while."

"You rest. I'll go and freshen up." Agnes stood. "I'll be right back. I have some coffee on the stove. Shall I heat up a cup?"

"No cream or sugar, remember."

"Right." Agnes hurried into the kitchen. She winked at Mildred, now perched on top of Katherine's toaster. "Shoo. Katherine won't appreciate you sitting there."

Mildred flapped back up to the tea-towel rack. Agnes gathered up the cloth beneath the rack and placed an old newspaper under the rooster. What was she going to do with four roosters? They would eat her out of house and home. The hope of eggs? Another folly.

She flicked a match against the burner, lit the flame, and slid the coffee pot onto the burner. She pulled two cups from the cupboard.

The old newspaper photograph under Chicken Mildred caught her eye. A man and a woman standing beside the bronze plaque outside the Newbury Emergency Room. She leaned over and peered at the picture. Gracious! Wasn't she the same woman Albert had called 'honey' at the casket warehouse?

Agnes read the caption beneath the picture. *Mr. and Mrs. Bernard Whistlemeyer Donate ER Plaque.* Mrs. Whistlemeyer? *You're kidding!*

Why would she be at the warehouse with Albert? She folded the newspaper, laid it on the kitchen table and placed another newspaper under Mildred. "Now, stay put." She shook her finger at the rooster.

Agnes hurried down the hall, freshened her lipstick and face powder and gave her hair a pat. Returning to the kitchen, she poured two cups of hot coffee, placed them on a tray alongside the newspaper and carried it into the living room.

Godfrey had pulled off his shoes and loosened his tie. He lay on the sofa, sound asleep. Little *putt-putt* noises burbled from his lips.

Agnes's heart stirred. How long had it been since a man lay snoring on her living room sofa? Over twenty-four years, before Douglas enlisted in that fool's errand, and died in that other pointless war. Best not to dwell on the past. She shrugged.

Dear Godfrey. Wasn't it just like a man to forget everything and fall asleep within five minutes?

Agnes set the tray on the coffee table, took the newspaper and her cup of coffee and sat in the sofa chair. She gazed at the photo of Mr. and Mrs. Whistlemeyer. Something Godfrey said niggled at the back of her mind.

He said that thousands of dollars of the Hawaiian citizens' money was sent to the mortuary to be destroyed, and was unaccounted for.

Oliver Finklebaum...

Mrs. Whistlemeyer cooing with Albert at the warehouse...

Godfrey's assignment to find missing ration books. Where was the connection? Maybe there wasn't any. Maybe it was just a series of singular events.

Ere er errr er. Over the sofa, Myrtle and Mrs. Whistlemeyer gurgled on the window curtain. They were as happy as a pair of sardines in a tin can.

Katherine was so mad. Would she want to move out?

Was there a chance Godfrey would propose marriage? And if he did, what would be her answer?

What about her reputation, already sullied, and soon to be

completely destroyed once the story about the watch tower fire got out? And, you could bet your bottom dollar it would get out.

She shook her head. There were so many things to worry about, she didn't know where to start. She put her hand over her eyes.

Godfrey stirred. "Hey, you." He grinned.

"Your coffee's getting cold, there on the table."

He reached for the cup and took a sip. "Just right. Thanks."

"Did you have a nice nap? I tried not to wake you."

"I wasn't exactly sleeping. I was thinking about Oliver Finklebaum. What if he is related to your friend, Albert? Even if that's the case, what is the connection between the money and Oliver and—"

"Wait a minute! Take a look at this." She thrust the newspaper into Godfrey's hand.

"What is it?" Godfrey glanced at the paper and then laid it down. "Mr. and Mrs. Whistlemeyer, from the mortuary? Isn't that where Katherine was working?"

Agnes nodded. "Mrs. Whistlemeyer was at the casket warehouse that night with Albert. Albert called her 'sweetheart.' Don't you think that's odd? I heard she divorced Mr. Whistlemeyer, but to take up with Albert? Very strange indeed."

"People sometimes get divorced. What's that got to do with anything?"

"I don't rightly know. I haven't worked it all out in my mind. It's just very odd." Agnes put up her finger and tapped her lips. "*Humm.* Let me see. If Oliver is related Albert...Oliver had access to the money that was supposed to be destroyed at the mortuary. Albert owns a coffin warehouse and his new girlfriend owns a mortuary. That sounds like there might be a connection, but I don't know what it is." Agnes set her cup on the table.

"First off, you're assuming that Oliver and Albert are related. We can't go off half-cocked without some proof."

"Then you should get some proof. Check his military records or have someone ask Oliver if he's related to Albert. At least it's a lead..."

The phone jangled. "Excuse me. I should get that. It might be Katherine." Agnes hurried to the kitchen, her stomach fluttering. "Hello?"

"Mrs. Odboddy? This is Bernard Whistlemeyer, down at the mortuary. May I speak to Katherine? It's rather urgent."

"I'm sorry. She's not here right now. Is there any message? She should be home shortly."

At least I hope she will. God willing and the creek don't rise...

"We have rather a situation down here. Clyde's daughter just came in on the bus from Omaha. You know, Clyde is the stiff...I mean... *heh heh*...the dearly departed that Katherine was working on when she fell."

"Okay."

"It seems we didn't know that we had a celebrity living right here in Newbury. Can you believe it? Clyde is Eleanor Roosevelt's second cousin, twice removed on her mother's side. Miss Opal, Clyde's daughter, that is, notified the White House about Clyde's sudden departure, and, what do you suppose? Mrs. Roosevelt just happens to be in San Francisco this weekend. The White House says if we can hold Clyde over until Sunday, she's agreed to drive up and attend his funeral."

My Mrs. Roosevelt? "Really? How exciting! She's the first real celebrity we—"

"We can keep Clyde in the cooler...I mean the *Celestial Breezes Chamber*, but waiting several days like that, and after his fall sort of messed up his... Katherine needs to come back and put on another layer of...well, you don't need all the details. I'll explain it all to her. There's so much to do before the First Lady arrives. I want to shampoo the carpets and...well, you don't care about all that either, do you?"

"I'll be sure and let Katherine—"

"My, I'm all a-twitter with the news. I can't seem to get my wits together. Imagine. Mrs. Roosevelt. Right here in Newbury at my establishment, no less."

Will the man never stop jabbering? I can't wait to tell Godfrey. "It's certainly exciting. I can understand your—"

"I want Clyde to look extra nice. It's a reflection on my establishment, you know. Not that I'd expect any further White House business, and I'm afraid he'll be a bit worse for wear with all this delay and his tumble and all. Any idea when Katherine could come down and work her magic?"

"*Umm*… I really couldn't say. I expect she could come down some time tomorrow. Would that be soon enough, if the funeral isn't until Sunday? Have you planned any refreshments for afterwards?" *We should have some cold salads and maybe finger sandwiches…*

"You might check with Mildred Haggenbottom about those details. I called the First Church of the Evening Star and Everlasting Light and they put me in touch with her. She volunteered the Ladies Benevolent Society to prepare a light luncheon following the service. Mildred said she would ask a few of the ladies to provide refreshments. Oh, I tell you, I'm just all a-twitter!"

"Mildred's in charge? Then I'm sure I'll be asked to assist. I'll let Katherine know you called. I'm so excited. I wouldn't miss it for the world. Mrs. Roosevelt is my heroine. I never thought I'd get to meet her in person."

"Then, we'll see you Sunday."

"Oh, Mr. Whistlemeyer. One more thing before you go. Do you know Albert Finklebaum?" *Of course he knows him. Albert is the jerk that just stole his wife.*

"Dear me, goodness. Why do you ask?"

"I have a friend who knows an Oliver Finklebaum in Hawaii." The lie tripped off her tongue like *greased goose liver*. Why hadn't she done as well lying about the watch tower fire? "We were just wondering if he might be related to Albert. Odd name, you know."

"True. No more so than Agnes Odboddy. *Heh heh!*. See how I made a joke there? I'm quite a witty fellow, when you get to know me. No one ever expects an undertaker to be droll, but I've been quite amusing on a number of occasions. Do you want to hear a very funny song I perform at parties? I could sing it for you, if you like."

"Mr. Whistlemeyer? I'm rather busy. Perhaps another time? About Oliver Finklebaum. Is he related to Albert?" *He sure changed that subject in a hurry, and rather well too.*

"Oh, yes! We were discussing Oliver, weren't we? I believe Albert has a son named Oliver by his first wife, Purity. She was a Mormon girl. They give their daughters such names. It's intended to inspire them spiritually, you see. Like Faith, Charity, Prudence…that sort of thing."

"Mr. Whistlemeyer? About Albert and Oliver?" She backed across the kitchen, unwinding the twisted telephone cord.

"Oh, yes. I've never met the son. I believe Oliver is in the military somewhere in the Pacific. I expect he's the one. Doubtful there'd be two Oliver Finklebaums in the military."

"And in the Pacific."

"Precisely."

"Thanks, Mr. Whistlemeyer. I'll let Katherine know you called. Good-bye."

Agnes hung up the phone, grabbed the coffee pot and returned to the living room. "Wait until you hear what I just learned." She smirked, as she filled Godfrey's cup and flopped down on the sofa beside him.

"What did you just learn?" Godfrey grinned.

"Albert has a son, Oliver, but we guessed that already, didn't we? Here's the prize in the Cracker Jacks. Mrs. Roosevelt is related to a local man who passed away. She's coming to town on Sunday for his funeral. I'm going to help with a luncheon afterward. I'll get to meet her. Isn't that thrilling?"

"Mrs. Roosevelt—here? That is news. I'll likely be asked to head up a security detail, since I'm already here in town. I should get going. They're probably trying to reach me at the motel to discuss it. I shouldn't keep them waiting." Godfrey stuffed the paper in his pocket and shoved his feet into his shoes. He stood and grabbed his coat.

"Aren't you going to stay and eat dinner with me?" Disappointment filled Agnes's chest. She drew in her breath.

Where had that come from? Did it really matter whether he stayed and ate chili beans and cornbread? Hadn't she been wracking her brain all afternoon for a way to discourage his amorous overtures? Now that he was leaving, she really wanted him to stay. To say that she didn't know her own mind was an understatement. It was more the behavior of a teenager in love, not a mature, sensible woman on a secret assignment for the government, and a warrior on the home front. Not to mention a self-appointed scourge of the underworld when the war was over.

Godfrey reached for the front doorknob. "I'll have someone look into Albert's financials. If he's showing any unexplained deposits, I can probably get a warrant for the warehouse. Might turn up something." Godfrey opened the door. "Give me a call if Jackson needs help in the morning. You've got my number at the motel." Godfrey leaned toward Agnes. His lips brushed her cheek with a touch as gentle as a butterfly landing on a rose.

Her heart surged. She caught her breath and stepped back. "Then, maybe I'll see you tomorrow?"

"I'll call you in the morning. Good-bye." Godfrey's little boy grin lit his face as he stepped out the door.

This was going to be harder than she thought, given her traitorous body's reaction to his touch. How long could she resist his advances? For that matter, did she really want to? Maybe she'd better have another chat with Chicken Mildred.

Chapter Twenty-Two

Saturday Morning—Newbury Daily Gazette Interview

Knock, knock.

7:20 A.M.? *Who could that be at this hour? Surely not Jackson.* He wouldn't come this early. Agnes pulled on her red flannel bathrobe and hurried into the living room. She tucked a strand of stray hair behind her ear.

It couldn't be Katherine. She had a key. She should be home soon. *I'll apologize. We'll talk and work things out. We always do.* This wasn't their first little tiff. What two women living under the same roof didn't fuss from time to time? They always apologized, and for the most part, got along well.

Katherine had called the night before about 10:00 P.M., stating she would spend the night at Myrtle's house. They were going to see the movie *Casablanca.* She still sounded angry when she said good-bye.

More pounding on the door rattled the window glass.

Whoever's here at this hour will just have to catch me in my nightgown. Agnes rubbed her eyes and opened the door. A flashbulb went off in her face. "What? What's this all about?" She shoved at the door, but a foot thrust into the jamb stopped it from closing. Her gaze traveled from the man's foot up to his face. "What's the meaning of this? Who are you?"

"Newbury Daily Gazette." The young man pushed open the door and stepped inside. "We've heard a rumor that you burned down the watch tower yesterday while you were on coast watch. You want to tell us all about it?" The other man moved inside and raised the camera. A second flashbulb flared in Agnes's face. *What in blue blazes is going on here? Right in the middle of my own living room.*

Her mouth pulled down. She put up her hand. "Both of you! Get out of my house before I call the police. Who do you think you are, coming in like this? I'm not even dressed. Don't you dare print that picture, young man!" She peered into the photographer's face. "Richie Haggenbottom? Aren't you Mildred's nephew? I should think you'd know better than to show up at a lady's front door at this hour of the morning and shove a camera in her face. Wait until I tell your aunt!" Agnes clenched her fists and glared at Richie.

Richie lowered the camera, his cheeks aflame. "Sorry, Mrs. Odboddy. It's my job to take pictures where the newspaper sends me." He pointed to his companion. "This is Harvey Littlejohn. He's our star reporter."

Agnes smoothed her hair back. "Well, you should have called for an appointment. Now that you're here, Harvey, I suppose you might as well come in. If you'll excuse me for a few minutes, I'll get dressed. I'd prefer to be interviewed with my clothes on. Have a seat." She gestured toward the sofa.

Myrtle and Mrs. Whistlemeyer moved sideways.

Ritchie glanced up. "What the heck—"

"That's another story, Richie. Mind your head. Mrs. Whistlemeyer is a particularly good aim. Myrtle—not so much." Agnes nodded toward the chicken on the left side of the curtain rod. "Oh, there's coffee in the kitchen. Go on in and serve yourself while I get dressed. You'll have to heat it up. It's from last night. I'll be right back."

Agnes scurried down the hall, into the garage and out the back door. She gathered up the hem of her nightgown and robe and raced next door, tails of her bathrobe flapping. She pounded on the front door. "Mavis! Open up. It's me. Agnes. I need to use your phone."

Mavis came to the door, rubbing her eyes. "What is it? Is it Katherine? Has she taken a turn for the worse? I knew I shouldn't have told that FBI guy where you were the other night. Hope that was okay." Mavis opened the screen.

Agnes rushed in. *Ah. So that's how Godfrey knew I was at the hospital.* "Where's the phone?" She gazed around the living room, a strand of hair falling across her forehead.

"Same place it's always been. In the kitchen. What's wrong? Is that FBI guy back? Your house on fire?" Mavis leaned out the door and gazed at Agnes's house next door. "What's the Newbury Daily Gazette truck doing here?"

Agnes waved her hand and hurried into the kitchen. She dialed the operator. "Operator? Connect me to the Boyles Springs military base. I need to speak to Colonel Farthingworth! It's an emergency." She tapped her foot. *Telling the family I'm to blame for the fire is one thing. Lying to the newspaper is something else again...*

Mavis stood in the kitchen door, her eyes wide. She whispered. "What's going on?"

Agnes shook her head. "Two men. At the house. No time to explain." She turned back to the telephone. "Colonel Farthingworth? This is Agnes Odboddy, from Newbury..."

Mavis disappeared down the hall toward the bedrooms.

"Yes. Mrs. Odboddy. What can I do for you?" Colonel Farthingworth huffed. He stifled a yawn.

Mavis re-emerged, a holster strapped around her bathrobe and a shotgun in her hand.

Agnes laid the phone on her shoulder. "What on earth are you doing, Mavis? They want to interview me, not murder me. Put that thing away." She moved the phone back toward her mouth. "Colonel? I've got a reporter in my living room, asking questions about the watch tower. I wondered what I should say. You see, my granddaughter is already mad at me because I told her...well, never mind what I told her. What should I tell the press?"

"We discussed this, Mrs. Odboddy. You agreed to take the blame for the fire, for the sake of national security. Are you having second thoughts? You know the importance—"

"I know, I agreed. I just wondered... I never expected the newspapers to get involved. The whole town is going to think I'm..." *Isn't that what they already think? Why should this be any different?* She shook her head. "Thank you, Colonel. Never mind. I'll handle it. Don't worry. I won't let you down. Good-bye." Agnes's shoulders drooped as she hung up the phone.

Mavis stood at the front window, the edge of the curtain pulled back, staring at the truck parked at the curb. The shotgun lay across her arms. She turned. "If you want me to run the fellers off, honey, Tilly and I will go over and speak to them." She patted her rifle. "Tilly is very convincing, don't you know. What do they want, anyway?"

Agnes tightened the belt on her bathrobe and opened the front door. "Now, don't you worry about it, Mavis. I've got everything under control."

"But, I heard you on the phone with the military. You said something about the watch tower. Agnes! Was that some of your doing out there?"

Agnes lowered her head. "You might as well know. I expect it will be all over the newspaper this evening, anyway. It was me. I burned the gol-blasted thing down. All by myself. Nobody else, okay? Thanks for letting me use the phone." She started down the sidewalk.

"Well, you don't need to get so huffy about it. I was just trying to help."

Agnes turned and looked back as Mavis disappeared into her house. *Now she's mad.* She raised her hand, then lowered it and shook her head. *I'll apologize later. I've got to get rid of these newspaper reporters first.*

Agnes pulled on a house dress, shoved her feet into black loafers and returned to the living room.

Richie and the reporter sat on the sofa, leaning forward, apparently to be out of the line of fire from the chickens. Ritchie set his coffee cup on the table and stood. "Mrs. Odboddy?" He glanced at his friend and raised an eyebrow.

"Sit, sit. I'm ready now. Fire away. What do you want to know?" Agnes settled into the sofa chair across the room.

Knock, knock, knock.

"Oh, excuse me, Ritchie. Someone's at the door. It's probably Jackson. He's come to build my chicken coop. You young fellows will excuse me for another minute, won't you? I have some business to attend to."

She pulled open the door, ran her hand over her flyaway hair and smiled. "Jackson. Come on it. I'll give you some money and the car keys."

Richie glanced at his watch. "We really don't have much time, Mrs. Odboddy. We were supposed to be back before 9:00 A.M. with the—"

"Well, I shan't be a minute." She turned back to Jackson. "You know what materials to buy, Jackson? Just wait here a minute." She hurried to the kitchen and pulled a $20 bill from the cookie jar, then brought it back to Jackson. "This should cover it. If not, give them my name. I'm sure they'll give you the material and I'll run down and pay them later."

"Yessum, Mrs. Odboddy. Sure will. I have a plan all drawed out and a list of things I needs to buy. Should be back in a hour or so and we'll get them chickens all fixed up." He glanced up at the curtain rod.

Myrtle and Mrs. Whistlemeyer gurgled. A little brown feather floated down and landed on Harvey's head.

"You have a..." She shook her head. *Serves him right if it sticks in his hair all day.*

"Never mind. Thanks, Jackson. Hurry back now." She closed the door behind him and turned to the young men. "Now, where were we?"

"Just a few questions and we'll be on our way." Harvey opened his notebook and licked the end of his pencil.

"Of course." Agnes straightened her shoulders, knit her brow, her gaze locked on Harvey's face. *Try to look like you're paying close attention, Agnes.* She leaned forward.

"Now, just exactly what caused the—"

"Can I get you some more coffee?" Agnes popped off the sofa and took a step toward the kitchen.

The reporter frowned. He took a quick breath and blew it out. "No, thank you, Mrs. Odboddy! Now, please tell me in your own words just what caused the fire at the watch tower. I understand you were alone when the fire started."

Mrs. Odboddy sighed, lowered her eyes and stared at her fingernails. She sat back down on the sofa chair. *Here we go. Shouldn't be too hard to convince them I was responsible.* "You see, I..."

For some reason, now that it was time to relate a lie and take responsibility for a foolish act, her mouth went as dry as a prairie cactus flower. She took a quick breath and tried again. "It was like this. I was watching the coastline and..." Her mind went blank. *What did we decide I was supposed to say? That's right. Kicked over the heater.* "I turned on the heater. There was this squirrel, see. It climbed up the legs on the watch tower, or maybe it climbed up the ladder. I didn't exactly see how it got in, but then it jumped over the wall. It startled me and I made a swipe at it with my purse and...and that's when I accidently knocked over the heater..." Agnes glanced at the reporter and Ritchie. Were they buying it, or not?

"A squirrel... At the beach? Then what happened?" Harvey's eyebrows touched the edge of his brow line. He wasn't buying her story.

I'd better beef it up a little. "Well, maybe it wasn't a squirrel. Maybe it was a...seagull. Now that I think of it, I'm sure it was a seagull. Anyway, I knocked over the heater and the spark ignited the kerosene and started the fire. I tried to put it out, but it spread too fast. I barely escaped with my life!" Agnes's heart thumped. She touched her nose with a shaking hand. In spite of the tingle at the end of her nose, it didn't seem to be growing like Pinocchio's.

"A seagull. Makes a little more sense. Why didn't you say that the first time?" The reporter glanced toward Ritchie.

Ritchie's hand covered his mouth. His shoulders shook.

Is he actually giggling? "I was embarrassed to say that a seagull startled me. You see, I've been terrified of seagulls ever since I was a baby and a seagull landed near my baby blanket and tried to pick... out...my...eyes..." *Good grief.* This blasted fib was spinning out of control with every breath. Why was this so hard? She'd been telling tall tales for years and never had so much trouble making the details sound right.

Harvey stood and glanced at his wristwatch. "So, let me get this straight for the newspaper story. In the middle of April, when it was close to 75 degrees at the ocean, a squirrel that wasn't a squirrel but was really a seagull came over the wall. You have a fear of seagulls because one tried to pick your eyes out when you were a baby, and when you tried to chase it away, you accidently knocked over the heater and the watch tower caught on fire. You couldn't put it out with the fire extinguisher hanging three feet away on the wall, and you barely escaped with your life. Is that about right?"

"You've got it! That's exactly how it happened. Are we done now?" Agnes jumped up from the sofa chair and opened the front door. "Thank you so much for dropping by. I'm looking forward to your story. Good-bye!"

Harvey and Ritchie stood and stepped onto the porch. "*Uhh.* Okay. Good-bye."

"Say hello to your aunt, won't you?" Agnes closed the door and leaned against it. She put her hand over her eyes. *Good grief!* Katherine was going to have a cat-fit when she saw that whopper in print.

Chapter Twenty-Three

*A*gnes put on an old house dress, a worn sweater and a pair of rubber Wellington boots. She took a hoe from the garage into the back yard where the Victory Garden awaited its weekly watering and weeding.

Ling-Ling pranced behind on little cat feet, pausing occasionally to sniff a weed or a flower drifting in the light breeze. She flopped down on the path, lifted her back foot and began to polish her left hip.

Agnes chuckled. "Ling-Ling. You should have seen that reporter's face when I told him how I burned down the watch tower."

Jackson came around the end of the house, carrying an armload of boards.

"Oh! You're back. Everything go okay? Did you have enough money?"

"Sure thing, Mrs. Odboddy. Wait till you sees what I got. They's using all that metal for submarines and such so I couldn't buy no chicken wire. I had to reconnoiter another way to hem them chickens in." Jackson dropped the boards and scurried back around the end of the house.

Oh, dear. Why hadn't she thought of that? No chicken wire? How would they keep the chickens confined?

Jackson reappeared with an armload of old fishing nets. "I'm gonna stretch this here net around the area we *desumgates* for the chicken yard. Won't that work fine?" Jackson grinned and wiggled like a Christmas puppy.

Agnes shook her head. "Maybe if you tacked it firmly up and down the posts, it might work." She smiled. "Good job, Jackson. That was an excellent idea. What can I do to help?" The hoe clattered as she tossed it to the ground.

Ling-Ling jumped and dashed up the apple tree.

"Sorry, Ling-Ling. Didn't mean to scare you." Agnes's gaze followed Ling-Ling to an upper branch where she clung, both front feet hanging over the edge.

"I don't need nothing right now, Mrs. Odboddy. I have a bit of measuring and cogitating to do here for a while. If I needs you, I'll call."

"I'll try not to get in your way. Godfrey volunteered to come over later and lend you a hand." Agnes unwound the garden hose from the hook and pulled it toward the tomato vines.

"'Bout the time I start settin' the posts, another pair of hands would be helpful. Maybe just before noon?" Jackson pulled a tape measure from his pocket. "You wants them right near the kitchen window, right?"

"Make the yard twelve foot square and they'll need a little shelter for the night time. Can you put a perch on the windowsill?" *I'll have a clear view of them when I work at the sink.* She had developed a fondness for the little buggers, particularly Chicken Mildred. "They are quite pretty, aren't they?" Mildred peered at them through the kitchen window from his perch on the tea towel rack.

"Yassum, they is, all gold and red and black. I'm not much fond of just any old chicken. Best way I likes them is crispy brown and fried up on a platter with mashed potatoes and gravy."

"Jackson! What a thing to say." She glanced toward the window. "Do you want Mildred to hear you?"

Jackson shrugged. "Don't rightly 'spect she'd care much what I says, bein' she's a hen and all."

"About that. Godfrey says that they aren't...Listen. Is that the phone?" Agnes turned off the water, dropped the hose and hurried into the house. "Hello?"

"Agnes? It's Mildred. How are you, dear? I've been meaning to call. I hope you aren't letting all the gossip get you down."

Agnes's stomach jittered. "Gossip? What specific gossip are you referring to?"

"Oh! Nothing special. I'm sure it's nothing to worry about. I didn't believe a word of it, anyway. Something about the fire out at the watch tower? *Umm…* You didn't have anything to do with that, did you?"

"What have you heard?"

"Just…that you were responsible for—"

"Mildred. Trust me. Don't believe everything you hear, okay? Is that why you called?"

"No. It's the funeral tomorrow. Can I count on you to help out with the luncheon for Clyde's…Mr. Hoffelmeister's funeral? I expect you've heard that Mrs. Roosevelt is coming. Very private, you know, for security reasons. Family and closest friends only."

"Wouldn't miss it for the world. Just think. Mrs. Roosevelt!"

"Of course, the ladies from the Benevolent Society providing the lunch will be there. Would you make your War-Time Cake? And, perhaps a large container of lemonade?"

"I can do that. *I'll wear my blue flowered shirtwaist and my pearls. And I'll borrow Katherine's blue hat.* "What time should I bring over the food?"

"Maybe around 10:15 A.M.? The service starts at 11:00 A.M. We can set up the luncheon during the service and serve immediately after. I'm sure Mrs. Roosevelt is on a tight schedule."

"Sounds good. I should go. Jackson's out back working on the chicken coop. I can't wait to get these chickens out of the house."

"What chickens? Whatever have you gone and done this time?"

"Hadn't you heard? The town is so busy gossiping about me, I figured everyone knew about my roosters. Long story. I'll fill you in later. See you…"

Agnes glanced up at Chicken Mildred on the tea towel rack. *What will Mildred think when she hears I've given her name to this rooster?*

"Should I bake that cake now or go back out and finish watering?"

Mildred gurgled.

"You're right. I'll do it now before it gets too hot to turn the oven on." Agnes opened a cabinet and found a Betty Crocker booklet she'd received in the mail. She flipped to the second page.

Hail to the women of America! You have strengthened your country's defense as plane watchers, as members of the armed forces, in war plants, in the Red Cross and other Civil Defense activities. Now you must heed the government's request to increase the use of available foods and save those that are scarce. Become women soldiers on the Home Front. Never has there been such an opportunity for American women to contribute. We salute you all.

Agnes put her hand to her heart. She was already a true soldier on the home front, committed to a national security secret. She would fight the war with the last bit of her breath, whatever the cost to her personal reputation. Let the newspaper print whatever they like about the watch tower. She would shoulder the blame like a soldier. *Humm... the Red Cross. Maybe I should give up the work at the Ration Stamp office and join the Red Cross... I wouldn't have to see Albert anymore.*

Agnes lit the oven and turned it to 325 degrees. She flipped through the little book to page 27. Here it is. "War-Time Cake—eggless, milkless, butterless. Let's see.

"Mix in saucepan, 1 cup brown sugar, 1¼ cups water, ½ cup shortening; 2 cups seedless raisins, ½ tsp nutmeg, 2 tsp cinnamon, and ½ tsp cloves. Boil for three minutes. Cool."

She glanced up at Chicken Mildred. "You won't be stuck on that towel rack much longer, baby. Jackson is making you a nice yard out back right this minute."

Mildred fluffed his feathers.

Agnes measured and stirred. The kitchen counter was soon littered with spices, raisins and various containers. "Now, what's next? Add 1 tsp salt, 1 tsp soda. Blend in 1½ cups flour and 1 tsp baking powder."

Agnes poured the batter into a greased and floured eight-inch pan and slid it into the oven. After setting the timer to 50 minutes, she dialed Godfrey's number at the motel.

His sleepy voice answered after several rings. "Hello?"

"Hey, Godfrey. Sorry. I didn't wake you, did I?" Agnes glanced at the black metal chicken clock over the stove. 10:15 A.M. Why was he still in bed?

"*Ohhh*. I've been up half the night. We got a warrant and made a raid on your buddy's casket company. The one he so cleverly calls *A Tisket, A Casket?*"

"Yes. I remember." *A night I'll never forget.* "So? What happened?" Agnes pulled her hankie from the front of her dress and dabbed it across her neck. Just the thought of that night was enough to... Was Albert really involved with the missing money? Oh, how she wished she had been a mouse in the corner when Godfrey rushed the warehouse.

She could see it now. A contingent of FBI raiders sneaks up to the warehouse, all padded up with vests, hard helmets, and guns at the ready. Godfrey pitches one of those tear-gas thingies through the window, shattering the glass. Another officer slams a battering ram against the front door, flattening it like it was made of Tinkertoys. Bullets fly back and forth as they rush the joint. One of the cops falls to the ground, but it's only a flesh wound... Probably has a wife and kids... He'll live.

Albert fires back with a machine gun and that hussy, Mrs. Whistlemeyer, faints dead away. Seeing that he's outnumbered, Albert throws down his gun, puts up his hands and they whisk him away in the paddy wagon. All the caskets are stuffed with the money missing from Hawaii. Godfrey is a hero and gets a medal for busting up the gang.

Agnes sighed. "So...tell me everything! What happened?" Just like Ellery Queen, her man had risked life and limb to bring the felon to justice. *And, I helped!* Her heart beat faster. She held her breath. *Oh, my! It's hot in here!*

"Oh. He was very cooperative. We looked around the office and the warehouse. Didn't find anything. It was just a hunch, you know.

Without a smoking gun, per se, our hands are tied."

"Oh, Lord!" The machine guns, paddy wagons and battering rams of her imagination sizzled and melted like butter in a skillet. She blew out her breath. "So, where do you go from here?"

"We'll look closer at his financials, but again, without proof, no way to nail him with a crime. Or for that matter, maybe we were just on the wrong track."

"I see. By the way, Jackson is here building my chicken coop. Are you coming over? He said he could use some help around noon."

"Are you going to feed me or should I eat first?" Godfrey chuckled. "No pressure. Just wondered."

"*Umm.* Why not? I still have that pot of beans and cornbread we didn't eat last night. If you should happen to see Katherine downtown somewhere, would you tell her…never mind. I'm sure she'll be back soon. I'll tell her myself. See you later."

"Good-bye, dear. Later." Godfrey hung up the phone.

The scent of cinnamon and spices filled the kitchen. Agnes checked her cake. Rising nicely, but not yet done. *I should have made two cakes.* One for lunch today and the other for Mrs. Roosevelt. She rinsed out the mixing bowl and began adding ingredients for a second War- Time cake. The first one was about done when she slid the second into the oven.

Knock, knock, knock.

Agnes glanced up at Mildred. "Must be Godfrey. How did he get here so quick?"

Chicken Mildred gurgled.

"I'm going to miss talking to you like this when you go outside, Mildred. Maybe I should get a canary bird." Agnes hurried into the living room, smoothing back her hair. She smiled and opened the door. "Come on in, God—Sophia! Oh! I was expecting…someone else." Her shoulders slumped.

"Agnes? Good morning. I've brought you a new bicycle, seeing as how I sort of squashed yours the other day. *Heh, heh…* I can't tell you how sorry I am. Shall I just park it here beside the door?"

"Well, thank you. That was very thoughtful of you. I really did miss my bicycle."

Sophia leaned forward and glanced into the living room. "I see you have one of those new radio and phonograph consoles. Mind if I come in and take a look? I'm dying to see how it works." She shoved a foot inside the door.

Agnes stepped back. "Come on in, I guess." *What choice do I have? You're already in!* "We got this one from Sears and Roebuck. My granddaughter is a Duke Ellington and Glenn Miller fan. She has most of Tommy Dorsey's records, too. She likes the big band music."

"How nice." Sophia flumped down on the sofa chair beside the phonograph and ran her hand over the mahogany finish. "By the way. Whatever happened out at the watch tower? I've heard rumors that you—"

"Whatever you heard was probably true. I did it, all by myself. Burned that sucker to the ground..." Agnes glanced at her wristwatch. "Now, if you don't mind, I—"

"Of course. About this record player. How do the records—"

Mrs. Whistlemeyer shifted overhead on the curtain rod.

Sophia glanced up. "What the heck are those things—?"

"They're called roosters! The female version lays eggs. The males just sit around on curtain rods and fluff their feathers. Really, Sophia, I hate to rush you, but, I don't have time to visit. Busy day, you know. I'm expecting company any minute now." Agnes moved to the front door.

Sophia stood and slowly moved toward the kitchen. "I should be going, too. *Umm...* Something sure smells good. Spice cake?" She poked her head through the kitchen door.

"It's a War-Time cake for the funeral tomorrow and another for my company...who should be here any minute..." Agnes put her hand on the door knob. "So...if there's nothing else..."

"Well, now that you mention it, I wonder if you'd do me a favor. Can you speak to Mildred on my behalf? You see, she didn't ask me to contribute to the luncheon, so I wasn't invited to attend poor Claude's funeral." Sophia's Rita Hayworth-lips turned down in a pout.

"I'm such a fan of Mrs. Roosevelt and I so wanted to meet her… and of course pay my last respects to my dear friend, Claude…

"Clyde. Clyde Hofflemeister."

"Yes, of course. Him. Clyde. Do you think you could put in a word so I might attend dear Clyde's services?" She folded her fingers together as if in prayer. "Please?"

Agnes sighed. "I'm supposed to bring the cake and lemonade. Could you prepare the lemonade and maybe a Jell-O salad? Perhaps if you have flowers blooming in your yard, you could bring a bouquet for the buffet table. I don't suppose it would be a problem if you're contributing to the luncheon. You're a member of the Benevolent Society, too. "

"Oh, Agnes. You're such a dear. I knew you'd help me. You're such a good friend."

Sure, I am. Now that you've finagled me into getting what you want. How could I say no?

Sophia peeked down the hall. "Do you suppose I could use your bathroom before I go? I hate to drive all the way home…"

"Just down the hall there. Don't mind the chicken on the shower curtain. I'll pop into the kitchen and see how my cake is doing." *Why didn't I just keep my mouth shut?*

Sophia disappeared down the hall.

Agnes shoved a toothpick into the cake. *Clean as a whistle.* She picked up a crocheted potholder and pulled the cake from the oven, set it on a metal trivet and covered it with a clean tea towel. "Don't get any funny ideas, Mildred. Sugar isn't good for you." She glanced up at the rooster on the tea towel rack. "Don't forget what happened to your poor brother, Clara, when he ate the lemon tarts."

Mildred shifted on the towel rack. *Err er er er!*

"Yes, I know you're anxious to get to your new home. Jackson should have everything ready by suppertime."

Sophia came back down the hall, straightening her skirt. She stopped at the edge of the kitchen and squinted at Mildred. "You really did have a chicken in the bathroom. Oh, here's another one in the kitchen. How droll! Now, I really must run. All sorts of errands, you know. I just wanted to pop over and bring you the bicycle. Again, so sorry about the accident." Sophia's smile would have melted the ears off a chocolate Easter bunny, right through the wrapper.

"Don't give it a second thought. Things happen."

"Good-bye, dear. See you tomorrow. *Ta-ta!*" Sophia scurried down the sidewalk to her black Packard, parked at the curb.

Agnes waved, a forced smile crinkling her cheeks. *Ta-ta yourself, you old bat. Shame, Agnes. That was mean-spirited. Why can't I admit I was wrong about her? All she's ever done is try to be my friend. She even brought me a new bicycle. I really must change my ways if I ever hope to get through the Pearly Gates.*

Agnes stood up straighter and shrugged her shoulders. "Tomorrow, I'll be so nice to Sophia, her head will spin right off her scrawny neck."

She laughed. *Now, there's a sight I'd like to see.*

Chapter Twenty-Four

Y oo-hoo, Grandmother. I'm home." Katherine closed the front door without a sound. Her heart did a little flip. Any second now, Grandmother would pop out of the kitchen.

I shouldn't have gotten mad and left the house yesterday. It was rather childish.

The voices coming from the back yard must be Jackson and Grandmother out by the new chicken coop. She glanced up. The curtain rod over the front window was bare. Except for the tiny feathers scattered across the sofa and coffee table and the tell-tale streaks down the curtains, it was hard to imagine that Mrs. Whistlemeyer and Myrtle had roosted there for three days. Katherine smiled. She felt bad that she wasn't here to help Grandmother and Jackson get the chickens off the curtains. What a sight that must have been.

She hurried into the kitchen. The rack beside the sink held a clean tea towel, but no Chicken Mildred. So, life with chickens in the house, as interesting as the last three days had been, had finally come to an end. Thank goodness. Now things could get back to normal, whatever that looked like. Living with Grandmother was never *normal*. Her stomach wrenched. She still had to make peace with her.

Katherine opened the back door and peeked outside. "*Yoo-hoo!* I'm home."

Agnes turned as the screen door screeched. "Katherine! You're back." She dropped the garden hose onto the mound of bean poles and walked with arms outstretched toward the porch.

Katherine stepped into her embrace. "Oh, Grandmother. I'm sorry. I shouldn't have gotten so mad. We should have talked things over." Katherine wiped a tear from her cheek and hugged her grandmother.

Agnes patted Katherine's back. "I never meant to hurt you. You know I'm just a foolish old woman."

Katherine looked up. "Hey, Jackson! Godfrey." Katherine smiled and waved at the men, attaching screws onto the gate. "Grandma and I are going in the house and have some tea."

Agnes beamed. "The guys are almost finished with the coop. Isn't it wonderful? Myrtle and the gang are already thrilled with their new home." The four roosters ambled around, gurgling and picking at bread crumbs Agnes had scattered across the ground to acclimatize them to their new yard.

"It must be a sight more comfortable than sitting on a curtain rod and a towel rack. I see you even got Sophia out of the bathroom. She looks happy."

Agnes put her arm around Katherine's waist. "You guys come on in when you're done. I'll heat up that pot of beans for your lunch." She and Katherine walked into the house. "So, are we okay, Katherine? I'm really sorry I offended you." Agnes lit the stove and set the tea kettle on to boil.

Katherine sat at the table and folded her hands. "And, I'm sorry I left in a huff. I should have explained why I was so upset. But, Grandmother, you've got to stop all this nonsense. Now, tell me. What really happened out at the beach? Did you start the fire?" *Maybe this time I'll get the truth.*

Agnes opened and closed her mouth a few times. Her face turned several shades of pink.

Katherine drummed her fingers on the table. *Now what's the problem? We've both apologized.* "Grandma? I'm waiting." Katherine clenched her fist and pulled it out of sight under the table. *Why can't she just tell me the truth, for once?*

"I don't want you to be upset with me, Katherine. I know you won't believe this, but I can't tell you what happened out there. I was sworn to secrecy and I—"

"So, that's the way it's going to be? More nonsense?" Katherine's chair squeaked across the linoleum as she stood. She placed both hands on the table and leaned toward her grandmother. "I wouldn't have come home if I thought you were going to keep spinning yarns."

"But, you have to believe me, dear. I want to tell you, but I promised!" Agnes spread her hands, tears sparkling in her eyes. "What can I do? You saw the soldiers bring back my car. I told you the truth. They took me to the military station and made me promise."

Grandmother lowered her head. "Alright. Have it your way. I knocked over the heater and started the fire. Burned down the blasted watch tower. Almost set fire to the entire Newbury County. Is that what you want to hear?" Tears trickled down her cheeks. "Believe whatever you like. I'm done!" Grandmother dashed down the hall and into the bathroom, her shoulders shuddering with sobs. She slammed the door.

Great! Now what shall I do? I shouldn't have pushed so hard. Katherine's hands tingled. Her hair clung to the back of her neck, wet with perspiration. Her heart pattered like a playing card pinned to the wheel on a little kid's bicycle.

What part was the truth? Some of it? Certainly, not all of it. The soldiers *had* brought back Grandmother's car. But, being sworn to secrecy? Ridiculous. She admitted knocking over the heater. That sounds more likely than anything, but, why would she have turned on the heater? What did the military have to do with it? Truth, half-truths and lies. *I just don't know what to believe. And I need to know.* Maybe Godfrey had some idea.

Katherine yanked open the back door. "Godfrey! Can I have a word with you?"

Godfrey laid down the screwdriver, wiped his sleeve across his brow and stomped up the steps, kicking dirt from his shoes. "I could use a cold drink." He turned back. "Jackson. Want a cold drink?"

"No, suh. I'm fine. Almost done here. I wants to finish up right soon and get on home. Today is my little girl's birthday and my wife baked a cake."

Godfrey reached into his pocket and pulled out a half-dollar coin. He pitched it toward Jackson. "Here you go. She can buy something nice down at the Five and Dime. Tell her we all wish her a happy birthday."

Jackson beamed and snatched the coin. "Why, thank you, suh. That's most generous of you." He turned back to the gate.

Godfrey sat at the kitchen table and looked around the kitchen. "Where's Agnes?"

Katherine poured him a glass of water from the icebox water bottle and set it on the table. She nodded down the hall. "I'm afraid we had another spat. I guess she's washing her face." She lowered her head. "I made her cry."

"Why? That doesn't sound like Agnes."

"I asked her about the watch tower. She's spinning such a wild tale, I still don't think she's telling the truth."

"Katherine, be patient with her. She must have her reasons."

Katherine walked down the hall and knocked on the bathroom door. "Grandmother, please come out. Godfrey's here. We want to talk to you."

Grandmother's voice was muffled coming through the door. "Maybe I don't want to talk to you. I'm through talking. You don't believe anything I say, anyway."

Godfrey knocked. "Agnes. Please come out. Come and see your chicken yard. Myrtle and Mrs. Whistlemeyer are asking for you. They want to say thanks." He grinned and winked at Katherine.

She smiled. Godfrey's remark should make Grandma smile, too. "Please, Grandma? Come out and have some lunch with us. The guys are done outside. I'm heating up the beans." She dashed back to the kitchen, pulled the beans from the icebox and scraped them into a saucepan. She lit the burner and hurried back to the bathroom. There, now it's true. Enough lies had been told today. She didn't want to add another one.

The door squeaked open and Grandmother peeked through the crack. "Can we not talk about the watch tower? One day, I'll tell you all about it, but not today, okay?" Her sad eyes looked ready to burst into tears again.

Katherine's heart melted and her anger washed away. Grandmother had done so much for her. She was more of a *mother* to her than her own mother, who had married three times and was too busy taking care of each *husband de jour* to care much about Katherine. What did it matter if Grandmother told a tall tale or two? Who cared how the watch tower burned down, anyway? Would it change anything to know the real reason? Katherine opened her arms. "Come here, Grandma."

Agnes flung open the door and rushed into Katherine's arms. "I'm so sorry. I love you so much." A glint of morning sun coming through the kitchen window glinted against the chopsticks in her hair.

"And I love you, too."

Godfrey put his arms around them. "And I love you both!"

Katherine laughed and wiped her eyes. "Let's go out and see our chickens."

Saturday Night

Agnes pulled down the living room drapes, sloshed them up and down in the bathtub with *Oxydol* laundry soap and hung them over the shower rod to dry. *Thank goodness, the chickens are in their coop, Katherine's gone to bed and Godfrey is gone.* The house was finally quiet. One last check in the kitchen to make sure everything was turned off and she was ready for bed.

Agnes turned on the back porch light and glanced through the kitchen window. The roosters gurgled, picking contentedly at shreds of lettuce and potato peelings left over from dinner.

She yawned. What a day! All she wanted to do was lay her head on her own pillow and go to sleep. "Good night, Katherine," she whispered outside her bedroom door.

"Good night, Grandma. Love you."

Agnes went into the bathroom and closed the door. Gritting her teeth like a Cheshire cat, she peered into the medicine cabinet mirror. Not bad for an old lady. Seventy years old and she still had all her teeth. She pulled the chopsticks from her bun, loosed the pins and let her hair fall around her shoulders. She ran a comb through her auburn tresses. *It's almost time to freshen the color.*

Agnes glanced around the bathroom. *Now, where are my diamond earrings?* She was sure she'd laid them on the edge of the bathroom sink, when she took them off to do the gardening work. Had she put them in the medicine cabinet? She opened the mirrored door. *No. Not there.* A rush of panic surged through her chest. Could they have fallen on the floor? Or into the toilet?

She moved the waste basket and lifted the corner of the bathroom rug. Her heart pattered as she remembered Douglas's smile, the day he brought them to the hospital on the day John was born. The precious memory was still as fresh as though it were yesterday.

Labor had been long and hard. Making his appearance in a breech presentation, John's birth was slow and tedious, painful and frustrating—a twelve hour ordeal.

When perspiration popped out on the doctor's brow, she sensed she was in trouble.

The terrifying thought that she might die in labor entered her head. Her body arched in another painful contraction. Exhausted by the time the spasm released, she lay gasping for breath, her cheeks dripping with sweat mixed with tears. She turned fearful eyes toward her doctor. "Why is this taking so long? What's wrong?"

"There, there. You're doing fine, Agnes. It won't be long now. But, I must warn you, the baby is presenting breech. There's always the possibility his legs may be dislocated or broken from the pressure of coming through the birth canal. We must be prepared for the worst."

"Thanks for the pep talk. Now, I have something else to worry…" Another contraction cut short her sarcasm and still another hour of excruciating labor finally resulted in the birth of her precious son. He had a shock of black hair. His face was red and pinched, but blessedly, he suffered no injury as a result of his difficult birth.

Agnes didn't fare as well. She was unable to have another child.

Douglas had presented her with roses and the beautiful diamond earrings to commemorate John's birth.

Where in blazes were they? Agnes flung things around the bathroom, in search of the illusive jewelry. A bath towel hit the floor. She dumped over the wastebasket and pawed through the contents. She got down on her hands and knees and reached behind the toilet. *Nothing there!* They were gone.

Hadn't that wretched Sophia Rashmuller come in here this afternoon? Agnes could almost see Sophia washing her hands, spotting her precious earrings on the side of the sink and stuffing them in her purse.

Tears prickled Agnes's eyes. A crushing sensation rose up in her chest—rage, despair and helplessness. If murderous thoughts could kill, Sophia would topple over in a dead heap. *As sure as kittens in the spring, Sophia has snitched my earrings.*

Agnes touched her ears. How naked they felt beneath her fingertips. She would likely never again feel the warmth of the silver or see them reflected in her mirror as she had for the past forty-three years. She wanted to jump in her car, drive to Sophia's house, fling her to the floor and demand the return of her jewelry. But, she knew she could never do such a thing.

Maybe she should call Chief Waddlemucker. He'd know what to do. She could imagine what he'd say. "No speculation, Agnes. Just give me facts."

What were the facts?

The earrings were here this morning.

Sophia was here this afternoon.

The earrings were gone tonight.

Common sense said Sophia took them. Circumstantial evidence said she took them. In her heart, Agnes *knew* Sophia took them. But, Chief Waddlemucker would say, "You got no proof, Agnes. Without proof, my hands are tied. There's nothing we can do about it."

Tears spilled down Agnes's cheeks. She tried to imagine seeing Sophia tomorrow at the funeral parlor. How could she face her, knowing she was a thief? Or next week in knitting circle? How could she deal with this...*woman* time and again in social settings and never speak out? Should she tell the other ladies what happened? Or...maybe... maybe...

Wasn't she a self-appointed scourge of the underworld? The righter of wrongs? A warrior on the home front, bringing truth, justice and the American Way to their little community?

Some dark night, very soon, maybe even tomorrow night, she and Jackson would drive across town to Sophia's house.

Jackson would boost Agnes through Sophia's bedroom window. She'd wear Douglas's raincoat and hat again in case anyone spotted them. She'd creep around Sophia's bedroom with a flashlight and check her bloomers drawer. That's where thieves hide their ill-gotten booty. It wouldn't be a surprise to find all kinds of jewelry stashed there. The woman was a thief. Maybe she *was* a Nazi spy like she'd first suspected. Maybe she stole jewelry to finance her nefarious organization. She probably stole something everywhere she went. Wouldn't Chief Waddlemucker be pleased when she brought back a pocketful of stolen—

"Grandmother? You're still up? What are you doing in here?" Wasn't Katherine a dear to be so concerned?

Should she tell Katherine about her plans to raid Sophia's house? Probably better not. Agnes dried her eyes, blew her nose, and opened the bathroom door.

"Why, Grandmother. What's wrong? You've crying again. I told you I was sorry we quarreled. "

"It's not that." Agnes dabbed her eyes with a tissue. "We've had a theft, but don't worry. I plan to take care of the matter very soon. She won't get away with it."

Katherine shook her head. "She, who? Who stole what?"

"It's that Sophia Rashmuller. I told you she was no good. She's stolen my diamond earrings. The ones your grandpa gave me the day your father was born. Sophia was in the bathroom this afternoon, and—"

"Stop! Sophia didn't take your earrings. I saw them on the sink when I came home. I was afraid they might fall down the drain, so I put them in your room on your dresser."

Agnes's cheeks felt like socks hung too close to the stove on a winter day. A sense of relief with a full measure of embarrassment coursed through her chest. "On my dresser? Really? Sophia didn't...?"

"No, Grandmother. She didn't."

"Oh." Agnes turned away from Katherine, for surely, her face was as bright as a Red Delicious apple. "Okay, thanks." She stepped back into the bathroom and closed the door. Dear God, when would she stop seeing *boogey-men* everywhere she looked? It was getting down-right humiliating. No wonder Katherine was upset with her. Fortunately, no one need ever know that she had accused Sophia of stealing her earrings and called her a Nazi spy. Again! *I'm not about to tell, and Katherine won't mention it to anyone.*

Agnes pulled off her glasses and laid them on the back of the toilet. She washed her face with a cloth, careful to remove the lipstick, and rouge from her cheeks. Her blurry reflection leered back in the mirror. Eyes—bloodshot from crying. Cheeks—shiny pink from scrubbing, and long auburn tresses hanging limp around her shoulders.

Agnes closed her eyes and sighed, lamenting the lost beauty of her youth. She would never again stand in front of this mirror, as she had once done, smile and turn from side to side, admiring her youthful figure, clear complexion and smooth skin.

If Godfrey could only see her now, he wouldn't be half so inclined to…whatever it was he seemed inclined to do.

Agnes wound her hair into two long braids and flipped them over her shoulders. She pulled her toothbrush from the holder on the wall, plucked the can of tooth powder from the medicine cabinet and shook some white powder into her hand. She added a little water, stirred it with her finger to make a paste, dipped her toothbrush into her palm and lifted it to her mouth. Her hand quavered. *Wait!* The consistency of the paste didn't feel quite right. Did it need more water? Or had she pulled the wrong can…

Laying her toothbrush on the edge of the sink, she washed the paste from her palm, opened the medicine cabinet and lifted out the can of tooth powder. Hadn't it been almost empty this morning when she brushed her teeth? Now it felt full. The shape and color looked right, but…

She put her glasses back on. The words on the label snapped into focus. *Waverly's Rat Poison. Contents—Arsenic.*

Her stomach rocked and stabs of pain shot through her eyes. *Oh, my stars! How on earth did this get in my medicine cabinet?* There ought to be a law against manufacturers making cans of rat poison that resembled hygiene items, like tooth powder. Imagine, if she or Katherine had brushed their teeth with it. *How could I be so stupid?* The cans looked so much alike, she must have picked up the rat poison at the grocery store by mistake.

It was undeniable. Old age and decrepitude had set in, and now she had almost killed herself by confusing rat poison with tooth powder. She might have even killed Katherine!

Cold chills paraded up and down her spine. Yet again, she berated herself for being too preoccupied with her conspiracies and wild accusations. *Scourge of the underworld, indeed.*

Should she tell Katherine about mixing up the cans? Better not. After the episode with the earrings, she was on thin ice with Katherine already. This story wouldn't help.

Agnes glanced down. Something white lay wadded up in the corner. She picked up a handkerchief embroidered with the initials SR. Sophia must have dropped it when she was in the bathroom. Agnes stuffed it in her pocket. She'd wash and iron it and return it to Sophia tomorrow afternoon. It was the right thing to do, particularly after falsely accusing her of stealing the earrings. Obviously, she had misjudged Sophia. She was a good friend. Hadn't Sophia brought over lemon tarts and a new bicycle when she accidently nearly ran her down?

Best thing was to put the rat poison on a high shelf in the garage. She wouldn't want anyone else to make the same mistake.

Chapter Twenty-Five

K atherine's shriek jarred Agnes from her slumber. *Holy potato chips! Katherine?* Agnes shot out of bed, grabbed her umbrella and hurried into the living room, her long flannel nightgown swirling around her ankles.

Katherine stood in the open doorway, staring at the folded Newbury Daily Gazette.

Agnes skidded to a stop, wielding the umbrella over her head. "What's wrong? You about scared me to death. Have the Japanese attacked? Did Ling-Ling get at the chickens?"

"The chickens are fine. Why didn't you tell me? I would never have…" Katherine's eyes sparkled as big tears gathered. She put her arms around Agnes and laid her head on her shoulder. "I'm so sorry. I shouldn't have doubted you." The newspaper crinkled against Agnes's back.

Agnes pulled away. "Whatever are you babbling about? *She's reading Ritchie and Harvey's newspaper story. She's going to hate me even more, now.*"

"Here in the paper. Read it yourself." Katherine thrust it in Agnes's face.

"I haven't got my glasses. What does it say?" *Is she actually buying the story about the seagull and the heater at the watch tower?* Agnes handed the paper back to Katherine.

"It's a long article. You can read it later. It says that Japan is arming air balloons with bombs and sending them to the U.S. across the jet stream, hoping they'll land here and cause panic. A woman and five children in Oregon found one at a picnic grounds. They didn't know what it was, so they touched it and it exploded. They were all killed. Oh, Grandma!" Katherine's tears spilled down her cheeks.

"That's terrible!" Agnes's thoughts crashed around in her head. Her heart raced. Her worst fears, realized. Now, people had been killed by the air balloons. Should she tell Katherine about the attack at the watch tower or keep faith with Colonel Farthingworth? "What else does it say?"

Katherine scanned the newspaper. "It says that the government kept a press black-out on the balloons for fear of panic. I guess now that people have died, they feel the public should be warned to stay away from them or there could be more deaths. The military base in Boyles Springs says that one of the air balloons crashed into the watch tower at the beach. That's your watch tower, Grandma. That's what started the fire, wasn't it? You didn't have anything to do with it."

Agnes hung her head. A little smile tickled the corner of her cheeks. *Well, what do you know?* Good old Colonel Farthingworth had come through and cleared her name. That should end the town's gossip.

"Grandma, why did you take the blame for the fire? First, you made up a stupid story and said you were responsible for the fire. Why didn't you tell me what really happened?" Katherine dabbed at the tears on her cheek.

"Colonel Farthingworth asked me to take the blame because they didn't want the public to know about the bombs. I was just doing my patriotic duty. You would have done the same thing under the circumstances."

"Wouldn't it have been better that people knew so they wouldn't go near the things? Those poor children in Oregon."

"The Colonel explained that the government thought if they kept it secret, Japan would never know what damage the balloons were causing. At that point, no one had been hurt. If Japan thought the

balloons weren't making it to the U.S., they might stop sending them."
Agnes leaned her umbrella against the edge of the sofa. "Now that
people have died, the public needs to know."

"Isn't that like locking the barn door after the horse is loose? At
least now folks know that you weren't responsible. Oh, Grandmother.
People have been saying terrible things about you, and I didn't even
defend you. I'm sorry. I should have known better."

Agnes's heart crumpled. She hated lying to Katherine, and it felt
so good to regain her trust. She waved her hand dismissively. "Oh,
pooh! I knew what people would say when I agreed to the plan. I'm
willing to do what needs to be done if it will end this war even one day
sooner. So what if people talk about me?" She shrugged. "It's not the
first time and I don't suppose it'll be the last. A little gossip never hurt
anyone."

"Grandma, you were so brave to take the blame like that."

"Any red-blooded American would have done the same." Agnes
nodded.

Katherine shook her head. "I'm not so sure they would have,
Grandma. I'm not so sure at all."

Katherine combed thick, green, scented gel through her hair and
pinched multi-teethed metal wave clamps across the crown of her head.
The scent of the gel reminded her of a meadow on a spring morning. The
clamps held her damp hair tightly in three-inch waves. In about thirty
minutes when her hair dried and she removed the clamps, deep ridges
would curve across the back of her hair where the clamps had been.

She pulled a wad of hair from her comb and stuffed in into the
end of a long hairnet *rat* resembling a sausage. Then she rolled her
long hair over the eight-inch long *rat* at her neckline, creating a tight
roll across the back of her neck and curving up toward her ears. Long
hairpins held the Victory Roll in place. She had just begun to wear

the hairstyle favored by factory workers and housewives, keeping long hair off *m'ladies* faces while they worked.

Katherine stepped into the kitchen where Agnes stood at the kitchen sink, wiping her hands on a tea-towel. "I'll be leaving for the mortuary pretty soon. Mr. Whistlemeyer asked me to come early, to give Clyde a final *once-over* on his hair and makeup before the service." Katherine giggled. "I shouldn't laugh. No doubt Mr. Whistlemeyer wants to put his best foot forward, or in this case, Clyde's best foot. He's trying to make a good impression on Mrs. Roosevelt."

Katherine peeked out the kitchen window into the chicken yard where Mrs. Whistlemeyer and Chicken Sophia fussed over an apple peeling Grandmother had tossed out earlier this morning. Weren't they cute? All brown and red and gold. Mildred and Myrtle sat perched on the top of their little house. Katherine smiled. *Don't tell me I'm getting attached to a bunch of Bantam roosters?* Only Grandmother could end up with four worthless chickens that will never lay an egg!

The telephone jangled. Katherine turned and picked up the receiver. "Hello?"

"Katherine? Good morning. It's Dr. Don Dew-Wright."

At the sound of his voice, Katherine's heart skipped a beat. A smile leapt to her lips. "What can I do for you?" She glanced toward her grandmother. *Is she watching? I'll never live this down if she sees me blush.*

"I hope I'm not intruding."

"Oh, not at all!" *Probably wants to comment on the newspaper story.*

Dr. Don coughed and cleared his throat. "I read about the Japanese air balloon strike at the watch tower. I'm curious. Wondered if there was anything out there left to see. By the way, I was glad to see the article cleared your grandmother's name." He chuckled.

"*That's what I thought.* Yes. We're pleased, too. All that gossip for nothing. They asked her to keep the balloon bombs and the cause of the fire a secret. I think folks owe her an apology."

"So, about this afternoon. Would you be interested in going out to the ocean with me? We could picnic and check out the watch tower." A little gasp came through the phone.

Dr. Dew-Wright really wanted to spend time with her? Katherine's pulse raced at the thought. "I'm sorry. Clyde Hoffelmeister's funeral is this afternoon. I do the hair and makeup down at the Whistlemeyer mortuary and...well, Clyde needs a touch-up after...you remember what happened."

"Well, lucky Mr. Hoffelmeister. Why does he get such special treatment from a pretty girl and I don't?" He chuckled. "I didn't mean to be disrespectful. Poor choice of words on my part."

"Have you heard that Mrs. Roosevelt is coming to his funeral? Grandmother and her group from the First Church of the Evening Star and Everlasting Light are serving luncheon afterwards. We're all pretty excited to meet Mrs. Roosevelt."

"Our Mrs. Roosevelt is coming...here?"

"Oh, yes. She's a distant relative of Clyde's, and she's in the area, so I guess its good publicity. Or, maybe not. I don't know. In any event, that's where I'll be this afternoon, so that's a no to a picnic. Maybe some other time?"

Katherine held her breath. She switched the receiver to the other hand and wiped her sweaty palm against her skirt. Would he think she wasn't interested? Was she interested? Katherine turned as Grandmother inched across the kitchen toward the phone, wiping down the counter with the dishrag. She wasn't even trying to hide an attempt to catch every word of the conversation, every innuendo, every sigh. *Isn't she a busybody today?*

"Katherine, are you there?"

Goodness. Had he suggested an alternative date and she hadn't even heard him? "What? What did you say?"

"I said you weren't going to get rid of me that easily. We can go out another time if you like."

So, he really did want to spend time with her. Hadn't she told

Grandmother just days ago that she wasn't interested in any man as long as the country was at war?

Maybe Dr. Dew-Wright was different. He was a doctor right here in Newbury. Didn't folks at home need doctors just as much as the troops? Surely they wouldn't leave the towns without doctors. But, wasn't it more likely that the younger doctors would go to the war zone and the older ones stay home? Perhaps it was only a matter of time until...

A knot formed in Katherine's throat. She hardened her heart against Dr. Dew-Wright or romance with anyone, for that matter. Lose another man to the war? Not on your tintype! Best to end it before it started. Katherine pursed her lips. Tears prickled her eyes. "Actually, come to think of it, Dr. Don, I'm pretty busy these days. But thanks for asking. Good-bye." She gulped and started to hang up the phone.

"Wait. Katherine. Don't hang up. What just happened? Did I get my signals mixed? I thought you and I...well, at least I felt...and I thought—"

"Oh, you didn't do anything wrong. I'm just not..." Tears stung her eyes. She fumbled in her pocket, searching for a handkerchief. From the corner of her eye, she saw Grandmother's hand waving a hankie toward her. "It's just that—"

"What is it, Katherine? Tell me. Do I need a breath mint? A closer shave? What's the problem?"

Katherine sniffed, dabbing Grandmother's hankie on her cheeks.

She would not risk another broken heart. It couldn't happen again. She wouldn't let it. "Oh, it's not you at all. With all my responsibilities, I really don't have time for socializing. But, thank you for thinking of me." She slammed down the phone before she could change her mind, rushed into her room, closed the door and twisted the lock.

Katherine slipped through the mortuary kitchen, past Grandmother, Mildred and Sophia carrying trays and food from their cars into the funeral home. "I'll come back and help you as soon as I can, Grandma."

She strolled into the *Serenity Chamber* where Jackson and Mr. Whistlemeyer stood over Clyde's plain white casket.

"Katherine, I just received a beautiful Koa wood casket from Finklebaum's *A Tisket, A Casket* warehouse this morning. I've decided to use it for Clyde instead of the one his daughter picked out. The other is so much nicer. Clyde *is* somewhat of a celebrity, after all. I'll make up the difference in the price, myself."

Mr. Whistlemeyer shoved Clyde's casket from the *Serenity Slumber Chamber* into the *Eternal Transportation Center* where the Koa wood casket was lined up in a row with other caskets of varying design and prices, awaiting candidates. "Come help us lift Clyde into his new cocoon of perpetual rest."

Katherine's mouth dropped open. "You want *me* to help move Clyde…" Cutting Clyde's hair was one thing. Making up his bruised and battered face was even more difficult, but lifting his body from one casket into another was something else again.

"Sure thing." Mr. Whistlemeyer clapped his hands. "You and Jackson take hold of his feet. I'll heft his shoulders. It'll be a snap, with him more or less rigid and all. We'll lift him right out of this one and tuck him snug as a bug in a rug into this hand-carved one. With our guest of honor attending, it's the special touch we need."

"Alright. If you're sure you guys can't handle him by yourself." Katherine laid her comb on Clyde's chest and moved to the end of the casket where Jackson gripped Clyde's feet. *Please don't let there be another mishap.* One tumble per customer was surely enough.

Jackson shook his head. "Miss Katherine, I doesn't think you needs to lift him any. We can manage. You just roll the casket out of the way when we lifts him up. That's just the best way you can help. Isn't that right, Mr. Whistlemeyer?"

Mr. Whistlemeyer's brows knit. "I suppose so. Yes, that will be fine. Are you ready? On my count. One, two, three, now!"

Mr. Whistlemeyer and Jackson lifted Clyde's rigid body.

Katherine whisked the casket away.

The men gently lowered Clyde into the satin-lined, Koa-wood beauty.

Mr. Whistlemeyer adjusted Clyde's jacket and straightened his hands across his chest.

"Now, I'll roll him into the chapel or *Heaven's Golden Gate* as we like to refer to it around here." The wheels on the roll-around moved soundlessly over the carpet into the parlor. "There, now maybe a touch more powder on his nose, Katherine."

Katherine leaned over the casket and patted the powder puff across Clyde's face. She took her comb off his chest and stood back. "He doesn't look any the worse for his tumble, does he?"

"He looks right genteel, Miss Katherine and that's a fact. If you is through with me, Mr. Whistlemeyer, I'll just leave before the crowd starts arrivin'. I'm not much comfortable in a crowd."

"Thanks for your help this morning, Jackson. The rugs look wonderful. You did a great job. I appreciate you working extra hours this weekend." He moved several baskets of flowers closer to the front of the casket. Tall flickering candlesticks at each end lent almost a cathedral atmosphere. "There now. Isn't everything just lovely?" He rubbed his hands together like a spider hovering over a fly. "And, just in time, too." He glanced at his watch. "The guests will be arriving shortly."

Jackson straightened a wrinkle from Clyde's tie. "Always glad to help you, Mr. Whistlemeyer."

Mr. Whistlemeyer nodded to Katherine. "If you'll excuse me. I have matters to attend to before Mrs. Roosevelt arrives." He scuttled into the back room.

"How is them chickens, Miss. Katherine? Is they happy in their new home?" Jackson grinned.

"They are. I don't know how to thank you. Did Grandmother pay you for the work yesterday?"

"No need. No need. Your grandma is a right nice lady. Always happy to help a widda' woman. Okay, I sees folks pulling into the parking lot outside. I'll be leavin' now." Jackson touched his forehead and left the chapel through the glass entry doors at the front of the building where his bicycle leaned against the wall.

Katherine glanced through the window. A large black Hudson touring car had pulled into the parking lot. She checked her watch. Could it be Mrs. Roosevelt's party, already? They weren't expected for another thirty minutes! Perhaps Grandmother could make Mrs. Roosevelt a cup of tea while she waited. Where was Mr. Whistlemeyer? He should be out there greeting his honored guest.

Katherine hurried down the hall, opening doors and peeking inside. "*Yoo hoo!* Mr. Whistlemeyer?" She had to find him, quick. She paused beside a door, hearing raised voices inside. She opened it a crack and listened.

"What do you mean it's too late? I'm telling you, you've used the wrong one. You're going to have to switch them." A man's voice—and he sounded pretty put out about something.

Katherine peeked through the door. *Albert Finklebaum?* What was he doing here? She pulled the door back a bit and put her eye to the crack.

"Are you crazy? I can't go out there and switch them now. Mrs. Roosevelt's car just pulled up out front. She's probably in there with him already." Mr. Whistlemeyer's voice raised a notch. "Do you think I can mess with everything, right in front of the President's wife?"

Katherine let the door slide nearly shut. *What's he talking about?*

"Whistlemeyer, listen to me. Somehow, things got mixed up at the warehouse. We sent the wrong one by mistake." Albert jerked his thumb toward the chapel. He clenched his fist, and raised it toward Mr. Whistlemeyer's face. "You need to do as I say. I've about run out of patience with you."

Mr. Whistlemeyer's face blanched. "What difference does it make, anyway? I'll pay the difference if that's what you're worried about. What's gotten into you? Isn't it bad enough you steal my wife? Now you want to humiliate me in front of Mrs. Roosevelt?" Mr. Whistlemeyer's voice turned cold. "This is the last straw. Get out of my establishment, Finklebaum! Now!" He raised his fist and took a swing at Albert.

Albert ducked and grabbed Mr. Whistlemeyer by the shoulders. "So, that's the way it's going to be, *huh*? Think you can take me, old man?" The two men rocked back and forth, exchanging punches that mostly went astray or bounced off the other's paunchy belly.

Katherine bit her lip. What were they thinking? Having a fist fight with the President's wife not thirty feet away?

Albert and Mr. Whistlemeyer continued throwing meaningless jabs at each other. If the present circumstances and location wasn't so ridiculous, their fight would have been almost comical.

"Stop!"

Katherine turned, as Godfrey rushed through the door at the rear of the room and grabbed Mr. Whistlemeyer's arm. "Stop this nonsense, you idiots! There's a celebrity in the parlor. Clean yourself up, Whistlemeyer. Get out there and greet your guests." He gave Mr. Whistlemeyer a shove toward the door where Katherine stood.

She stepped aside as Mr. Whistlemeyer barreled past her toward the men's room.

"And you, Finklebaum. You've got no business here. Get on your way." Godfrey pointed toward the rear door, his menacing scowl more threatening than his words.

"I got a right to be here. I got business with Whistlemeyer." Finklebaum took a step back. "Don't think this is over!" He scuttled out the door, rubbing his nose, which had begun to swell and turn purple.

Katherine stepped inside. "Godfrey, what's going on? They were shouting something about the funeral parlor and Mrs. Roosevelt. None of it made any sense."

"Don't worry your pretty head about it. They probably started drinking to celebrate Mrs. Roosevelt's arrival and things got out of hand. Is your grandmother here yet? Mrs. Roosevelt is already in the chapel. Someone needs to greet her. I should connect with her security detail." Godfrey hurried into the chapel.

Katherine followed him to the door and peeked inside. *She's here! What a smart suit.* Mrs. Roosevelt and her secretary stood beside Clyde's casket. Mrs. Roosevelt dabbed a lace handkerchief at her eyes. Her companion placed an arm around her shoulder.

The driver and Mrs. Roosevelt's body guard stood at attention by the front door.

Godfrey approached them just as Pastor Lickleiter and his wife from the First Church of the Evening Star and Everlasting Light walked through the front door.

Mr. Whistlemeyer hurried down the aisle, his face flushed and an angry red blotch just below his eye where Albert's fist must have accidently connected with his cheek. He shook hands with the pastor, took his arm and strode down the aisle toward the casket. "Mrs. Roosevelt? I'm Bernard Whistlemeyer, the proprietor of this establishment. So sorry to meet on this sad occasion." His shoulders drooped theatrically. He lowered his head, looking for all the world as if he, too, had just lost his best friend. "Dear Clyde. What a loss to our fair community. *Tsk Tsk.* This is Pastor Lickleiter. He'll be conducting the services today. Pastor?"

Mrs. Lickleiter released her husband's arm, glanced around and then sat down near the front of the chapel. No one had introduced her to Mrs. Roosevelt. Her expression suggested she was used to being the invisible woman in the room. *Poor thing does look a tad mousey today.*

Pastor Lickleiter shook Mrs. Roosevelt's hand. "What a pleasure. We're so honored by your presence, sad as the occasion is. God rest his soul. Won't you have a seat?" He glanced up and saw Katherine. "And, here's our Miss Katherine. Come and meet Mrs. Roosevelt." The pastor glanced at his wristwatch. "We are all a bit early, aren't we?"

Mrs. Roosevelt stood beside her secretary, next to Clyde's casket.

Katherine hurried over. "Pleased to meet you, ma'am. Could we bring you a cup of tea before the service starts? I'm sure we have time before the others arrive." *My, she looks older than her pictures. I don't think she's wearing a stitch of makeup.*

"That would be lovely, Katherine. I am a bit weary from the drive. Is there a ladies room I might visit? It feels like hours since we left San Francisco. How about you, Tommy? Care to join me?" She smiled at her secretary. "Oh, I should introduce you. Tommy, this is Katherine. What is your last name, dear?"

"Katherine Odboddy." She ducked her head and glanced up at Tommy through her long lashes.

Mrs. Roosevelt's eyes crinkled with a smile. "Tommy is my loyal companion and secretary. She's my right arm and manages my life. I couldn't go anywhere without her."

"Pleased to meet you, Tommy." Katherine extended her hand. *Are they wearing their skirts that short in Washington?* "If you'll follow me, I'll show you to the ladies room." *I can almost see her knees.*

"Thank goodness. I don't think I could wait much longer." Tommy dug in her purse and pulled out a package of cigarettes. She shook one into her hand. "Do you mind if I smoke?" She put the cigarette to her lips and lit it with silver lighter, inhaled deeply and blew out a stream of smoke.

"Well, I…I rather think it would be best if you stepped outside." Katherine cheeks warmed. Was the woman born in a barn? Wouldn't you think she'd have more respect for Mrs. Roosevelt's cousin twice removed, lying in his casket?

Katherine walked the women into the connecting hallway. "Here's the ladies room. That door will take you to the parking lot, Tommy. You can smoke out there." She turned back toward the chapel. "I'll go and see about some tea. Can you find your way back inside, ma'am?"

"I'm sure we can, Katherine. Thank you." Mrs. Roosevelt shoved on the bathroom door and disappeared inside.

She looks just like a regular woman. Not at all what I expected. I guess President's wives pull their corsets on like everybody else. Won't Grandma just die when she sees the length of Tommy's skirt? She'll have to get out her sewing box and turn up her hems all over again!

Chapter Twenty-Six

Mitzie Steals the Show

Agnes pulled the top off her cake pan and slid the cake onto her mother's favorite cut glass cake plate. She turned as Katherine came into the kitchenette. "Hey. Everything okay out there? Did you get Clyde fixed up and presentable?"

"He looks great." Katherine glanced at her wristwatch. "Mrs. Roosevelt and her party arrived already. Can you fix her and her secretary a cup of tea before the service starts?"

Agnes grabbed the teakettle and filled it with water. "Certainly! I think we can put together a plate of cookies, too."

Sophia hurried over, her gaze darting from Agnes to Katherine. "She's right there in the next room? I didn't think I'd ever get such a chance... I mean...to meet her."

Agnes raised an eyebrow. *Odd. She looks so anxious.* "What's wrong, Sophia? Are you nervous about meeting a celebrity?"

"What? No! No! Of course not. Just overwhelmed with this... opportunity." Sophia's cheeks flamed pink. "I'll check the teakettle." She turned her back to Agnes and Katherine.

Agnes shrugged and pawed through the cups and saucers in the cupboard, looking for some without chips or a scratch. She made her selection and wiped the plate and several cups with a tea towel, then pulled open a drawer where the tablecloths and napkins were stored. "I wish I'd thought to bring down some freshly pressed linen napkins. These look so wrinkled." She chose the best of the lot that matched, laid them on the table and ran her hand across them to smooth out the wrinkles.

"These will have to do. Is it just the two of them? How about the driver?"

"I'll ask when we serve Mrs. Roosevelt." Katherine filled the tea ball infuser with loose tea and dropped it into a yellow teapot with a crack running down the side. "Is this is the best teapot he's got?" She opened several cupboard doors and shook her head.

"We're lucky Whistlemeyer has a teapot down here at all. I doubt he ever expected to entertain the President's wife. It will have to do, cracks and all." Agnes poured boiling water into the pot while Sophia arranged the cups, saucers and cookies on a tray with the napkins.

"Who's going to take it in to her?" Sophia's breathing quickened as she glanced from Agnes to the chapel door.

"I think I should." Katherine picked up the tray. "She'll be expecting me. Don't worry, Sophia, you and Grandmother will get a chance to meet her later, after the service."

Agnes opened the door and Katherine carried the tray through. "Isn't this exciting? Who thought we'd ever have a chance to meet Mrs. Roosevelt face to face?"

"How are you feeling, Agnes? You look a little peaked." Sophia's expression resembled a cat that just snatched a treat from the party-snacks. "Do you have a headache, or cramps or any dizziness?"

What an odd question. Agnes pushed a loose strand of hair behind her ear. "Of course not. Perhaps I'm a bit tired. Why do you ask? Do I look sick?"

"Oh, no, just concerned, you know. After all, a woman of your age…well, you're likely susceptible to all kinds of things, aren't you?" Sophia shoved the plates and cups around the counter. "Arthritis, rheumatism, blurry vision, forgetfulness…"

Agnes put her hands on her hips. "What? I'm not that old! I'm…" She remembered last night's commitment to be nice to Sophia. "*Uh…* Mildred should be here with the salad, any minute now." *What an odd remark. It's almost as if she expected me to be sick.* "Oh, here's Mildred and Edith now."

Agnes held the door for Edith, carrying in a casserole wrapped in a towel. Mildred followed with a large salad bowl. "Here, Edith, let me take that casserole. Do we need to heat it up some?" *She looks so mousey today. You'd think she'd be more concerned with her appearance, being Colonel Farthingworth's wife. It's obvious she doesn't get her hair done at Katherine's shop.*

Edith shook her head. Grey-streaked hair drawn straight off her face into an unbecoming bun made her look older than her years. "I just pulled it from the oven and brought it straight over. I don't think we'll need to heat it anymore."

Edith removed her sweater and hung it on the coat rack near the door. She hugged Sophia. "Hello, dear, how are you today? Did Mr. Puddles come home? I could hardly sleep a wink worrying about him last night."

Sophia patted her shoulder. "I shouldn't have bothered you. I just had to talk to someone. Mr. Puddles came home during the night. End of lost cat story! It was so sweet of you. Thanks for being there for me." She turned to Agnes and Mildred. "My cat ran away. I needed to cry on someone's shoulder and Edith was such a comfort to me."

Now isn't that...special? Sophia and Edith are just the chummiest pals. "Our pets are such babies, aren't they? Did I tell you we got some chickens?"

Sophia snickered. "You can say that again. They're roosting all over her house. Looked like a zoo over there. In the living room and the kitchen—"

"Sophia! That wasn't nice." Mildred glared at her. "I'm sure that's not true." She glanced at Agnes for confirmation.

Agnes shrugged. "It was true when Sophia stopped by. Jackson built us a coop yesterday. We didn't plan..." Agnes's face warmed. What more could she say? There really wasn't a good reason for having chickens in the living room and kitchen for three days. Certainly, neither

Sophia nor Edith would have done it. Why was Sophia being so mean? First, the comment about looking sick, and now the crack about her chickens. *And I was planning to be nice to her today. The old battleax.*

Katherine swung the door open and held it ajar. "Are you ladies coming in for the service? The guests have arrived and Pastor Lickleiter is almost ready to start."

Bless Katherine. She came just in time to change the subject.

Agnes followed Katherine, Mildred, and Edith into the parlor. She and Mildred moved toward the center pew and Katherine and Edith walked further down the aisle. Sophia turned down the hall towards the ladies room.

Agnes gazed around the chapel. Clyde's daughter sat weeping in the front row, beside her husband. *I don't believe I've ever seen her face in Newbury over the past ten years.* Wasn't it a shame how children live three states away, never visit their parents until they lay dead in their casket, and then weep their heart out on the front row of the funeral parlor? Maybe they were tears of shame, rather than tears of love and loss.

Obviously still feeling responsible for her neighbor's death, Mrs. Turnbull wept alongside Clyde's daughter. What was in that box at her feet? *Surely, it's not her cat, Mitzie!* The corner of the lid lifted, revealing a pink nose and a black ear. By golly, it was. Guess Mrs. Turnbull figured since Clyde died trying to save Mitzie's life, she should pay her respects at his funeral.

Mrs. Lickleiter sat in the back row, though it was doubtful Clyde had ever darkened the door of the First Church of the Evening Star and Everlasting Light. Apparently it was the duty of the pastor's wife to attend every service her husband ever held, be it christening, wedding or funeral. And, Mrs. Lickleiter was a good pastor's wife, if she was nothing else.

She wore a black and white printed dress with short sleeves and a matching braided belt. Quite out of style this year. Hemline was much too long. Poor woman had no fashion sense at all. Maybe it was time to approach the board about giving Pastor Lickleiter a raise. If his wife's appearance was an indicator, he desperately needed it.

Several other neighbors made up the remainder of the guests, along with Mrs. Roosevelt, her secretary, driver and her body guard. Mildred, Katherine and Edith sat near the back.

Where was Sophia?

Mrs. Roosevelt sat beside Tommy in the front row across the aisle from Clyde's daughter and husband.

Mr. Whistlemeyer sat closer to the hallway.

Pastor Lickleiter began the service with a prayer and spoke about Clyde's good points. They were few. And, his achievements in life; they were fewer.

He spent a good deal of time describing the details of Clyde's final attempt to save Mrs. Turnbull's cat. All eyes turned toward the box jiggling at Mrs. Turnbull's feet.

At the mention of the cat, Clyde's daughter broke out wailing.

Mrs. Turnbull wailed even louder, drowning out Clyde's daughter's heaving sobs.

Pastor Lickleiter paused, giving the ladies time to compose themselves. After several sniffles and a good deal of nose blowing, he continued. He had just opened the Bible and began to read an encouraging verse when Albert Finklebaum walked up the side aisle and sat down beside Mr. Whistlemeyer.

Mr. Whistlemeyer glared at him and shifted over several inches, putting more space between them.

Agnes glanced toward Mrs. Roosevelt. How was she holding up? Just behind her row, the door into the hallway leading to the restrooms squeaked, then opened about three inches and stopped.

Some twelve minutes later, Pastor Lickleiter concluded his final prayer. "Now, I'll invite any who wish to come forward to share your remembrances of Clyde."

Mrs. Roosevelt stood and walked to the pulpit. She looked very comfortable at the podium, as she'd had plenty of practice over the past year, going from one fundraiser to another and heading multiple political and charitable events.

Mrs. Roosevelt looked out at the crowd and began to speak. "Clyde and I were great friends when I lived in the Hudson River Valley during my preteen years. Clyde was a distant cousin on my mother's side. But, during those impressionable years, he was more than a friend. He was like a brother to me. We played in the river, climbed trees and built forts from scrap lumber. Clyde was always the leader, whether he pretended to be a swashbuckling pirate, or a sheriff in the Old West. He always made me the captain's mate or the Indian that died by his hand, but I didn't mind.

"Clyde was lots of fun, and he was a great animal lover. He had a little black and white spotted dog that followed us everywhere. Sometimes, Clyde would add him to our gang and we'd pretend the dog was the dead Indian and he'd let me be the deputy sheriff. When we grew older, I lost track of Clyde, but from what I remember about him, I'm not surprised that Clyde risked his life, trying to save Mitzie."

Meow!

As Mitzie responded to her name, all eyes swiveled to the box at Mrs. Turnbull's feet.

Mrs. Turnbull burst into a fresh frenzy of weeping at the cry from the cat carrier. She leaned down, unsnapped the lid and pulled Mitzie into her lap. Mitzie wiggled and then settled in her lap with another plaintive *Mew!*

Mrs. Roosevelt paused, and then spoke again. "Farewell, dear Clyde, until we meet again." She stepped out from behind the podium and returned to her seat.

The silence in the room was palpable. Most of the guests dabbed their eyes, whether they had ever given old Clyde much thought before or not, because in death, Mrs. Roosevelt made him more lovable than he had ever been in life and to a man, they grieved his loss.

Agnes wished she had known him better. Who else lived nearby, quietly and with few friends, perhaps on her very own block, who needed a friend? She vowed to meet the neighbors that she barely knew down the street.

Mrs. Roosevelt had touched her heart and from the sniffles and tear-filled eyes around her, Agnes guessed that many of the others had experienced the same wake-up call.

Pastor Lickleiter invited others to speak, but who could follow Mrs. Roosevelt after the speech she made? There were no takers, not even his daughter or Mrs. Turnbull.

"Then I'll invite you all to stand," instructed Pastor Lickleiter, "and come forward if you wish to extend your final farewell to our friend and neighbor, followed by luncheon in the next room."

Godfrey stood near the hall door, close to Mr. Whistlemeyer and Albert Finklebaum.

Mrs. Turnbull jumped from her seat with Mitzie cradled in her arms. She moved into the line behind Clyde's daughter and her husband. They paused beside the casket, glanced at Clyde and moved back to the front row.

Mrs. Turnbull wailed as she stepped up to the casket with Mitzie clutched to her breast. She leaned over the casket, tears dripping from her cheeks onto his lapel. Then, she held Mitzie up until her furry front feet hovered over the edge of the casket. What was she doing? Allowing Mitzie to pay her last respect?

Agnes gasped as Mrs. Turnbull lowered the cat into the casket. *Surely, she doesn't plan to put her into the...! Oh, my Stars!*

Whatever was Mrs. Turnbull's intention, Mitzie wanted none of it. Had her feline intuition perceived Mrs. Turnbull's plan, that she should escort Clyde to his final reward? Perhaps her Egyptian forefathers and foremothers were okay with an unintended journey to the afterlife, but being a modern-day puss and not the least bit appreciative of Clyde's failed attempt to save her life, she had no intention of joining him on his voyage to the Field of Reeds.

A collective gasp erupted from the audience when Mitzie clawed her way up Mrs. Turnbull's suit jacket and onto her hat. The shriek that bellowed from her moggy bosom sent chills down Agnes's spine.

Mitzie teetered on Mrs. Turnbull's hat for a moment, then vaulted off the end of Clyde's casket and onto the floor, plunged down the aisle toward the front door.

Mrs. Roosevelt's driver opened the front door and Mitzie was last seen heading down the block toward Wilkey's Market.

Horrified by her thwarted attempt to honor Clyde with her sacrifice, Mrs. Turnbull collapsed onto a chair in the front row and resumed her wailing. From the fuss she made, one would think she was the grieving widow rather than Clyde's next door neighbor. Doesn't guilt make us act in the most peculiar ways?

For a moment, the crowd froze, unable to believe their eyes. *What just happened?* Katherine, Mildred and Edith covered their mouths to stifle the giggles and scurried back to the kitchen.

But, life, and in this case, death, must go on. As soon as Mrs. Turnbull had somewhat regained her composure, and the tabby distraction had disappeared around the corner, Agnes moved again toward the beautifully carved Koa wood casket to bid the *dearly departed* a hasty farewell. She peered at Clyde. *My, didn't Katherine do a fine job.* He never looked better.

A fly dithered around Clyde's head and then settled on his nose. Agnes leaned forward to shoo it away. As she straightened back up, her diamond earring slipped from her right ear and slid down beside Clyde's arm and disappeared next to the satin lining.

Oh, my stars!

Chapter Twenty-Seven

Warrior on the Home Front

*A*gnes scanned the faces of the crowd. Had anyone seen what happened? Now, what was she to do? Announce to the guests that she'd lost her earring in the casket or pretend to give him a kiss while she reached down to retrieve the trinket? Who would believe she wanted to kiss the old fellow? On the other hand, she wasn't about to send Clyde to his eternal rest with her precious jewels.

Perhaps if she pretended to straighten his tie, she could casually slide her hand between his arm and the satin lining. She reached forward, her heart in her throat, and pawed beside Clyde's arm. Nothing! She slid her hand back and forth along Clyde's arm. *What's that?* Something bulged in the lining, but it was too big to be her earring.

Agnes panicked. Where had it gone? She glanced back toward the audience. The short line of guests stood nearby, sighing and shuffling their feet. No doubt they wished she'd move on so they could pay their respects and get on with the free lunch. But, she couldn't move on. Not with her diamond earring wedged somewhere between Clyde and the here-after. Maybe it hadn't gone beside his arm. Maybe it went inside his jacket! *Oh, how can this be happening?*

Agnes slid her hand inside Clyde's coat, first on one side and then the other. She patted his chest and ran her finger under his collar and down around the neckline of his shirt.

The guests began to mumble.

Godfrey appeared at her side. "What on earth are you doing?

Everyone is staring," he whispered. "What's wrong?"

Agnes whispered back. "My diamond earring fell into the casket. I can't find it!" She slid her hand alongside Clyde's arm again and patted the bulge in the lining. "Something's here, but it's not my earring."

"Let me see." Godfrey ran his hand along the bulge beside Clyde's arm. His head jerked up. His eyes were wide as his gaze swept across the room to Albert and Mr. Whistlemeyer. Pushing Agnes to the side, he turned to the people in the line. "FBI business. If you'll all please return to your seats…"

Godfrey took a penknife from his pocket and slit the casket lining. He reached into the lining and pulled out stacks of hundred dollar bills, twenties and tens. "Just as I thought!" He gestured to the bodyguard at the door. "Security. Restrain those two men." Godfrey pointed at Albert and Mr. Whistlemeyer.

Albert began shoving and stumbling from his aisle toward the hallway.

"Hold them both for questioning," Godfrey shouted.

"What's going on?" Mrs. Turnbull bellowed, tears streaking down the grooves and wrinkled in her mascara-stained cheeks.

"Oh, poor Daddy! The disgrace of it," Clyde's daughter wailed.

"Most peculiar funeral I've ever attended," Tommy muttered.

"Does this mean we won't get lunch?" An unidentified voice called from the back of the room.

"Agnes," Godfrey grinned. "Thanks to you, we solved the case. This is the missing Hawaiian money I've been looking for."

"So, the money was in the casket all the time?" Agnes put her hand to her cheek. "But, you searched Albert's casket warehouse and didn't find anything."

"We suspected him from the beginning, since his son was on the Hawaiian money detail. Now that we've found the money in the casket from Finklestein's warehouse, we can charge him with conspiracy and theft and whatever else the FBI can think up. Charges against his son and the casket manufacturer in Hawaii probably won't be far behind."

Godfrey's eyes gleamed as he pulled more money from the lining, licked his thumb and flipped through the bills.

"I can't believe Mr. Whistlemeyer was involved, too. He looks so harmless." Agnes glanced at the two culprits in the back row, hunched in the back row with a security guard standing over them. Albert looked miserable. Mr. Whistlemeyer looked dazed and confused.

Godfrey stopped counting and nodded toward Mr. Whistlemeyer. "I suspect he was involved. We'll know more when we question him. Didn't you tell me you saw Mrs. Whistlemeyer in the warehouse the night you were there? Sounds like they were all in cahoots. They're as guilty as a fox in the henhouse."

Agnes reached into the casket again, and ran her hand between Clyde's arm and his torso. "Here it is!" She held up her missing earring. "If I hadn't dropped my earring, you never would have found the money. Did you say there was a reward?" She giggled and screwed her earring back onto her ear.

Godfrey shoved the stack of bills into his pants pockets and into the inside and outside pockets of his jacket. "Agnes, I'm headed to Sears and Roebuck to buy a suitcase. I need something to carry all this money in, so if you'll excuse me, I'll be back as soon as I can." He patted the unbecoming bulges in his jacket.

He waved to the security men guarding Albert and Mr. Whistlemeyer. "Please hold these gentlemen in your car until the police arrive." He looked up and caught Katherine's eye. "Will you call Chief Waddlemucker? Tell him to pick up these guys and take them downtown for questioning.

"So, if you'll excuse me…" Godfrey leaned forward and whispered in Agnes's ear. "I love you." He kissed her cheek, and headed for the kitchen.

Agnes felt as if cold fingers had traced a pattern down her neck and then up into her hairline. She rubbed the back of her neck. *Now, what brought that on?* Before she could call him back, Godfrey disappeared through the door.

Agnes glanced toward Mrs. Roosevelt. She had apparently taken all the excitement at the casket in stride. Considering her life at the White House and all the spectacular events she attended, how could a bit of confusion at a funeral parlor upset her? She sat quietly in the front row, watching the comings and goings and whispering to Tommy.

Agnes rushed to her side. "Are you ladies alright? Sorry for the confusion."

Mrs. Roosevelt stood and extended her hand. "We don't quite understand what just happened? Who are you?"

Agnes curtsied. "I'm Agnes Odboddy, one of your most ardent admirers. I think you already met my granddaughter, Katherine?"

"Charming girl."

"Thank you. I quite agree. They don't come any better than Katherine. She's—"

"Mrs. Odboddy. About the commotion around Clyde's casket?" Perhaps Mrs. Roosevelt was losing patience with the chaos after all.

"Oh, of course. It's rather complicated. You see, Godfrey…Agent Baumgarten…is with the FBI. He's been following the case of some stolen Hawaiian money. These two men had smuggled it into the U.S. in the caskets made in Hawaii." She turned and gestured to Clyde's beautiful Koa wood casket. "Then, I dropped my earring into Clyde's casket, and while I was looking for it, I felt the money in the lining."

"Your earring…"

"Yes, the ones my husband, God rest his soul, gave me the day my son was born. They were diamonds, you see, and I couldn't bear to lose one of them. I was sure that Clyde wouldn't want me—"

"Please go on. About the money in Clyde's casket?"

"Godfrey knew right away that Mr. Whistlemeyer…he owns the mortuary and Albert, from the casket company, must be in cahoots with Albert's son, there in Hawaii. Oh, never mind the details. Everything's going to be alright now. Let's go into the other room and have some lunch. The ladies from the First Church of the Evening Star and Everlasting Light have prepared a wonderful luncheon."

Agnes looked up and noticed that the chapel was nearly empty. What with all the pandemonium at the casket, most of the guests had either given up on paying Clyde their last regards, or thankful for the confusion, used it as an excuse not to look at his dead body.

Clyde's daughter still sat in the front row, her head leaning on her husband's shoulder.

The security guard and driver had moved the two culprits to the car, to wait for Chief Waddlemucker. Katherine, Edith and Mildred were likely in the kitchen serving up the food.

Where on earth was Sophia? She hadn't been seen since before the service started. And, after she made such a fuss about meeting Mrs. Roosevelt, too.

Mrs. Roosevelt picked up her purse and followed Agnes toward the kitchen when the hallway door burst open and Sophia rushed in. She held a gun in her hand, and pointed it at Mrs. Roosevelt.

What the heck? Agnes stopped and stood between Mrs. Roosevelt and Sophia. "What on earth has possessed you, Sophia?"

"Get out of the way, you stupid cow. You can't stop me. I'm going to kill Mrs. Roosevelt." Sophia pointed the gun toward Agnes's head.

Well, Agnes, you're in for it now. Talk about being a warrior on the home front. Doesn't this just take the cake? "Don't be ridiculous. There's no way you're going to shoot the President's wife! You'll have to shoot me first." Agnes threw out her arms, shielding Mrs. Roosevelt. She glanced through the window toward Mrs. Roosevelt's car. Where on earth was the body guard? *Seems like this is his job, not mine.* "What's this all about, Sophia? Have you lost your marbles?"

Sophia rose up on her tiptoes and tossed her head back. "Don't call me Sophia. I am Officer First Class Sophia Rashmuller of the Gestapo. I've been undercover for the past year. You'd be surprised how much you can learn from a foolish woman married to a Colonel."

Agnes gasped. Poor Edith Braithwaite. She must have spilled her guts to her friend, Sophia, a Nazi spy, and all the information went straight to the Nazis. *Wait a minute! Didn't I tell Chief Waddlemucker that Sophia was a Nazi spy? And, he called me a meddling old woman?*

"Sophia. Let's talk this over. You'll never get away with killing Mrs. Roosevelt." Agnes raised her voice, in hopes she could attract the security guard. Was he deaf as well as incompetent? What good was a security guard that didn't guard his client? She could see him through the window, leaning against the Hudson, smoking a cigarette and chatting with the driver like a couple of schoolgirls.

"There's an FBI agent in the kitchen and a security guard right outside!"

Mrs. Roosevelt tried to move around Agnes. "Let me try to reason with her."

Agnes pushed her back. "Stay back. She'll shoot you. She's a Nazi spy, just like I thought."

"Yes you did, Agnes," Sophia sneered. "You're either the smartest woman in Newbury or the luckiest. I've tried to get rid of you three times since Chief Waddlemucker told me that you suspected me."

"What are you talking about? You really are losing your mind, Sophia. Put the gun down. You need a long vacation. I think there's a room with a view in Sing-Sing with your name on it."

Agnes reached back with her left hand, as though to straighten her hair. She pulled a silver chopstick from her bun, and then moved her arm slowly down her back, concealing the chopstick in the folds of her skirt. Now, with at least the semblance of a weapon, she took a step forward. "Why don't you tell us how you tried to get rid of me? I'm afraid I never noticed."

Sophia took a step back. "Stay where you are, you nit-wit. How did you manage to survive the poisoned lemon tarts? And the rat poison in your medicine cabinet. You weren't even hurt when I ran down your bicycle. You fool. Did you really think that was an accident?" Sophia laughed.

Agnes mouth dropped open. "You put poison in the lemon tarts?" Poor Chicken Clara. Not dead from too much sugar, after all. He died from eating the poisoned lemon tarts. Was there a chicken Heaven for chickens that save their master's life? As sure as God made little green apples, if Clara hadn't eaten the lemon tarts, she and Godfrey and Katherine would have eaten them. They all could have died. The woman was the devil! And, she had a gun!

Agnes gripped the chopstick, feeling the cold steel between her fingers. Sophia was still too far away. If she tried to rush her, Sophia would get off a shot that might hit Mrs. Roosevelt. *I can't let that happen! I have to get closer.* She stepped forward.

"Sophia. Tell me. Why did you come to America? What did we ever do to make you want to hurt us? Didn't we welcome you to the knitting circle? Wasn't Edith your best friend?" She took another step toward Sophia, being careful to stand between Sophia and Mrs. Roosevelt.

Sophia's laugh was that of a madwoman. "I have no friends. I've got a job to do. I befriended Edith Braithwaite when I learned she was married to the Colonel. Wasn't she just a wealth of information?" Sophia chuckled again. "The Gestapo never gave me enough credit. They never dreamed I'd have the chance to kill the First Lady. It doesn't matter what happens to me, now. My name will live forever in the Third Reich as the woman who killed Mrs. Roosevelt. Don't you see? Now, get out of my way." She stepped forward, now only an arm's length from Agnes.

"I told you, I can't let you..." Agnes rushed at her, screaming, "Help! Godfrey! Where in blazes are you?" She jabbed her chopstick straight into Sophia's shoulder.

Sophia jerked back and fired. The shot went wild.

Agnes grabbed Sophia's arm and grappled for the gun.

Tommy rushed forward and threw her body against Sophia, sending the three of them tumbling onto the floor. Arms and legs twisted as they struggled. Sophia still had the gun. Another shot rang out.

Agnes pitched back and lay still. Faces whirled and spun. *Katherine. Godfrey. Chief Waddlemucker. Mrs. Roosevelt.*

She closed her eyes. *I can't do this anymore. I need to rest...*

"Grandmother? Can you hear me? It's Katherine."

Agnes stirred and opened her eyes. Had she fainted? Her arm ached. Nausea surged through her stomach at the sight of blood seeping through the tea towel wrapped around her upper arm.

She lay on the floor; the sickening scent of lilies and carnations swirling around her head. Something was wrong. Something was always wrong when the scent of lilies filled the air. Like when Douglas died and she sat like a stone in the front row at the funeral parlor, avoiding Godfrey's glance every time he tried to catch her eye... *Just let me rest for a minute.*

She closed her eyes. Voices pulled her back. *Mrs. Roosevelt! Sophia! The gun!* She swallowed what felt like a rock in her throat and tried to speak. "Is Mrs. Roosevelt alright?" Her voice sounded like Chicken Mildred when she pulled a worm from the ground. Was that just this morning? Too much had happened. It was hard to sort it all out. *So tired...*

"Mrs. Roosevelt is fine. She called the White House and they want her away from here as soon as possible, so they skipped lunch. They were afraid Sophia might have an associate who would try again. You saved her life. You're a hero, Grandma."

Agnes smiled. "I suppose I am. Maybe I'll get a medal." A warm glow of satisfaction filled her chest. She *was* a true warrior on the home front, wasn't she? Agnes shrugged. "Where's Godfrey?"

"I haven't seen him since...actually I don't know where he is."

"How about Chief Waddlemucker?"

"He's out front with the security guard. They'll take Sophia, Albert and Mr. Whistlemeyer down to the police station for questioning in a few minutes. How do you feel? The ambulance should be here any minute. I guess you know you've been shot." Katherine's lips quivered as she held back tears, and pressed a towel even tighter against Agnes's shoulder.

"So I see." Agnes flexed her arm and grimaced. "But, you said Mrs. Roosevelt is alright. That's the important thing."

Katherine nodded. "She wanted me to thank you and tell you good-bye."

"Then I guess I'm ready to go to the hospital. My arm aches like thunder, and…and…I think I'm going to be sick." Agnes turned to the side and…retched on the carpet.

Poor Jackson would have to shampoo the carpet all over again.

Chapter Twenty-Eight

G odfrey opened the door to Agnes's hospital room, his arms full of yellow daisies. "May I come in? How are feeling, dear? They said you were out of surgery and everything went well."

Well, there he is, finally! Her heart did a little jig. "Just a little sore, but no worse for wear. Did you get everything all wrapped up down at the mortuary?"

"Indeed. I got all the bills out of the casket and Clyde is on his way to his eternal rest." Godfrey smiled. "I bought a small duffle bag for the money. I'll be leaving right away, Agnes. I wanted to see you before I left."

"I understand, Godfrey. You have to get back to Washington and report the attack on Mrs. Roosevelt. Do you suppose I'll get a medal or something? Finally, I was able do my part for the war effort. Who would have thought I would save the President's wife?" Agnes leaned her head back against the pillows and sighed.

"I don't think there's a medal in it for you, Agnes. In fact, I expect there will be a press black-out on Sophia's attempted assassination. Think how demoralizing it would be to the country to know that some nut-job almost killed the First Lady? No, I don't believe they'll allow even one word in the papers. I expect they'll make everyone at the mortuary swear to never repeat a word of anything they saw at the funeral, including finding the money. It is a shame, isn't it? I'm sorry."

A cold chill paraded through Agnes's belly. "Why am I not

surprised?" She sighed. "When I mess up, it's headlines, but when I do something good, it has to be a press black-out. I'm getting used it."

Godfrey chuckled. "That's not always true. I saw your name in the paper just this morning. You've been cleared of setting the watch tower fire. Everyone knows you took the blame for national security reasons. They mentioned your bravery during the air attack. That's good, isn't it?"

"At first, I had to explain a reason for the fire. Now, how am I going to explain this?" She moved her arm and grimaced. What kind of story was she supposed to make up to explain a bullet in her shoulder? "So, you're leaving to take the money back to Washington, right? Are you coming back?"

"No."

"What do you mean, 'no'?" She lifted her head. "You're not taking the money to Washington? Or you're not coming back?" Agnes put her hand on Godfrey's arm and leaned forward. "I had hoped—"

"Neither, Agnes. I'm not going to Washington and I'm not coming back to Newbury."

"I don't understand," Agnes whispered. "Why not?"

"This is the way I figure…Everyone's money in Hawaii was replaced with script last December. All the real money was scheduled to be burned and the government put a press black-out on its disappearance." Godfrey chuckled. "The way I see it, only the folks at Clyde's funeral know that the money was found, and because of the attempt on Mrs. Roosevelt, they're all sworn to secrecy. So, you see? Nobody knows about anything."

The chill in Agnes's stomach raced up her chest and into her throat. She coughed. *He couldn't mean what I think he means.* Her eyes held his gaze. "Go on."

Godfrey leaned over the bed and took her hand. His sweaty palms felt cold against her hand. "I've spent thirty years in the FBI working for peanuts. I figure I can use this money more than the government can. If I turn it in, it will be destroyed.

"I'm leaving the country with the money. Don't you see, Agnes? There's enough to set me up for the rest of my life."

Agnes gasped. She felt the blood rush to her head. *Godfrey? Stealing the money?* She couldn't believe her ears. She shook her head. It wasn't possible. Not the Godfrey she knew. The Godfrey she *thought* she knew. "You can't do this. You're not a thief. You're a loyal, hard-working FBI agent." Her fingers kneaded the coverlet like a kitten treading on a soft afghan. "It's your duty to turn in the money. How can you even consider such a thing?" She grabbed his arm and shook it. She wanted to take him by the shoulders and shake him until his teeth rattled, but it wasn't possible with one arm in a sling.

Godfrey gazed out the window for a moment. He turned back toward the bed, his deep blue eyes boring into her soul. "Think about it, Agnes. I counted it. "There's $982,550 dollars here. If you had a chance to take a million dollars, tax free, and no one would ever know you took it, wouldn't you be tempted? Well, this is the chance of a lifetime and I'm going to take it."

Was this the young man she had loved twenty-four years ago? He had the same glint in his eyes. The same Cheshire Cat grin on his face. But, did he have the same heart? She grieved the choices she had made, her lost youth and her chance for love. Standing now before her, the second chance for love she thought might become a reality, was being snatched away by his greed. It was a quality in Godfrey she would never have guessed.

As a self-appointed scourge of the underworld, a hometown patriot, how could she let him do this terrible thing? Tears stung her eyes. The pain in her heart was almost palpable. "They'll come after you. You'll be a hunted criminal…a fugitive. Please Godfrey, I thought you and me…that we might have… I thought—"

"I'm going to Australia. They don't extradite from there. The U.S. can't touch me. With almost a million dollars, what a life we could have. I'll buy a cattle ranch. We'd be rich. Come with me, Agnes. Just you and me and a suitcase full of free money. Wouldn't it be grand?"

It would be grand, indeed, wouldn't it? Every ounce of her being cried out to throw caution to the wind, step out in faith and follow her heart. Except…except…

Outside the window, a rooster crowed. She remembered her imaginary conversation with Chicken Mildred. *This is your home, Agnes. Everything you love. You can't run off with Godfrey. You hardly know the man, even if he does turn your knees to butter every time he aims those baby-blues your direction.*

Chicken Mildred was right. Her stomach churned with an overwhelming need to throw up. Agnes turned away. "I can't, Godfrey. I can't leave Katherine. She needs me."

Godfrey put his hands on Agnes's face and kissed her cheek. "Katherine's a grown woman. She doesn't need you. Come away with me."

"What about my chickens? Who would take care of Ling-Ling?"

Godfrey backed away. His smile faded. "Wouldn't Katherine take care of the chickens? You're turning down a million dollars for four roosters and a cat? I thought I meant more to you than that."

"You mean a lot to me, Godfrey, and I have thought about us growing old…*er*…older…together, right here in Newbury. Don't do this, please. Stay here with me."

Agnes clutched his arm. Tears trickled down her cheeks. Her heart throbbed. What a crazy turn of events. All week she had rejected Godfrey's advances. Now, here she was, begging him to stay.

"Agnes, come with me. We'll be on a boat to Australia before they know we're gone."

For half a second, her determination wavered. She saw herself spending the rest of her life with the man of her dreams, a new life in Australia, and a million dollars to spend. Images filled her mind. Vast plains filled with longhorn steer, supper on the patio beneath a flaming sunset and waking to a pink dawn in the arms of the love of her life. A smile crept across her face.

Wait. Taking the money was wrong. They'd be on the run from the

law, never able to return to the United States of America, her home in
Newbury. Never able to see Katherine happily married and someday
bounce great-grandbabies on her knee. Leaving behind everything she
loved; her home, friends and the life she'd built in her community, even
the folks who thought she was a little bit nuts. No, it was too much to
ask. She couldn't do it.

"I'm sorry, Godfrey. I care deeply for you, but I can't go with you.
Will you write to me when you get settled? I'd like to know where
you are."

"Of course." He patted her hand.

Was that Katherine and Mildred's voices just on the other side of
the door? "You'd better go, Godfrey. Sooner or later, someone will ask
questions about the money and you'd better be long gone when the
subject comes up. If they catch you, it's Leavenworth."

"They're not going to catch me. Good-bye, Agnes." Godfrey
leaned down and kissed her hard on the lips.

Even now, she had the power to stop him. She reached for the
nurse's call button. The nurse could call Chief Waddlemucker and he'd
alert the FBI. They'd probably catch Godfrey before he boarded the bus
or surely be waiting at the San Francisco airport. The blood throbbed in
her forehead, knowing the power she held in her hand. And yet...and
yet...because she loved him, she would not betray him.

Love! The equalizer of our moral compass; a moral equivalent
between how much we love and how much evil we are willing to tolerate.
Every evil we could never accept, the blackest of sins overlooked when
the offender is someone we love. No. She would not betray him. The
FBI would know the money was gone soon enough. Let them discover
it on their own.

"I love you, Agnes."

She put her arm around his neck. "I know. Now go. Go!"

Godfrey waved and hurried out of the room, and out of her life.

Chapter Twenty-Nine

*G*gnes closed her eyes. His departure seemed to suck the air from the room. His loss felt almost unbearable. Opening her eyes at the sound of the door creaking open, she blinked back tears. *Katherine and Mildred.* She dashed tears from her cheeks. *I will not let them see me cry.*

"Why, you look just fine, Grandmother. Are you feeling better?" Katherine's hands were full of pink and yellow roses arranged in Agnes's favorite carnival glass vase.

"Why, you've brought roses from the bushes beside the driveway. Thank you, dear."

"We passed Godfrey in the hallway. He seemed to be in a hurry." Katherine ran water from the sink into the vase and set the roses on Agnes nightstand.

"Oh, I see he brought you some flowers, too." She moved Godfrey's daisies alongside her vase of roses. "Is Godfrey coming back later, or did he have to leave for D.C.?"

"*Umm*…he's…gone. He had all that money to deal with. I have no idea when we'll see him again. He came to say good-bye." Agnes dabbed her hankie at her eyes.

"Oh, don't worry. It's obvious that he's crazy about you. I don't think he's going to disappear now." Mildred tugged the coverlet on Agnes's bed and smoothed the wrinkles.

Agnes turned away. No point in letting Katherine or Mildred read anything from her face.

"Thank you for coming, Mildred. Did everything go alright at the mortuary? Mrs. Roosevelt got off okay? I'd hoped to talk with her over luncheon."

"She couldn't stay long, but we all had a chance to chat with her for a few minutes. She's really a lovely woman. Even after the terrible scene with Sophia, she chatted with us like nothing even happened."

"She was sorry she didn't have a chance to thank you, Grandmother," Katherine said.

"Speaking of Sophia." Mildred lowered her voice. "We're all in a state of shock. A Nazi assassin, right under our noses and we didn't even know it. Poor Edith is beside herself. Who knows what she told Sophia over the past year? Edith is so distraught she's gone home and taken to her bed. The doctors had to give her a sedative."

Agnes scooched up against the pillow and put up her nose. "Didn't I tell you Sophia was a Nazi spy? I knew it from the minute I met her. That phony red hair was a dead giveaway."

"But, Agnes, you have...I mean, your hair..." Mildred dropped her gaze.

"Excuse me!" Agnes picked up her chopsticks from the nightstand and shoved them into the back of her flaming red hair. "My hair color is quite natural!"

Katherine smiled. "Of course it is."

The door opened and Dr. Don walked in. "How is my favorite pat... Oh, Katherine. I'm glad you're here. I don't believe we finished our conversation this morning."

Katherine's cheeks turned lemonade pink. "Dr. Dew-Wright. This is not the time nor is it the place to discuss—"

"Oh, I disagree. This is exactly the time and place. I have witnesses." He smiled at Agnes and Mildred.

Agnes turned away and examined her flowers. *Poor Katherine. She's in for it now. I can't wait to see how she wiggles out of this one.*

"Ladies? Will you be the jury? I promise to abide by your decision. This morning, I asked Miss Katherine to step out with me and she turned me down. Now, Katherine, you must tell me the truth. Why won't you go out with me?"

Tears puddled in Katherine's eyes. She wrung her handkerchief in her hand. "I just can't go through this again. What would I do if you went off to war and died? I couldn't bear it, not again. Better we shouldn't start something we can't finish. "

"Aha!" Dr. Don laughed. "I thought it might be something like that. But, you didn't give me a chance to explain. I won't ever be going to war. I had scarlet fever as a child and it left me with weak lungs. I'm classified 4F, which keeps me out of the military. Thank goodness, with my medical degree, I can still contribute to the war effort here at home. So, if that's all that's bothering you..." He turned again and gazed at Mildred and Agnes. "Ladies of the jury. Can either of you think of a reason I shouldn't pick Katherine up next Sunday about 11:30 A.M.?"

Agnes grinned and shook her head.

Mildred giggled and clapped her hands.

"Katherine?" Dr. Don reached for her hand.

"Guilty as charged." Katherine dashed tears off her cheeks. "I'll accept the verdict. It sounds pretty wonderful. Not the fact that you have weak lungs, mind you, but the fact that you won't be going to war. I'd be happy to step out with you, Don. Is it okay if I call you Don?"

"I wouldn't have it any other way."

The door creaked open again and Chief Waddlemucker stomped in, carrying a potted cactus. "Is there someone in here pretending she's sick?" He set the cactus on the night stand beside the two vases of flowers. "Katherine, Mrs. Higgelbiggel."

"Haggenbottom." Mildred squinched up her nose.

"Of course. So sorry. Mrs. Haggenbottom." Chief Waddlemucker's cheeks reddened. "Just came by to thank you, Agnes, for today. You saved Mrs. Roosevelt's life and that's a fact.

"Sophia spilled her guts at the station. The Nazis' have her head so scrambled, she would have gladly died trying to kill Mrs. Roosevelt. She's not even sorry. Says she's proud that she took the chance, even if she didn't finish the job." The chief stuck his hands in his pockets and rocked back on his heels.

"Unfortunately, we can't file attempted murder charges against her, because Washington wants to keep a lid on the whole attempted assassination. They don't want the public to know that we came *that* close to losing our First Lady." He snapped his finger. "But, since she shot you too, Agnes, we plan to charge her with your attempted murder."

"Sophia's really not a very good spy, you know." Agnes frowned. "She claimed she'd tried to kill me three times already this week. Guess this makes it four misses."

"Three times? I can't understand why you never mentioned this before, Agnes. You're so prone to share your concerns about everything else." Chief Waddlemucker smirked.

Agnes snorted. "You're the one who spilled the beans about me saying she was a Nazi spy. I suppose she tried to get rid of me before anyone could take me seriously and start investigating her." Agnes rearranged the sling and repositioned her arm.

Chief Waddlemucker looked up. "That's right! The other day, when she ran down your bike! You know, I thought there was something fishy about that at the time. So, it wasn't an accident." He dropped his gaze. "I'm sorry, Agnes. I should have guessed. But, what else did she do?"

"Yesterday, when she came to my house, she switched my can of tooth powder with a can of rat poison. I came close to brushing my teeth with it. I thought I'd bought the can myself by mistake, so I didn't mention it to Katherine." Agnes turned toward Katherine with a wan smile.

Katherine's face paled. "You should have told me, Grandma."

Chief Waddlemucker wiped his brow with his handkerchief. "And, the third time?"

Agnes nodded. "A few days ago, Sophia brought over a plate of lemon tarts. Our Chicken Clara got into them, so I threw them out. We all thought Clara died from eating too much sugar. Sophia admitted she'd poisoned the tarts."

"Poor Chicken Clara. She saved your life," Katherine whispered.

Chief Waddlemucker turned to Mildred. "Agnes claimed that Sophia tried to poison you with lemon tarts at your society meeting. That's probably why she thought it was poetic justice to poison Agnes's tarts. What made her think she could get away with it if she had succeeded? I would have connected the two incidents. What a stupid woman."

"Sophia is an evil woman," Katherine said, "but, she's not very smart. She's not in her right mind."

Chief Waddlemucker looked up. "Say…Where's Godfrey? I thought he would bring the money down to the station, but he never showed up. I suppose he took it directly back to Washington, instead.

"By the way, he was right about Albert's son in Hawaii. Albert confessed how his son sneaked the money out of the convoy before it got to the mortuary. Then he bribed the Koa coffin maker to slip it into marked caskets headed for the casket warehouse here in Newbury."

"That's odd. Then, how did it end up in Clyde's coffin? Why didn't Albert remove the money at the warehouse?" Katherine asked.

Chief Waddlemucker shrugged. "Somehow, the card on the container marked with an X got switched to another container. When Albert didn't find the money in the marked casket, he tried to call his son, long distance. You know how the phone lines overseas are these days. They didn't make connections until this morning. When Albert figured out the cards must have gotten mixed up and the wrong casket was sent to Whistlemeyer's, he hurried over, but by then, Clyde was already in the casket with the money."

"I heard them arguing about something in the back room. It must have been about the mix-up," Katherine said.

"Oh!" Agnes's hand flew to her mouth. "I just remembered something. I know what happened. The night I was in the warehouse hiding behind the coffins… A label with an X fell off one of them. I must have stuck it back on the wrong carton. Oh, that's funny." She giggled. "If I hadn't followed Albert thinking he'd stolen the ration books and mixed up the card, we never would have found the money."

"Well, Agnes, I have another surprise." Chief Waddlemucker patted her arm. "Remember, you claimed someone was stealing ration books? Well, it was true! Albert admitted everything. Said Mrs. Whistlemeyer came up with the plan to steal the books. When she heard that Albert was managing the Ration Stamp office, she left her husband and took up with Albert. She talked him into the ration book scheme.

"That's how she learned that his son was part of the Hawaii project. She masterminded the plan to steal the money and ship it here in the coffins. She's a regular Mata Hari. Of course, Albert claimed she manipulated him and he had to *go along* with her to keep her happy.

"Apparently, poor Mr. Whistlemeyer didn't have anything to do with the smuggled money. He's lucky to be rid of such an evil conniving woman."

"So, Mrs. Whistlemeyer was behind everything? Is she in custody?" Katherine took Agnes's hand and gave it a squeeze.

"We got a search warrant for Albert's house and found a box of old ration books hidden in his garage. Mrs. Whistlemeyer is in the pokey and Mr. Whistlemeyer was released pending further investigation, but I suspect he'll be cleared." Chief Waddlemucker stood.

"The District Attorney was contacted about Sophia's charges. You should hear from him in a few days, Agnes. As soon as Godfrey gets back to Washington and turns the money over to the FBI, we can start prosecution proceedings against Albert and his accomplices."

Agnes closed her eyes. The money wasn't ever going to reach Washington. Not if Godfrey had anything to do with it. She smiled.

It wasn't likely that Albert or Mrs. Whistlemeyer would ever have smuggling charges brought against them, either. Without the money, and with all the witnesses at the mortuary sworn to secrecy, there would be no way to tie them to the Hawaiian money theft.

The ration book theft was another story. Albert might see the inside of Alcatraz yet. And, Mrs. Whistlemeyer? The California Institute for Women in Tehachapi probably had room for one more inmate.

Chief Waddlemucker picked up his jacket, preparing to leave. "I guess Mrs. Whistlemeyer decided to ditch her husband and make off with the small funny elves."

Agnes's head jerked up. "What? What did you say about Albert and small funny elves? I don't understand."

Chief Waddlemucker turned at the door. "I didn't say anything about small funny elves. I said I guessed Albert and Mrs. Whistlemeyer were going to make off with *all the money themselves*. Really Agnes, I've told you before. You must get your hearing checked."

Agnes's face warmed. Every time she talked to Chief Waddlemucker... "You must speak with a lisp. It's the only explanation. There's certainly nothing wrong with my hearing."

Katherine laughed. "Grandmother. You're just tired. We should leave and let you rest. I'll come back later tonight. Dr. Don said you can go home in the morning." Just the mention of Dr. Don's name and her cheeks turned the same color as the pink roses in the vase beside Agnes's bed.

There's bound to be a wedding before long and grandbabies shortly thereafter or my name isn't Agnes Agatha Odboddy.

"Katherine, what we need is a vacation. When this blasted war is over, how would you feel about a long ocean voyage?"

"That sounds wonderful, Grandma. Where should we go?"

"Oh, I don't know." Agnes turned toward the window. Outside, the color of the sky reminded her of Godfrey's blue eyes. The clouds were the color of the shock of hair that fell across his forehead. She sighed, her heart full of love. Somehow, she was sure they would meet again. "Any place is fine with me, dear. Just off the top of my head, I'm thinking... Why don't we visit Australia?"

A Special Thank-You

Thank you to the following friends and family who made this book possible.

To Londa Faber for suggesting the character and personality of Agnes Odboddy.

To my Inspire Christian Writers Critique group for helpful hints and suggestions: Sheila Alford, Dee Aspin, Erin Bambery, Sherry Bergmann, Ellen Cardwell, and Sandra Heaton.

To Wanita Zimmerman and Ellen Cardwell for sharing their personal WWII experiences that found their way into Agnes's story.

To my patient husband, Lee, for patience and technical support. Without his help, I would have tossed the computer against the wall more than once.

To Donna Harper for the wonderful illustrations in the book.

To Julie Williams for her editing, mentoring, and technical finesse. You bring it all together.

To Lois Parrish and Sherri Bergmann for final editing and graphic contributions.

To Elk Grove Publications for unlimited support.

And

To every fan that reads my books and asks, "When is the next one coming out?"

About Elaine Faber

Elaine Faber is a member of Sisters in Crime, Inspire Christian Writers, and Cat Writers Association. She lives in Northern California with her husband and four house cats. She volunteers at the American Cancer Society Discovery Shop and is a board member of the Elk Grove Friends of the Library.

Elaine started writing poetry and short stories as a child. She has completed five novels. Many of her short stories are published in magazines, on-line weekly magazines and in at least eight short story collections (anthologies). She favors writing in the cozy mystery and humorous mystery genre.

Elaine's novels are available on Amazon in print and e-book.

Black Cat Mysteries Series
Black Cat's Legacy ~ http://tinyurl.com/lrvevgm
Black Cat and the Lethal Lawyer ~ http://tinyurl.com/q3qrgyu
Black Cat and the Accidental Angel ~ http://tinyurl.com/07zcsm2

Mrs. Odboddy Series
Mrs. Odboddy: Hometown Patriot
Mrs. Odboddy: Cross-Country Courier **(Coming Soon)**
Crossing the country by train to join Mrs. Roosevelt's Pacific Island Tour, Agnes carries a package to President Roosevelt. Despite facing daunting circumstances and a Nazi spy intent on stealing her package, she reaches Washington D.C. only to be met by J. Edgar Hoover, who is determined to sabotage her journey.

Elaine's Website ~ http://www.mindcandymysteries.com
Share your thoughts about Mrs. Odboddy or the Black Cat series on an Amazon Book Review.

Elaine is available for speaking engagements at your club or organization. Email her with your questions or comments at Elaine.Faber@MindCandyMysteries.com.

Also by Elaine Faber

Black Cat's Legacy

Elaine Faber

Black Cat's Legacy

A tale of intrigue and murder with a touch of whimsy.

Thumper, the resident Fern Lake black cat, knows where the bodies are buried and it's up to Kimberlee to decode the clues.

Kimberlee's arrival at the Fern Lake lodge triggers the Black Cat's Legacy. With the aid of his ancestors' memories, it's Thumper's duty to guide Kimberlee to clues that can help solve her father's cold case murder. She joins forces with a local homicide detective and an author, also researching the murder for his next thriller novel. As the investigation ensues, Kimberlee learns more than she wants to know about her father. The murder suspects multiply, some dead and some still very much alive, but someone at the lodge will stop at nothing to hide the Fern Lake mysteries.

Black Cat and the Lethal Lawyer

With the promise to name a beneficiary to her multi-million dollar horse ranch, Kimberlee's grandmother entices her and her family to Texas. But things are not as they appear and Thumper, the black cat with superior intellect, uncovers the appalling reason for the invitation. Kimberlee and Brett discover a fake Children's Benefit Program and the possible false identity of the stable master. To make matters worse, Thumper overhears a murder plot, and he and his newly found soul-mate,

Noe-Noe, must do battle with a killer to save Grandmother's life.

The further Kimberlee and her family delve into things, the deeper they are thrust into a web of embezzlement, greed, vicious lies and murder. With the aid of his ancestors' memories, Thumper unravels some dark mysteries. Is it best to reveal the past or should some secrets never be told?

Elaine Faber

Black Cat
and the
Lethal Lawyer

A tale of betrayal and greed with a splash of fantasy.

Black Cat and the Accidental Angel

Elaine Faber

Black Cat
and the
Accidental Angel

A tale of memories lost and love found with a touch of the divine.

When the family SUV flips and Kimberlee is rushed to the hospital, Black Cat (Thumper) and his soulmate are left behind. Black Cat loses all memory of his former life and the identity of the lovely feline companion by his side. "Call me Angel. I'm here to take care of you." Her words set them on a long journey toward home, and life brings them face to face with episodes of joy and sorrow.

The two cats are taken in by John and his young daughter, Cindy, facing foreclosure of the family vineyard and emu farm. In addition, someone is playing increasingly dangerous pranks that threaten Cindy's safety. Angel makes it her mission to help their new family. She puts her life at risk to protect the child, and Black Cat learns there are more important things than knowing your real name.

Elaine Faber's e-books are available on Amazon for $3.99. Print books. $16.00.

Cover photo *Black and White Cat*: © vivienstock, http://us.fotolia.com/id/46333972 (halo added)

Mrs. Odboddy: Cross-Country Courier

gnes dodged puddles across Wilkey's Market parking lot, struggling to balance her purse on her wrist, her umbrella and a bag of groceries in each arm. She lowered her head and aimed for her yellow and brown 1930 Model A Ford, parked two rows over and three puddles down. Why hadn't she let Mrs. Wilkey's son, George, carry out her bags when he offered? Maybe Katherine was right. *I'm too independent.* No harm in accepting a little help from time to time. Let the kid learn the joy of helping others.

As she approached her car, a black Ford edged up and stopped alongside her. She glanced up just as the side door opened and a man stepped out.

"You Mrs. Odboddy?" He reached up and ran his hand through his greasy black hair. A scar zigged and zagged across the back of his hand.

Agnes's stomach did a little twist. "Depends. Who's asking?" She took two steps toward her car. "Who are you and what do you want?" Her gaze roamed the parking lot. Not a man in sight, except the thug standing between her and her car.

The man reached out and grabbed her arm. "I want you to come with me."

Blood surged into Agnes's face. She caught her breath. Wouldn't you know it? Kidnapped in broad daylight and not a gol-darned cop in sight! No wonder, with every able-bodied man off fighting the war, leaving defenseless women and children victims of rapists and murderers. In less time than it took to think what to do next, she dropped her grocery bags, wielded her umbrella and smacked it across the man's shoulders.

"Hey! What's the big idea? Smitty! Give me a hand. The old broad's putting up a fuss." Scar-hand grabbed the umbrella from Agnes and shoved her toward the car.

Oh, good grief. What shall I do?

Smitty ran around the end of the car. Despite her struggles and a few well-aimed kicks, the two scoundrels shoved Agnes into the back seat and tossed her umbrella onto the floorboards. "Don't give us any trouble, Mrs. Odboddy," Smitty growled, rubbing his shins. "You're coming with us, like it or not, you hear?"

Agnes scooted across the mohair seat, huddled into the corner as far from Smitty's leering grin as she could get. "What do you want with me?"

Smitty and Scar-Hand jumped into the car. Smitty gunned the engine and lurched through the parking lot toward the street. He glanced over his shoulder. "Don't try any funny business. We were told to bring you to the boss and that's where you're going."

"I don't have any money if you're holding me for ransom." Agnes's heart pounded. How much was one old lady worth? She didn't have much money in the bank and with both her son and husband gone since WWI, her granddaughter, Katherine was about the only person who might be willing to pony up some cash, but no luck there, either. As a working girl, they didn't have a hundred bucks between them. No one in town would care much if she disappeared from the face of the earth. The thought made her stomach roil.

Was she about to vomit? It would serve them right if she puked all over their fancy Ford. The car headed down Main Street and out of town. She turned and waved frantically out the rear window at the car following behind. Maybe, if she could get his attention...

The man in the car smiled and waved back.

No! Can't you understand? I need help. I'm being kidnapped! No use. He thought she was just being friendly. She grabbed Scar-Hand's shoulder. "Where are you taking me?"

He shrugged and stared straight ahead.

Agnes ran her hand over her face. *Alright, calm down and think.* She had to have a clear head to make a plan. She took three deep breaths. *Assess the situation. Consider your options. Make a plan and execute.* She blew out her breath. *One thousand one, one thousand two...*

The odds of two against one weren't in her favor, racing down the road at the break-neck speed of thirty-five miles an hour. Opening the door and jumping out would be risky at the ripe old age of seventy-one. She'd probably break her neck or at the very least, her leg. Then, they'd stop and drag her back, broken leg and all. Forget that. Bad idea.

She reached for her umbrella! She could smack Smitty over the head again... No. He'd likely run the car off the road and the result could be the same as jumping out the door. Again, not a good plan. Maybe she could charm them. Hadn't she always prided herself in being able to handle any man with sweet talk and cookies?

"Smitty. What's your favorite hobby? Do you like to fish?" That's the ticket. Get him to talk about himself. Create a rapport. *People don't usually murder people they like.*

Smitty glanced back over his shoulder. "I like to shoot things. Squirrels, deer, dogs that dump over my garbage cans. That sort of thing. Why do you ask?"

Agnes's heart tumbled. "No reason. Never mind." So much for sweet-talk. Guess she'd have to bide her time. Maybe she could figure out an escape plan when they got where they were going. She shrank down in the corner and began to recite the Lord's Prayer under her breath.

Scar-Hand reached over and punched Smitty's shoulder. "Hey! Isn't that the kid right there?" He pointed out the window. "That one! In the blue striped tee-shirt. I'm sure that's him."

"You're right. He won't get away this time. Let's get him."

The killers weren't through yet. Now, they wanted Agnes and a teenage boy!

CPSIA information can be obtained
at www.ICGtesting.com
Printed in the USA
FSHW021628050920
73507FS